Praise for *An Unnecessary Woman*

"*An Unnecessary Woman* is a meditation on, among other things, aging, politics, literature, loneliness, grief, and resilience. If there are flaws to this beautiful and absorbing novel, they are not readily apparent." —*New York Times*

"Irresistible . . . [the author] offers winningly unrestricted access to the thoughts of his affectionate, urbane, vulnerable, and fractiously opinionated heroine. Aaliya says that when she reads, she tries to 'let the wall crumble just a bit, the barricade that separates me from the book.' Mr. Alameddine's portrayal of a life devoted to the intellect is so candid and human that, for a time, readers can forget that any such barrier exists." —*Wall Street Journal*

"*An Unnecessary Woman* is an antidote to literary blandness." —*Newsday*

"[The novel] throbs with energy . . . [Aaliya's] inventive way with words gives unfailing pleasure, no matter how dark the events she describes, how painful the emotions she reveals." —*Washington Post*

"[An] opaque self-portrait of an utterly beguiling misanthrope . . . Aaliya notes that: 'Reading a fine book for the first time is as sumptuous as the first sip of orange juice that breaks the fast in Ramadan.' You don't have to fast first (in fact it helps to have gorged on the books that Aaliya translates and adores) in order to savor Alameddine's succulent fiction." —*Boston Globe*

"I can't remember the last time I was so gripped simply by a novel's voice. Alameddine makes it clear that a sheltered life is not necessarily a shuttered one. Aaliya is thoughtful, she's complex, she's humorous and critical." —NPR.com

"A restlessly intelligent novel built around an unforgettable character . . . a novel full of elegant, poetic sentences." —*Minneapolis Star Tribune*

"[A] powerful intellectual portrait of a reader who is misread . . . a meditation on being and literature, written by someone with a passionate love of language and the power of words to compose interior worlds." —*Cleveland Plain Dealer*

"Beautiful writing . . . sharp, smart, and often sardonic . . . an homage to literature." —*The National*

"Reading *An Unnecessary Woman* is about listening to a voice . . . a fun, and often funny, book . . . rich in quirky metaphors . . . *An Unnecessary Woman* is not a game, though; it is a grave, powerful book. It is the hour-by-hour study of a woman who is struggling for dignity with every breath. . . . The meaning of human dignity is perhaps the great theme of literature, and Alameddine takes it on in every page of this extraordinary book." —*Washington Independent Review of Books*

"Aaliya is a formidable character. . . . When *An Unnecessary Woman* offers her what she regards as the corniest of conceits—a redemption arc—it's a delight to see her take it." —*Christian Science Monitor*

Also by Rabih Alameddine

*Koolaids: The Art of War*
*The Perv: Stories*
*I, the Divine: A Novel in First Chapters*
*The Hakawati*

# An Unnecessary Woman

# Rabih Alameddine

Grove Press
*New York*

Published simultaneously in Canada
Printed in the United States of America

ISBN-13 978-0-8021-2294-0
eISBN 978-0-8021-9287-5

Grove Press
an imprint of Grove/Atlantic, Inc.
154 West 14th Street
New York, NY 10011
Distributed by Publishers Group West

www.groveatlantic.com

14 15 16 17 18   10 9 8 7 6 5

*To Eric, with gratitude*

From my village I see as much of the universe as you can
    see from earth,
So my village is as big as any other land
For I am the size of what I see,
Not the size of my height.
    —Fernando Pessoa as Alberto Caeiro, *The Keeper of Sheep*

Perhaps reading and writing books is one of the last defences
human dignity has left, because in the end they remind us
of what God once reminded us before He too evaporated in
this age of relentless humiliations—that we are more than
ourselves; that we have souls. And more, moreover.
    Or perhaps not.
        —Richard Flanagan, *Gould's Book of Fish*

The cure for loneliness is solitude.
        —Marianne Moore, from the essay
        "If I Were Sixteen Today"

Don Quixote's misfortune is not his imagination, but
Sancho Panza.
    —Franz Kafka, *Dearest Father: Stories and Other Writings*

You could say I was thinking of other things when I shampooed my hair blue, and two glasses of red wine didn't help my concentration.

Let me explain.

First, you should know this about me: I have but one mirror in my home, a smudged one at that. I'm a conscientious cleaner, you might even say compulsive—the sink is immaculately white, its bronze faucets sparkle—but I rarely remember to wipe the mirror clean. I don't think we need to consult Freud or one of his many minions to know that there's an issue here.

I begin this tale with a badly lit reflection. One of the bathroom's two bulbs has expired. I'm in the midst of the evening ritual of brushing my teeth, facing said mirror, when a halo surrounding my head snares my attention. Toothbrush in right hand still moving up and down, side to side, left hand reaches for reading glasses lying on the little table next to the toilet. Once atop my obtrusive nose they help me see that I'm neither a saint nor saintly but more like the Queen Mother — well, an image of the Queen Mother smudged by a schoolgirl's eraser. No halo this, the blue anomaly is my damp hair. A pigment battle rages atop my head, a catfight of mismatched contestants.

I touch a still-wet lock to test the permanency of the blue tint and end up leaving a sticky stain of toothpaste on it. You can correctly presume that multitasking is not my forte.

I lean over the bathtub, pick up the tube of Bel Argent shampoo I bought yesterday. I read the fine print, squinting even with the reading glasses. Yes, I used ten times the amount prescribed while washing my hair. I enjoy a good lather. Reading instructions happens not to be my forte either.

Funny. My bathroom tiles are rectangular white with interlocking light blue tulips, almost the same shade as my new dye. Luckily, the blue isn't that of the Israeli flag. Can you imagine? Talk about a brawl of mismatched contestants.

Usually vanity isn't one of my concerns, doesn't disconcert me much. However, I'd overheard the three witches discussing the unrelenting whiteness of my hair. Joumana, my upstairs neighbor, had suggested that if I used a shampoo like Bel Argent, the white would be less flat. There you have it.

As I understand it, and I might be wrong as usual, you and I tend to lose short wavelength cones as we age, so we're less able to distinguish the color blue. That's why many people of a certain age have a bluish tint to their hair. Without the tint, they see their hair as pale yellow, or possibly salmon. One hairstylist described on the radio how he finally convinced this old woman that her hair was much too blue. But his client still refused to change the color. It was much more important that she see her hair as natural than the rest of the world do so.

I'd probably get along better with the client.

I too am an old woman, but I have yet to lose many short wavelength cones. I can distinguish the color blue a bit too clearly right now.

Allow me to offer a mild defense for being distracted. At the end of the year, before I begin a new project, I read the translation I've completed. I do minor final corrections, set the pages in order, and place them in the box. This is part of the ritual, which includes imbibing two glasses of red wine. I'll also admit that the last reading allows me to pat myself on the back, to congratulate myself on completing the project. This year, I translated the superb novel *Austerlitz*, my second translation of W. G. Sebald. I was reading it today, and for some reason, probably the protagonist's unrequited despair, I couldn't stop thinking of Hannah, I couldn't, as if the novel, or my Arabic translation of it, was an inductor into Hannah's world.

Remembering Hannah, my one intimate, is never easy. I still see her before me at the kitchen table, her plate wiped clean of food, her right cheek resting on the palm of her hand, head tilted slightly, listening, offering that rarest of gifts: her unequivocal attention. My voice had no home until her.

During my seventy-two years, she was the one person I cared for, the one I told too much—boasts, hates, joys, cruel disappointments, all jumbled together. I no longer think of her as often as I used to, but she appears in my thoughts every now and then. The traces of Hannah on me are indelible.

Percolating remembrances, red wine, an old woman's shampoo: mix well and wind up with blue hair.

I'll wash my hair once more in the morning, with no more tears baby shampoo this time. Hopefully the blue will fade. I can just imagine what the neighbors will say now.


For most of my adult life, since I was twenty-two, I've begun a translation every January first. I do realize that this is a holiday and most choose to celebrate, most do not choose to work on New Year's Day. Once, as I was leafing through the folio of Beethoven's sonatas, I noticed that only the pen-ultimate, the superb op. 110 in A-flat Major, was dated on the top right corner, as if the composer wanted us to know that he was busy working that Christmas Day in 1821. I too choose to keep busy during holidays.

Over these last fifty years I've translated fewer than forty books—thirty-seven, if I count correctly. Some books took longer than a year, others refused to be translated, and one or two bored me into submission—not the books them-selves, but my translations of them. Books in and of them-selves are rarely boring, except for memoirs of American presidents (No, No, Nixon)—well, memoirs of Americans in general. It's the "I live in the richest country in the world yet pity me because I grew up with flat feet and a malodorous vagina but I triumph in the end" syndrome. Tfeh!

Books into boxes—boxes of paper, loose translated sheets. That's my life.

I long ago abandoned myself to a blind lust for the written word. Literature is my sandbox. In it I play, build my forts and castles, spend glorious time. It is the world outside that box that gives me trouble. I have adapted tamely, though not conventionally, to this visible world so I can retreat without much inconvenience into my inner world of books. Transmuting this sandy metaphor, if literature is my sandbox, then the real world is my hourglass — an hourglass that drains grain by grain. Literature gives me life, and life kills me.

Well, life kills everyone.

But that's a morose subject. Tonight I feel alive — blue hair and red wine alive. The end of the year approaches, the beginning of a new year. The year is dead. Long live the year! I will begin my next project. This is the time that excites me most. I pay no attention to the Christmas decorations that burst into fruitful life in various neighborhoods of my city, or the lights welcoming the New Year. This year, Ashura falls at almost the same time, but I don't care.

Let the people flagellate themselves into a frenzy of remembrance. Wails, whips, blood: the betrayal of Hussein moves me not.

Let the masses cover themselves in gold, frankincense, and Chanel to honor their savior's birth. Trivia matters naught to me.

Beginnings are pregnant with possibilities. As much as I enjoy finishing a translation, it is this time that tickles my marrow most. The ritual of preparation: setting aside the two versions of the book of choice — one English, the other French — the papers, the notebook that's to be filled with actual notes, the 2B graphite pencils with the sharpener and Pearl eraser, the pens. Cleaning the reading room: dusting the side table, vacuuming the curtains and the ancient armchair, navy chenille with knotted fringes hanging off its arms. On the day of genesis, the first of January, I begin the morning with a ceremonial bath, a rite of scrubbing and cleansing, after which I light two candles for Walter Benjamin.

Let there be light, I say.

Yes, I am a tad obsessive. For a nonreligious woman, this is my faith.

This year, though, for the first time in quite a while, I'm not certain about the book I want to work with. This year, for the first time ever, I might have to begin a translation while having blue hair. Aiiee.

I've decided on Roberto Bolaño's unfinished novel *2666*, but I'm nurturing doubts. At more than nine hundred pages in both versions, it is no small feat, or no short feat. It will take me at least two years. Should I be taking on such a long-term project? Should I be making accommodations for my age? I'm not talking about dying. I am in good health, and women in my family live long. My mother is still going insane.

Let's put it this way: I don't hesitate when buying green bananas, but I'm slowing down. *2666* is a big project. *The Savage Detectives* required nineteen months, and I believe my work rate isn't what it was then. So I balk.

Yes, I'm healthy, I have to keep reminding myself. During my biannual checkup earlier this week, my doctor insisted that I was in sturdy health, like iron. He's right, of course, and I'm grateful, but what he should have compared

me to was rusty iron. I feel oxidized. What was it that Yourcenar, as Hadrian, wrote about physicians? "A man does not
practice medicine for more than thirty years without some
falsehood." My doctor has been practicing for longer than
that. We've grown old together. He told me that my heart
is in good shape, talked to me with his face hidden behind
a computer printout of my lab results. Even I, a Luddite,
haven't seen such archaic perforated printouts in years. His
mobile phone, a BlackBerry lying on the desk next to his left
elbow, was definitely the latest model, which should count
for something. I do not own one. But then, I have no need
for a phone, let alone a smart one; no one calls me.

Please, no pity or insincere compassion. I'm not suggesting that I feel sorry for myself because no one calls
me or, worse, that you should feel sorry. No one calls me.
That's a fact.

I am alone.

It is a choice I've made, yet it is also a choice made with
few other options available. Beiruti society wasn't fond of
divorced, childless women in those days.

Still, I made my bed — a simple, comfortable, and adequate bed, I might add.


I was fourteen when I began my first translation, twenty dull
pages from a science textbook. It was the year I fell in love
with Arabic — not the oral dialect, mind you, but the classical language. I'd studied it since I was a child, of course, as
early as I'd studied English or French. Yet only in Arabic
class were we constantly told that we could not master this
most difficult of languages, that no matter how much we

studied and practiced, we could not possibly hope to write as well as al-Mutanabbi or, heaven forbid, the apex of the language, the Quran itself. Teachers indoctrinated students, just as they had been indoctrinated when younger. None of us can rise above being a failure as an Arab, our original sin.

I'd read the Quran and memorized large chunks of it, but all that studying didn't introduce me to the language's magic—forced learning and magic are congenital adversaries.

I was seven when I took my first Quranic class. The teacher—a wide, bespectacled stutterer—would lose her stutter when she recited the Quran; a true miracle, the other teachers claimed. She had it all committed to memory, and when she recited, her eyes glowed, her scarf-covered head swayed on a shaky neck, and her pointing stick twirled before her. In the first row we covered our eyes whenever the pointer came too close—to this day, when I sit in the front seat of a car during a rainstorm, I'm afraid the windshield wipers might poke my eye. The teacher's stick may have appeared dangerous, but it was not what she beat us with. If we made a mistake in reciting, if a girl forgot a word or had trouble recalling a line, the teacher's cheeks contracted and glowed, her lips pursed and shrank; she'd ask the child to come to the front and extend her hand, and would mete out punishment using the most innocuous of implements, the blackboard eraser. It hurt as much as any inquisitor's tool.

As if forced memorization of the Quran—forced memorization of anything—wasn't punishment enough.

"Listen to the words," she exhorted, "listen to the wizardry. Hear the rhythm, hear the poetry."

How could I hear anything when I was either in excruciating pain or fearing that I might soon be?

"The language of the Quran is its miracle," she used to say.

Consider this: In order to elevate the Prophet Moses above all men, God granted him the miracle that would dazzle the people of his era. In those days, magicians were ubiquitous in Egypt, so all of Moses's miracles involved the most imaginative of magic: rod into serpent, river into red blood, Red Sea into parting. During the Prophet Jesus's time, medicine was king. Jesus healed lepers and raised the dead. During our Prophet's time, poetry was admired, and God gifted Muhammad, an illiterate man, with the miracle of a matchless tongue.

"This is our heritage, our inheritance — this is our magic."

I didn't listen then. The teacher frightened faith out of my soul. I didn't care that the Quran had dozens of words for various bodies of water, that it used rhythms and rhymes that hadn't been heard before.

Compared to the Quran's language and its style, those of the other holy books seem childish. It is said that after one glance at the Bible, the Maréchale de Luxembourg exclaimed, "The tone is absolutely frightful! What a pity the Holy Spirit had such poor taste!"

No, I might be able to poke fun at the Quran for its childishly imperious content, but not for its style.

It was finally poetry that opened my eyes; poetry, and not the Quran, that seared itself into the back of my brain — poetry, the lapidary. I'm not sure that the discovery of love is necessarily more exquisite than the discovery of poetry, or more sensuous for that matter.

I recall the poet who ignited the flame, Antara, the jet-black warrior-poet. I remember the shock of a doomed language being resuscitated.

*And I remembered you as spears quenched their thirst*
*In me and white swords dripped with my blood*
*So I longed to kiss the blades that recalled*
*The gleam of your smiling mouth to my mind*

Then again, maybe it was Imru' al-Qays. He and Antara are my preferred of the seven included in the legendary
Suspended Odes.

*But come, my friends, as we stand here mourning, do you see*
*the lightning?*
*See its glittering, like the flash of two moving hands, amid*
*the thick gathering clouds.*
*Its glory shines like the lamps of a monk when he has dipped*
*their wicks thick in oil.*
*I sat down with my companions and watched the lightning*
*and the coming storm.*

The language—we hear it all the time. News anchors
speak classical Arabic, as do some politicians, definitely
Arabic teachers, but what sputters out of their mouths
sounds odd and displaced compared to our organic Lebanese tongue, our homemade, homegrown dialect. Television and radio announcers sound foreign to my ears.
Those early poems, though, they are alchemy, something
miraculous. They opened my ears, opened my mind, like
flowers in water.

Yet my first translation was not a poem but twenty dull
pages. In the school I attended, the sciences were taught in
French. Rarely was Arabic used for physics, chemistry, or
mathematics in any of the schools of Beirut, whose main
curriculum has always been community conformity. It seems

that Arabic is not considered a language for logic. A joke
that used to make the rounds when I was a child, probably
still going strong: the definition of parallel lines in geometry
textbooks in Saudi Arabia is two straight lines that never
meet unless God in all His glory wills it.

The twenty pages were a curiosity; I wished to see for
myself. My first translation sounded odd and displaced as
well.

The translations that followed improved, I hope.

By improved, I mean that I no longer felt as awkward
about writing my name on what I translated as I did in the
beginning.


My father named me Aaliya, the high one, the above. He
loved the name and, I was constantly told, loved me even
more. I do not remember. He passed away when I was still
a toddler, weeks before my second birthday. He must have
been ill, for he died before impregnating my mother with
another, as he was supposed to, expected to, particularly
since I was female and first. My country in the late 1930s
was still trying to pull itself out of the fourteenth century. I'm
not sure if it ever succeeded in some ways. My father was
barely nineteen when he married and twenty-one when he
died, my mother a widow at eighteen. They were supposed
to spend aeons together. It was not to be.

What to do with a young widow? The families con-
vened. My mother's family, having thought they had one
fewer mouth to feed, now had two more. It is said that my
maternal grandfather hinted that they were given a defective
model. The families decided that the young widow would

be married off to her husband's brother and try once more, except she wouldn't receive a second dowry, her wedding gift. Three months after my father passed away—a three-month canonical period—my mother knelt obsequiously before a sheikh and watched as her father and second husband signed the contracts.

In time I was presented with five half siblings, none of whom I was particularly close to. Six children, one room, three narrow, lumpy mattresses on the floor; horizontal martial arts battles during the night, yawning bruised bodies in the morning.

My uncle-father was kind, if not particularly loving or affable. He paid little attention to his children, even less to me. I'm unable to recall much about him. I have no pictures of him, so in my memory his face is always obscured. In every evocation of a childhood scene, my stepfather's face is the least detailed, the most out of focus; when I think of him my memory's eyes have cataracts.

His sole remarkable trait was his unremitting passing of gas, which he had no inclination to control. Lunches and dinners, as the family sat on the floor surrounding him, were unbearable. The boys loved it, but I could barely eat after he broke wind. That's probably why I've been skinny all my life. To this day, there are certain human smells that make my stomach swirl.

At his deathbed, on a night drunk with cicadas, as the family sat in his room, he called on each of his children to offer final wisdom, but he forgot to call on his youngest daughter or me. The youngest was devastated, and all tried to comfort her. They surrounded her, cooed to her, smothered her with mollifying maxims, passed her their handkerchiefs. I wasn't distressed and none comforted me. No one passed me a handkerchief, not even a tissue. He had no wisdom to offer me; no one in my family did.

I am my family's appendix, its unnecessary appendage.

I was married off at sixteen, plucked unripe out of school, the only home I had, and gifted to the first unsuitable suitor to appear at our door, a man small in stature and spirit. Marriage is a most disagreeable institution for an adolescent. We moved into this apartment and it took fewer than four years for him to stand before me, as the law required, and declaim the most invigorating of phrases: "You are divorced." Nothing in our marriage became him like leaving it.

The impotent insect stepped out the door, and these floors never had to feel his feet again. Young as I was, I shed not a tear. I did what my nature demanded. I cleaned and scrubbed and mopped and disinfected until no trace of him remained, no scent, not a single hair, not a touch. I removed the nails on the wall where he used to hang his dirty hat and his pungent pipes that he thought made him distinguished. With a needle and spool of thread I repaired every hole in the doilies singed by the cinders of his pipe. I soaked the mosquito net in bleach.

I did not wait for the smell of him to dissipate on its own. I expunged it.


Before leaving this world, the listless mosquito with malfunctioning proboscis remarried twice and remained childless.

"Woman, you are divorced." Of course, he could have married over me and brought a second wife into our crumbly nest. Having more than one wife wasn't common in Beirut even then. He'd have been the only one in the neighborhood with two wives, but he could have done it.

My mother wanted me to be grateful. He may have rejected me as superfluous waste, he may have treated me as merely the dispensable product of his rib, but still I should be appreciative. "He divorced you. You can remarry a gentle widower or maybe a suitor of women more seemly who has been rejected a few times. Consider yourself fortunate."

Fortunate? For my mother, being a pathetic suitee was a cut above being a neglected second wife. She couldn't conceive of a world in which my husband didn't hold all the cards. In her world, husbands were omnipotent, never impotent. Mine thought of me as the cause of his humiliation and probably continued to blame his other wives. He couldn't risk having his women talk to one another.

I would have loved to chat with his second wife, or his third. Did he continue to wear his ridiculously large hat that cruelly emphasized his small head? I could have asked, "In all the years of marriage, did you ever see his penis? Did that shrively appendicle ever reach half-mast? When did he surrender? When did he end his fumbling humiliation in the dark? Was it a year, six months, a couple? I hazard it was merely a month. He pursued the charade for seven months with me."

In *The Science of Right,* Kant wrote, "Marriage is the union of two persons of different sexes for the purpose of lifelong mutual possession of each other's sexual organs."

Kant obviously hadn't met my husband.

Of course, like Descartes, Newton, Locke, Pascal, Spinoza, Kierkegaard, Leibniz, Schopenhauer, Nietzsche, and

Wittgenstein, Kant never formed an intimate tie or reared a family.

As a young woman, I was so frustrated never to have seen a man naked that I used to wait until my husband snored before lifting the covers, lighting a match within the enveloping womb of the mosquito net, and examining his body under his buttoned cottons. Ah, the disappointment of discovering a worm in place of the monster. Of this I was supposed to be afraid? This, the forge of fertility? Yet I couldn't rein in my curiosity. Ecce homo. I looked every chance I had, by the light of a match, not a candle, because when quickly extinguished its smoke was not as incriminating. The steady snores, the deep breathing, the lost world of sleep. Never once caught, never discovered.

Fifteen years ago, at sixty-one, my husband died, a solitary passenger on a public bus, his head leaning at an awkward angle against the murky window. The bus drove two full routes, passengers ascending and alighting, before the driver realized he was keeping company with a lifeless man. Sometimes death arrives quietly.

Wanting to put him to rest once more, I attended his burial, his final interment. No keening or wailing at his funeral. In the open casket, he lay dead. Someone had combed his hair flat and awkward, as if he'd just taken off his imbecilic hat. Seated all around me, the mourning women could not help but giggle and gossip. He had died with an erection that would not relent, priapism in the final throes, an irony worthy of Svevo.

In death Eros triumphed, while in life Thanatos had. My husband was a Freudian dyslexic.

Death is the only vantage point from which a life can
be truly measured. From my vantage point, as I watched
men I didn't recognize carry my ex-husband's coffin away,
I measured his life and found it wanting.

I realize that I haven't mentioned my husband's name.
It isn't intentional. It's just that I can call him *my husband*
and that defines him.

There are many reasons for not naming a character
or someone you're writing about. You might want to have
the book be entirely about the main narrator, or maybe you
want the character to remain ephemeral, less fully fleshed.

I have no such reasons, I'm afraid. He was Sobhi Saleh,
a leaden sound, unwieldy. Unfortunately, I still carry his
last name like a cross, nailed to it, you might say. His first
you can forget. We can jettison it under sea swells, bury it
under the silt of the Mediterranean.

Sobhi. Tfeh!

When I first married, though, life had possibilities. Beirut,
and this building, looked different in the early fifties. A
frangipani, long since disappeared, babbled mischievously
before the building, spilling fragrance and flowers as I entered. Across the street was a locust tree that has also van-
ished, uprooted. In the early evening, the neighborhood's
chatter of starlings hadn't yet been silenced. Among the
many definitions of *progress*, "enemy of trees" and "killer of
birds" seem to me the most apt.

When we moved in, the owner of the building, Hajj
Wardeh, his pale face sporting sunglasses, a bristle mustache, and at least three worthy warts, turned out with his

family to welcome my husband and me with rice pudding and rose water—an inappropriate double dose, I thought, since the pudding had more rose water than was necessary, and many a rose was beheaded for that dessert. I remember his perfectly tapering fingernails. I remember the first words out of his little daughter's mouth: "But she's much taller than he and skinnier." Fadia, forever long-tongued, was six then. I remember her father's embarrassment, her mother covering Fadia's mouth.

Hajj Wardeh said, "Welcome, family."

His title was recently and proudly acquired: he'd just returned from Mecca.

My black shoes were dyed earth red; I'd lugged two suitcases and several bundles, everything I owned, across town through a parasol pine thicket. Everything I owned including my trousseau: three dresses, one pair of shoes, three pairs of socks (not hose), underwear, two scarves, one gold chain, one bracelet, a brooch of crocheted cherries, two cooking pots, a serving dish that was slightly cracked, five plates, a copper and tin tureen and its ladle, a complete set of silverware for three people, my father's few things, and two textbooks from that year, which I knew I'd not use again.

I felt so rich then. The apartment seemed so wide and spacious. I look back now with longing.

From Pessoa: "Ah, it's my longing for whom I might have been that distracts and torments me."

Aaliya, above it all, separated, disentangled.

Many Muslim and Christian hajjis are masters of pious dissimulation who covet the title but not the path. Not Hajj Wardeh; he earned his title. He lived by Javertian principles. He was generous and neighborly at first, but once my husband walked out, he wanted nothing to do with me. I might as well have worn a scarlet letter. He forbade his children to interact with me. Fadia, who used to spend all her time in my apartment, began avoiding me, turning her back when I walked by. If she had to talk to me, she employed a haughty and authoritative tone, as if I were her scullery maid. She was only ten or eleven, already an autocrat. Just a bit of that belligerent childhood despotism passed into her adulthood — well, maybe a little more than a bit.

Even though Hajj Wardeh refused to acknowledge my existence in person, he took my side when it came to the apartment. My husband's family wanted it, claiming I had no right to it. My own family demanded it, suggesting that any of my brothers was more deserving of it. Hajj Wardeh would brook none of this. The apartment belonged to my husband, and unless my husband himself claimed it, or possibly his future sons, he would not release it to anyone. My husband, of course, could risk no such thing. As long as I paid my rent, Hajj Wardeh considered me his tenant.

My home, my apartment; in it I live, and move, and have my being.

My husband's family forgot about the apartment, but mine didn't. My mother couldn't look at me without trying to convince me to leave. My half brothers had large families living in small apartments. They needed it more than I did. They had more difficult lives, they deserved it. It was my familial duty. I was selfish, insensitive, and arrogant. Did I not know what people were saying about my living on my own? My mother was the young United Nations: leave your home, your brothers have suffered, you have other places you can go to, they don't, get out.

More than once, my half brothers cursed me. More than once, each one banged on my door in an attempt to terrorize me. Terrorized I was, particularly in the beginning when I felt most vulnerable and the fear of losing my home nibbled at me. I would be in the apartment eating or reading when banging and curses would suddenly erupt from behind the door. My heart would skip, my body would tremble. At times, during the early years of being alone, I felt as if my soul was withering, like a chestnut drying within its shell.

All that—the banging, the harassing, my brothers' demands—stopped years and years later, in 1982, during the Israeli siege of Beirut. Many inhabitants of the city had fled and squatters quickly took up residence in the empty homes. Those of us who remained, those who had nowhere else to go, were emotionally weary, fed but not nourished by fear and adrenaline. Thinking that no one was home, three men broke into my apartment in the early dawn. I hopped out of bed, still in my nightgown. There'd been no water for weeks; neither my hair nor my nightgown had been washed in ages. I picked up the AK-47 that lay next to me on the right side, where my husband used to sleep all those years earlier. It kept me company in bed for the whole civil war. Barefoot, I rushed out, brandishing the assault rifle. The men in fatigues took one look at the attacking madwoman and ran out the door—not silently, I might add. I chased after them, but only to the landing, since they'd already reached the ground floor, running in an unathletic manner—twelve independent limbs jerking and flailing haphazardly—a stampede of cartoon cows.

A shot fired from the fourth floor frightened me out of my hysteria. Fadia had aimed at one of the sandbags at the end of the street. Like me, she only intended to scare them, but she actually fired her rifle.

"Don't you dare come back," she shouted. "This is the smallest gun I have." Then, to her kids, "Get back inside. There's nothing to see here."

She too hadn't washed her Medusa hair or her tattered nightgown for quite a while. She probably looked as much a fright as I, but as usual, her fingernails were impeccably manicured. From two floors below, I was able to note the finely shaped scarlet nail of her forefinger pressing the trigger. From inside the apartment her husband shouted that she was insane. She blinked red eyelids at the limpid blue sky. I told her not to shoot anymore or the Israelis would bomb the building. It took her a moment to recognize me.

"That's a big gun you have there," she said.

Once the story of the crazy women went out, the maenads and their semiautomatic thyrsi, my half brothers stopped demanding the apartment.

Aaliya, the above, the crazy one.


I turn on the light in the reading room. Though it is barely seven thirty, the dark outside is oppressive. Winter is calling.

Ever since I retired, my dinnertime changes with the season. When I worked at the bookstore, I used to eat when I returned home, always at a fixed time. Since then, I'm not sure why, I feel hungry as soon as the sun sets and evening begins to fall. My stomach has its own circadian rhythm.

I feel tired, but it's too early for bed.

I decide against making myself a cup of tea. Caffeine in the evening throws my system off kilter, and I can't abide herbal infusions or the bland taste of the decaffeinated kinds. I say this as if my system were well balanced otherwise.

Of all the delicious pleasures my body has begun to refuse me, sleep is the most precious, the sacred gift I miss the most. Restful sleep left me its soot. I sleep in fragments, if at all. When I was planning for my later years, I did not expect to spend every night in my darkened bedroom, lids half open, propped up on unfluffable pillows, holding audience with my memories.

Sleep, the lord of all gods and of all men. Oh, to be the ebb and flow of that vast sea. When I was younger, I could sleep anywhere. I could spread out on a couch, sink into it, forcing it to enfold me, and disappear into the somnolent underworld. Into a luxurious ocean I plunged, into its depth I plummeted.

Virgil called sleep death's brother, and Isocrates before him. Hypnos and Thanatos, sons of Nyx. This minimizing of death is unimaginative.

"Nothing is less worthy of a thinking man than to see death as a slumber," wrote Pessoa. Basic to sleep is the fact that we wake up from it. Is waking then a resurrection?

On a couch, on a bed, in a chair, I slept. Lines would melt away from my face. Each quiet tick of the clock rejuvenated me. Why is it that at the age when we need the curative powers of slumber most we least have access to it? Hypnos fades as Thanatos approaches.

When I was planning for my later years, I hadn't considered that I'd be spending sleepless nights reliving earlier years. I hadn't thought I'd miss the bookstore as much as I do.

I wonder at times how different my life would have been had I not been hired that day.

I love Javier Marías's work. I've translated two of his novels: *A Heart So White* and *Tomorrow in the Battle Think on Me*. I'll consider a third after I read the French translation of the final volume of *Your Face Tomorrow*, although at more than thirteen hundred pages, I'll probably balk at that as well.

But I digress, as usual.

In one of his essays, Marías suggests that his work deals as much with what didn't happen as with what happened. In other words, most of us believe we are who we are because of the decisions we've made, because of events that shaped us, because of the choices of those around us. We rarely consider that we're also formed by the decisions we didn't make, by events that could have happened but didn't, or by our lack of choices, for that matter.

More than fifty years ago, on a gloomy day when hope followed my shrimp of an ex-husband out the door, or so I thought at the time, my friend Hannah led me by the hand to a bookstore owned by one of her relatives. The relative, a second cousin once removed, had opened the bookstore as a lark, a ground-floor store with an inadequate picture window in a distressed building off a main street and no foot traffic. There were more stupid stuffed toys than there were books, and everything was covered with dust. The bookstore had as much chance of making it as I did.

Yet of all things, the flint that sparked a flame in my soul was the huge, darkly stained oak desk where the owner sat. To a practically penniless twenty-year-old divorcée,

sitting behind such a desk seemed so grand, so luxurious —
something to aspire to. I needed grandeur in my life.

Hannah told her relative he should hire me, and he
informed her that he wanted to hire someone with more
experience and, just as important, with more class. He spoke
as if I weren't there, as if I were invisible, as if his face were
hidden behind a perforated printout. Hannah, my champion,
wouldn't accept defeat. She explained that I loved books
and read constantly, that I knew more about them than he
ever would, and, just as important, that I could dust and
clean and scrub and mop. He'd have the cleanest bookstore
in the city, I piped up, the most sparkling, a diamond. I
would rid it of its acrid and musty odor. He pretended to
mull over the offer before deciding to hire me for the time
being (still talking to Hannah and not me), until he could
bring in someone else to be the face of the bookstore.

What I didn't know at the time was that the first face
he offered the job to belonged to a pretty girl whose family was so classy that they immigrated to Brazil and one of
their scions had recently become the governor of São Paulo.
The girl left without ever showing her countenance in the
bookstore. The second didn't show up either; she married
and no longer needed or wished to be employed.

Had either of these women made an appearance, my
life would have been altogether different. I didn't realize
how the fate of those two had influenced mine until a few
years ago when the owner mentioned it in passing. He hadn't
thought for a moment that I could do the job. He credited
my success to his diligent training.

I worked for the paperback dilettante for fifty years, and
mine was the only face anyone associated with my bookstore.

❀   ❀   ❀

That huge, darkly stained oak desk I once longed for now sits comfortably in my reading room, behind it a window letting in early evening darkness, and next to it my overfilled bookcases. When the owner, my boss, died four years ago, his family closed the bookstore, sold the books and inventory for a pittance. I ended up with my desk.

How safe I will feel once I begin my translation, how sheltered, seated at this desk in the dark night, as Sebald as Jacques Austerlitz described, seated at this desk "watching the tip of my pencil in the lamplight following its shadow, as if of its own accord and with perfect fidelity . . . from left to right" — right to left, in my case — "line by line, over the ruled paper."

On this oak magnificence I place the new notepad, next to the pencils, next to the pens. I unscrew the primary pen, an old Parker, and inspect the ink. The walnut-shaped inkwell, a fake antique of porcelain and copper, is lushly full. It is always a delicious thrill when I prepare for a new project. I feel at home in my rituals.

The real antique on the desk is a comic book, an illustrated *A Tale of Two Cities* in Arabic, wrapped in red cellophane. Its value is sentimental only. It was woefully damaged — four pages missing, two torn, others water stained — when I received it some sixty years ago.

It was summer, I was ten. My mother took her children to the public garden of Beirut. I had only three half brothers by then, I think, the youngest still in the pram. I may not remember my siblings clearly, but I do the day and I do the dress I was wearing, my best one, a blue taffeta with white trim. It came with a white plastic handbag that wouldn't unsnap and was, in any case, too small to hold anything but a lonesome stick of gum. I remember clutching it to my right hip at all times. I remember the sky as clear and breezy, the whitish sun lazy and indifferent, neither too warm nor too bright. My mother—hunched over, her knees touching, both feet on the ground—sat on a wooden bench that was painted an overworked brown and was missing a board in its backrest. My half brothers and I clustered around her, planets orbiting our tired star. *Shoo, shoo.* She wanted us away. We weren't used to being around strangers.

In tentative steps with tiny feet I did separate, slowly and hesitantly, but I did.

A chestnut-haired boy, plump and pale, with eyes the color of newly pressed olive oil, sat forlorn, all alone on a bench, longingly watching gaggles of dizzyingly loud children rush about on bicycles, tricycles, and those topless, floorless miniature red cars. The lonely boy looked a few years younger than I. Rolled up in his hand was the comic book that lies on my desk right now.

I envied him. I wanted that comic book more than I'd ever wanted anything.

I asked him if he wanted to play. I used the word *play*, I remember that, giving him the option of choosing what game he wanted. He lit up, flushed as if he'd drunk a glass of Bordeaux. He did want to play, most certainly he did. He nodded and nodded and nodded. I asked if he was willing to share his comic book. He didn't mind at all, he let me hold it. My dress had no pockets because it came with a purse that didn't open. I gave it to him, my purse. A fair trade, no? He laid it on the bench and neither one of us noticed or cared when it disappeared. We played tag. My half brothers joined us, and others did as well. He had a good time. He left us grasping his mother's hand and waving wild good-byes, a wide smile turning his double chin into a triple. I remember his jolly face, his joy, and his lovely smile to this day. There must be a reason that this survives so clearly in my imagination.

I went home with my comic book, my mother giving me a tongue-lashing for losing the plastic handbag.

How would I ever grow up to be a proper lady?

There's another relic on the desk, though not as ancient, a souvenir from the war years in Beirut: a copy of Calvino's *Invisible Cities*, scorched in the lower right corner, but just the back cover and the preceding twenty-two pages. The front isn't damaged. I was reading the book by candlelight while people killed each other outside my window. While my city burned, I had an incendiary mishap, something that seems to have happened regularly to Joseph Conrad—the incendiary mishaps, not the burning cities.

The burning city, what a time. I have to mention here that just because I slept with an AK-47 in place of a husband dur-ing the war does not make me insane. Owning an assault rifle was not an indicator of craziness. You had to consider the situation. In the early days of the civil war, I used to descend to the garage beneath the building next door when the shell-ing began; our building didn't have one, being a decade older. I hated those nights. Residents of the neighborhood, anx-ious and sleep deprived, sat around the rodent-resplendent garage in inappropriate dress: nightgowns, boxer shorts and undershirts, holey socks. I spent many a night there in the beginning of the war, until one day in 1977, while I was underground, a group of Palestinians broke into the apartment, rummaged through my belongings, and one of them defecated on the floor of the maid's bathroom. That was the first break-in.

You might think that the Palestinian chose not to use the toilet because I had no running water. He might have felt it was beneath him to use the bucket filled with blue water — I'd hung toilet cleanser inside it — to flush. Not so; it was not uncommon for men to do such things. Israelis left their shit in houses they broke into; Palestinians left their shit; the Lebanese, the Iranians, the Syrians; Christians, Jews, Muslims. For man, this urge, which had been deposited in his cells at Creation, would forever be bestially liberated during war. It said: *I was here, like it or not.* I am told that toddlers in China do not wear diapers; their pants have a vertical opening along the seat making it easier for them to crouch and excrete. All soldiers should wear pants with slits.

Someone shat in my home. I procured a Kalashnikov.

I waited for a lull. After the incident, I was unable to sleep for three days, and no longer descended into the bowels of the neighboring building when the shelling gained heft and weight. I would choose to die with my apartment rather than live without it. In the margins of morning, I crouched behind my window and observed teenage Thanatophiles with semi-automatics running cockroachy zigzags. Moonlight on hand-me-down rifle barrels. As nebulae of flares colored indigo skies, I saw stars blinking incredulously at the hubris below. Set on low, my kerosene lamp murmured all night, acting as white noise. I waited and waited, kept company by a ticking clock whose dials glowed a phosphorescent lime green in the dark. I sat by the window, household chores not done. On my bulky couch next to the bulkier television, I watched my city, my necropolis, broil and crumble.

On the morning of cease-fire number 53,274 (the earlier one lasted all of thirty seconds, the one before that probably even less—okay, okay, so I exaggerate, but there certainly were more than one hundred cease-fires by 1977, two years into the war), I changed out of my nightgown into a pink tracksuit and espadrilles. Across the street, the Dexedrined Thanatophiles were playing poker, with matchsticks as chips, on a green felt folding table with slender legs, in front of Mr. Azari's grocery store, the true litmus test of whether a cease-fire would hold—the store, not the card game, for Mr. Azari was intimately connected to various militia leaders. The store was the war's weather vane. If its poison-green shutters were shut, no one ventured out of the house. If they were open, the neighborhood wasn't in imminent danger. By my count, there were five bullet holes scattered across the metal shutters. Mr. Azari waved at me, obviously wanting to talk, but I only nodded in his direction and rushed past. I berated myself for not being friendlier, for not trying harder to make him like me, since he hoarded food and water from his meager stock and offered it to his preferred customers. I reasoned that I would never be one. His favorites offered him home-cooked meals, and I was a mediocre cook. I was lucky, though; Fortune watched over me. Fadia was by far the best cook in the neighborhood, and fed him constantly. Since the war began, he had gained fifteen kilos. I may not have been Fadia's favorite person, but I was her neighbor and tenant (she'd inherited the building after her parents' deaths).

A few mornings a week, I'd wake to find on my doorstep a couple of bottles of water, maybe a sack of rice, sometimes a bag of fresh tomatoes or a few oranges. After nights when the clashes were fiercer than usual, she'd leave a dish of the same meal she offered Mr. Azari. With the first bite, I would turn devout and pray for her welcome into Paradise or God's bosom or any beauty spa she chose.

Instead of going to open the bookstore, I took a bedraggled jitney to Sabra. No Lebanese car would drive into the Palestinian camp's labyrinth once the civil war erupted, so I got out at the entrance. I had the need of Theseus and the knowledge of Ariadne, no ball of yarn for me, so I sought the Minotaur, not to kill him, but to ask for his help. I sought Ahmad.

Ahmad's mother lived in a shack, or, to be more precise, a jerry-built structure consisting of a concrete wall onto which three sidings of asbestos and corrugated iron were jammed, with a tin roof on top. Its door, also of shingles, was not hinged; you simply removed it to walk in or out and replaced it when through. No lock needed since neighbors were atop one another; if anything went missing, all knew which neighbor had borrowed what. I'd been there once before, years earlier, at which time six people lived within the structure. I only had to deliver a book, a present for Ahmad's seventeenth birthday, and didn't enter even though his mother, kind and gentle at the time, kept insisting that I honor her with my presence in her household.

What was difficult before the war, navigating the maze of alleys, had become tribulation. Puddles that used to form

only after rainfall had become permanent lakes of sewer-
brown, the stench suffocating. My thighs were sore from
being unnaturally stretched with each lake-avoiding step. I
had to maneuver my way around heaps of discarded furniture, rotted beams, broken plates, and twisted silverware.
A giant eucalyptus, seemingly the only living thing in sight,
added to the confusing aromas (shit and Vicks); it flourished
in its exotic environment, dwarfing the surrounding shacks
of brick, of cement, of aluminum siding, even cardboard.
A happy and content immigrant, proud of its achievement
and splendor, the tree would probably have laughed off any
suggestion of returning to Australia. Its sadly hued green
appeared bright against the poverty of color, all faded grays
and dirty whites. If only someone had planted a bougainvillea; it would have flourished in these fecund crannies.

When Ahmad's mother, who'd metamorphosed into a
small bundle of jerky gestures and imprecations, answered
the shingles door, she said that her ungrateful son hadn't
lived there for years. I should tell the coldhearted mother-
hater that the woman who conceived him, the woman who
carried him for nine painful months and cared for his every
need as he grew up, needed bread.

Ahmad had moved up in the world, out of Sabra.


Forgive me a brief digression here. It's only to offer you a
fuller idea of Sabra.

Years later, after the war, in the midnineties, a local artist asked me to help him sell prints of a map of Beirut and its
suburbs that he had lovingly painted by hand. He was obviously smitten with our city. He'd painted Beirut as if it were

the whole world, complete within itself, each neighborhood a different country with its own color, streets as borders, the tiniest road documented, every alley, every corner. He'd even drawn in little hydrographic symbols (fleurs-de-lis) where all the water wells are supposed to be — Beirut, whose name is derived from the word *well* in most Semitic languages because of the abundance of its belowground water.

A complete sphere, Beirut as the total globe, the entire world. The painter even created a Greenland effect, stretching the longitude lines at the top and bottom, with increasing distortion of size as one moved north or south of the city. In the map, Beirut existed outside of Lebanon, apart, not part of the Middle East. It was whole.

As a Beiruti through and through who in a long life has spent only ten nights away from the suckling breasts of her city (Grünbein: "Travel is a foretaste of Hell"), I considered the map a chef d'oeuvre, a stunning, glorious work of inspiration. The more I lauded, the wider his smile. We stood side by side in my bookstore, staring at the print I had hung on the wall. He tried to light a cigarette, but his hand shook too much. I told him he couldn't smoke inside. He confessed nervousness. I led him outside, carrying the map. "Let's see it in Beiruti daylight." In front of the store window, he shrugged off his uneasiness and regained confidence. I noted that the streets of Sabra were not named and were less delineated than the other streets.

"I tried," he said, "but everything worked against me. The streets were impermanent, transmogrifying at night into something else as if to trick me." The books behind the glass window were witnesses to what he said next: "The streets and alleys of Sabra multiply at night like rats — like rats, I tell you."

He had painted the Sabra camp a very light blue, like
the Siberian tundra in some maps. The cartographer must
have been loath to include the camp in his map. I considered giving him Bruno Schulz's book, which negotiates a
similar situation. Schulz wrote: "On that map . . . the area
of the Street of Crocodiles shone with the empty whiteness
that usually marks polar regions or unexplored countries
of which almost nothing is known."

Ah, *Cinnamon Shops* is still one of my favorite books.
That map of Beirut still hangs on my bedroom wall.

Sabra? I haven't been back there.


Back to Ahmad. I first met him when he was a timid teenager in 1967, lanky and wispy, a character out of a Chekhov story, with peach fuzz and kaffiyeh, trying to emulate
his hero Yasser (George Habash and the Popular Front,
which was beginning to form that same year, wouldn't come
into his life for a while yet). He wore bone-framed glasses
that were too big for his face. I didn't notice him standing
before my desk until he ahemmed. I was confronted by
the smell of licorice and anise, his tooth-crushing candy
drops. He was sent to me by another bookstore in the city,
told that no one else could help him. He was looking for
a book by an Italian, but couldn't remember the title or
the name of the author. He had to give me a little bit more
to go on, I told him. Italians had been writing books for
hundreds of years.

He said, "The hero of the book was not a hero, he killed
many lizards."

I didn't laugh, but my eyes must have betrayed me. He blushed and backed up a step. I walked him over to a stack and handed him *The Conformist*.

"The lizards are in the early pages of the book," I said. He held it in his hands as if it were the Quran. Did I have it in Arabic? I didn't think it had been translated (I wouldn't translate it because I found it didactically dull, not that I would have showed him the translation had I done one). His English wasn't very good.

"I'm not a teacher," I said. "Reading a book would definitely help your English."

Was it all right with me if he examined it to see if he could read it?

I returned to my desk. He sat on the floor leaning against a bookshelf, his legs splayed before him, the rubber soles of his shoes facing out, conspicuously visible. Three books faced out as well, *As I Lay Dying*, *Goodbye, Columbus*, and *A Moveable Feast*, the last two having recently arrived in Beirut. Separated by the spines of other books, they formed a triangle that floated atop his head. It was only then that I understood he couldn't afford to buy a book, any book. The army pants he wore were neither a fashion nor a political statement—they were inexpensive.

I asked if he had killed lizards when he was a boy. He asked for the meaning of the word *magpie*, the word *austerity*, and the word *covet*.

I liked him.

He loved the book, finished it in twenty-three days (the bookshop wasn't open on Sundays). He appeared every afternoon, sat in the same spot. On the infrequent occasion

that I had a customer when he arrived, he'd sheepishly wave
and tiptoe to Moravia's book, which he'd returned to its
position the day before. By the second week he began to
do little things around the shop, by the fourth he was sign-
ing for deliveries. I tried to have him hired, but the owner
refused. I needed the help. I was the only employee. If I was
sick, the bookshop didn't open.

"Give him part of your salary," the owner replied. "The
bookshop isn't a moneymaking enterprise. It's a labor of
love."

Not exactly. I provided the labor, I provided the love,
and he enjoyed the fugitive cachet of owning a bookstore.
Ahmad worked in the shop without pay for four years. He
didn't seem to mind. He helped me whenever he could, sat in
his spot and read during slow periods. He came and went
as he pleased, may not have been punctual, but he was fer-
vently devoted to the bookstore, to his reading, desperate
to educate himself. When I apologized for working him
without pay, he replied that sons always worked without
recompense.

One day he decided to paint the interior of the shop.
He'd ended up with free cans of light lavender paint. It seems
someone at the refugee camp had bought them for a bargain
before realizing that no one would want their walls that
color. Ahmad left the spaces behind the stacks unpainted
because we didn't have enough cans. I loved the color and
kept it till the bookshop closed and I retired.

I relied on him. A few young men used to trickle into the
bookstore before his arrival, solitary and in groups, without
any intention of buying books. With a single woman working at the store, a boy could practice flirting, try his luck. I

dealt with them by ignoring them. They were harmless, but I found them irritating. My friend Hannah, who often visited me at the store, found them amusing. She didn't interact with them, but her face lit up whenever one of the lads walked in. Ahmad, on the other hand, considered them offensive. He glared, followed them around until the offenders left the bookstore. One time after he chased two teenagers out, Hannah asked him if he was sure that they were not going to buy anything.

"They only wish to harass respectable ladies," he said.

"Are you sure respectable ladies don't wish to be harassed?" she said. "I don't know about Aaliya here, but maybe I want to talk to a handsome young man, just a few words here and there."

He looked up at both of us and smiled for the first time that day, his glasses sliding a little along his nose as he did so.

"If you talk to one," he said, "you wouldn't be able to get rid of him. He would never leave."

He left me sometime in 1971 because the traumatic events of Black September the previous fall forced him to reevaluate his priorities. The killings in Jordan probably convinced him that books would not open the door to his cell. In this world, a cause could—a cause could swing prison doors wide open. I mourned his loss.

Even though I believe that the choice of a first book, the book that opens your eyes and quickens your soul, is as involuntary as a first crush, I still wish he'd chosen a different one. He loved *The Conformist* and saw himself as utterly unlike its protagonist, but in light of what he would mature to become

in later years the choice now seems so pathetically predictable, almost a cliché. The Popular Front for the Liberation
of Palestine, as Marxist-Leninist as it may have considered
itself to be, was a mirror image of Mussolini's Fasci Italiani di
Combattimento. Political parties may argue, yell and insult,
punch and kick each other, launch grenades and missiles; it
is naught but Narcissus's silly gesturing at the pool's image.

Ahmad was sure he was different from Marcello, the
protagonist of *The Conformist*, who has no moral core, who
is a follower, who has no independent personality. Ahmad
claimed to be an individualist.

There is none more conformist than one who flaunts
his individuality.


Let me revisit the events of Black September, not so much to
paint the political or historical landscape, important though
that may have been in changing Lebanon and sending it into
the abyss of civil war, but to show the changes in Ahmad. I
wish to paint the transformation of his face.

I am familiar with only the broad strokes of his background. His family hailed from a small village east of Haifa,
expelled by the Yishuv during the Nakba of 1948 (his terms,
not mine). The village was leveled and erased from all but
the villagers' memories. He was born in Sabra. His family,
uncles and aunts, were dispersed across refugee camps in
southern Lebanon, Jordan, and the West Bank.

In September 1970, Jordan was in turmoil. Palestinian fedayeen were launching operations from that country, and Israel was retaliating—excessively, as has always
been her wont—by bombing Jordan. The Palestinians were

practically running the country, a state within a state. Feeling threatened, King Hussein of Jordan declared war upon them. Scores and scores perished. The conflict, the death and dying, lasted until July 1971 with the expulsion of the PLO and thousands of Palestinian fighters to Lebanon.

Lucky us.

During those months, Ahmad changed. He considered the king an Israeli agent, an American lackey. If brother could kill brother, then anyone was suspect, anyone and everyone. He was devastated. Already taciturn, he turned practically mute. He wasn't sullen as a teenager, but became so. He withdrew unto himself. His skies clouded with black.

But his face.

His face.

Joseph Roth once wrote: "It takes a long time for men to acquire their particular countenances. It is as if they were born without their faces, their foreheads, their noses or their eyes. They acquire all these with the passage of time, and one must be patient; it takes time before everything is properly assembled."

Ahmad acquired his countenance during Black September. His eyebrows wove together, almost becoming one, giving him an expression of permanent starkness. There was no need for patience before everything was assembled. Once the transformation began, it was quick and hurried. I could almost see each eyebrow hair stitch across the bridge of his nose. Disappointment hid in the tiny furrows of his forehead, fury in the corners of his mouth. The eyes darkened, the skin tightened; he lost what little baby fat he had, and the bones beneath his face grew more defined. The peach fuzz became a beard.

For a while, he still showed up at the bookstore, but he was no longer accessible. It was as if I became part of the problem, someone to mistrust, the other. We shared the same space, but no longer the attentiveness, the empathy, or the companionship. We were like a married couple. I didn't understand why he kept returning for those few months after Black September, but I wanted him to. I felt he needed me to be there in some inexplicable way.

One day he entered the bookstore in high sulk, and I noted that the transformation was complete. He reeked of testosterone. I also noted that the army pants were no longer the cheap kind. I felt crushed.

I looked him up and down, from the boots to the kaffiyeh. He smirked, turned around, showing me his back, and exited the bookstore.

He left me.

A few years later I went looking for him.

Yes, Ahmad had moved up in the world, out of Sabra, out of Siberia. By 1977, when I knocked on his door, he was living in a lively neighborhood of Beirut, far from the camp. He was still a vivacious picture of youth, but there was nothing peach-fuzzy about him. I had to remind myself that the peach fuzz was already gone the last time I saw him. At twenty-six or twenty-seven, he was in his prime, and amid a frenzied civil war, he was in his milieu: the slacks pressed and tailored, the white shirt fitted and expensive, the face smiling and clean-shaven. A zebra skin on the floor of the entryway greeted me, and it felt

as though Ahmad had flayed the prey before breaking
his fast that morning. The anteroom was bigger than his
mother's shack.

I was slow to understand, it took me a few minutes,
that he was relishing what he considered a role reversal.
Of course he'd help me. Whatever I wanted. I had always
been kind to him. Sit, sit in the majestic living room, plush
seats. I sat ensconced within a room of Balzacian embel-
lishments — a cloverleaf of small Lalique ashtrays, Lladró
and Hummel figurines approximating a modernist Nativity
scene, a grandfather clock, a rug that might have been twice
my age at the time.

He inquired whether I'd had breakfast. "Yes," I replied,
"I ate two days ago."

"Wonderful," he cheered, "wonderful."

Did I care for coffee?

A maid from the Philippines brought out the coffee. I
couldn't disguise my surprise.

"It must be worse where she comes from," he explained.
"They have their own wars."

One sip and I cut to the point. I told him I wanted to
protect myself. I'd had intruders in my home. He lit up,
happy to help. He suggested the AK-47: cheap, reliable,
never jams, easy to use, lightweight. They were flooding the
market; he had three of them in his apartment. I wanted to
pay for one. He couldn't take my money, but I could give
him what he'd always wanted.

What did he want?

"You know what I want," he kept repeating, "you know
what I want."

It seemed suddenly as if the two Ahmads, the young shy one and the older rough one, were struggling, a soul battle. He'd grown both more confident and more bashful. He'd only briefly look at me before his gaze dropped to his loafers. When nervousness used to smite him years earlier, his gaze would drop to my shoes, not his.

"You know what I want."

I didn't. I racked my brain. What was he talking about? He always used to want books, but not in a while. He couldn't blurt out what he wanted from me, could not enunciate desire. I stared, thought, actually scratched my head. Finally, as if inspiration had descended from above, I asked the most inconceivable of questions: "You want sex?"

It was what my Ahmad wanted.

"With me?" It was my turn to keep repeating—"With me? With me?"—like a silly Swiss cuckoo clock.

Why? I was a mess. I stank of sewage. I looked like the witch from Hansel and Gretel. I was forty. I was wearing a pink tracksuit, with swirling sequins no less. I didn't even have lipstick on.

He had a shower.

"A shower?"

He nodded.

"Hot water?"

Ahmad must have killed many a lizard. During the war in Beirut, the powerful had power, but only those with true power had water.

I laughed, a bit nervously, dislodging air and apprehension from the nooks of my lungs—laughter of agreement. He met my eyes, more confident, delighted, having read the signs of my capitulation. They say laughter is the ultimate conjoiner.

I knew what Ahmad was. I'd heard rumors, mysterious stories, most too strange to be believed. One of the war's preeminent torturers, he was called Mutanabbi (he could make a mute speak, a variation on the poet's most famous stanza), an apropos literary nom de guerre, while other torturers chose generic names like Kojak, John Wayne, Belmondo, Jaws, or Cowboy. I knew the rumors to be true the instant I saw the apartment, and if not the apartment, every rumor would have been confirmed by the bathroom — marble, stainless steel, hard lines (to use Nabokovian and not Balzacian descriptions).

I knew, and I agreed to what he wanted. It was probably I, not Marcello or Ahmad, who had no moral code.

I wanted a gun. I wanted a shower. I made a choice. This could be a problem, being intimate with an almost intimate, but I decided to let him worry about things, let him contemplate if he chose to do so. I would not. I refused to be embarrassed. The water called my name.

The shower felt like a monsoon: hot, succulent, and baptismal. As filth dissolved off my skin, as grime emigrated, I felt rejuvenated, I was reborn. The near-scalding water changed my body from rigid to supple, turned my skin the color of a pink peony. My senses were sharpened. I used Ahmad's razor to shave.

Drying myself with the luxurious towel was as close to a religious experience as I was ever likely to have. He waited for me in the bedroom; he fully dressed, I wrapped only in luxury. Excessive light. The Lladrós on the nightstand were bathed in molten sunlight gold. I nodded my head toward the translucent curtains. Ahmad rushed to draw them, plunging the room into demidarkness. The Ahmad I knew had momentarily returned, astonishingly sensitive, servile and compliant, content and optimistic. Toward the bed I tiptoed barefoot like a thief wishing not to be discovered, wishing not to arouse noise or echoes.

Before I unwrapped, I turned the Lladrós around. He must have thought it was excessive shyness. It wasn't. I preferred not to have ugliness stare.

He said I was beautiful. I told him the figurines weren't. He moved around the bed and scooped them all into the wastebasket. Once more, he lied and said I was beautiful. I told him I was alive.

From Donne:

*Love's mysteries in souls do grow,*
*But yet the body is his book.*

Ahmad was not the first, nor would he be the last. He was surprised I didn't lie down like a corpse. I wished to tell him that though I was by no means an experienced lover, I had been intimate with a few. I had studied Georges Bataille and Henry Miller, submitted to the Marquis, devoured the racist *Fear of Flying*, and cavorted with lewd Arab writers of the golden age who constantly thanked God for the blessing of fucking, al-Tifashi, al-Tijani, and al-Tusi, ibn Nasr, ibn Yahya, and ibn Sulayman; so many had taught me. I wanted to tell Ahmad that he shouldn't have interrupted his studying. I wanted to tell him that it was Moravia, his deflowerer, who had written about the natural promiscuity of women. I did not, none of it.

How can one describe the ephemeral qualities of sex beyond the probing, poking, and panting? How can one use inadequate words to describe the ineffable, the beyond

words? Those salacious Arabs and their Western counterparts were able to explain the technical aspects, which
is helpful, of course, and delightful. Some touched on the
spiritual, on the psychological, and metaphor was loved
by all. However, to believe that words can in any way mirror or, alas, explain the infinite mystery of sex is akin to
believing that reading dark notes on paper can illuminate
a Bach partita, or that by studying composition or color
one can understand a late Rembrandt self-portrait. Sex,
like art, can unsettle a soul, can grind a heart in a mortar.
Sex, like literature, can sneak the other within one's walls,
even if for only a moment, a moment before one immures
oneself again.

I was intrigued enough by the strangeness of the situation that my memory retained a few palimpsests of the
lovemaking, early images, when everything was technical or
mechanical. Memory chooses to preserve what desire cannot
hope to sustain. The images I retain, though, couldn't have
happened. In my memory, I can see myself with Ahmad, as
if a part of me participated in the encounter and another
floated high in the air, near the ceiling, and witnessed with
disinterest.

Aaliya, the high one — Aaliya with the bird's-eye view,
above the mud and muck and life's swamps.

What seeped through the mortar of my walls was not
his technique (adequate) or his ardor (more than). I was on
my knees facing away, he behind me still smelling of licorice
and anise, engaged in an age-old rhythm. He slowed, and his
fingers explored the topography of my lower back. I could
feel his face descending, examining a tiny city on a map. His
fingers squeezed gently before he removed them. At first,

I tried to dismiss this interruption, considered it a possible sexual quirk, but his fingers resumed the exploration of the region, lower back and upper derrière. His fingers squeezed once more, and this time I realized what he was doing, I recognized the feel of a blackhead being extruded. When he removed a third, I looked back, and it was more likely that I'd have turned to butter than to salt. He apologized, begged my forgiveness. It had been unconscious. He couldn't see a blackhead on his own skin without removing it and didn't realize he was doing the same with me.

I asked him not to stop. I loved it.

His fingers happily reconnoitered my entire back, delicately, gently, and ever so slowly turned my skin into a smorgasbord of delicious feelings. I was touched. I buried my face in the pillow to hide my ecstasy and my tears.

My heart had momentarily found its pestle.

Ecstasy and intimacy are ineffable as well, ephemeral and fleeting. Ahmad and I didn't repeat our interlude, never resumed the exploration. He won what he wanted, as did I.

Yeats once said, "The tragedy of sexual intercourse is the perpetual virginity of the soul."

We lie down with hope and wake up with lies.

When the warlords ended their interlude a few days after, I felt protected within the walls of my apartment, sat vigil with the Kalashnikov close to my bosom.

Aaliya, the high one, the separate.

I, Aaliya, the aged one, should get to bed—lie in my bed, call upon the gods of rest, instead of sitting at my desk remembering.

The receding perspective of my past smothers my present.

Remembering is the malignancy that feasts on my now.

I feel tired and weary, my mind leaden, my hair still blue.

And so the days pass.

My bedroom is quiet except for the flapping of laundry in the breeze, sails of minor ships in soft gusts; the building behind me has verandahs on every floor (ours has none), and each has multiple laundry lines. I don't mind these night sounds; I call them organic white noise. My bedroom has quieted over the years as Joumana's family upstairs and Marie-Thérèse's downstairs grew up and the rambunctious children departed. For as long as they lived below, Mr. Hayek had unidirectional screaming sessions with Marie-Thérèse at least once a week, throughout their marriage, until he died last year. I heard Fadia once say that you can tell how well a marriage is working by counting the bite marks on each partner's tongue. Mr. Hayek had none. He held nothing back. You can't do anything right. You always say the wrong thing. Why can't you do what I tell you? You're so frustrating. It was like listening to a less witty *Who's Afraid of Virginia Woolf?* with a mousy, mute actress playing Martha.

It is much quieter now.

It's much easier to sleep now, if only I could.


I had a troubling night. I must have dozed off briefly, because in the early morning my heart found itself disquieted by a short unrestful dream — not one with my mother, the protagonist of my most disturbing dreams, but one about Hannah, probably the woman my mother disrespected most in life, and in death.

How does this memory of mine work? How it betrays me. What thunderous ministorms of neurons were fired in my mind during the dark of morning, what ghosts!

While I dozed, Hannah materialized—healthy, younger, in her late thirties—and it seemed irrelevant at first that she was much younger than I. My almost sister-in-law appeared corporeal and sturdy, yet somehow askew, resembling a posthumous oil portrait more than herself. She wore one of her familiar unshapely dresses, fine linen and purple. There was an affectionate formality in the way the arms of a black sweater crossed around her shoulders, in the care of the woolly knot's placement and position. Her shoes, not her face, were furrowed with wrinkles. Her gaze was kind, open, and amused.

"Sweetheart," I said softly, extending my hand toward her cheek. "No one wears her hair like that anymore." She grinned and I answered with my usual smile that begged forgiveness. She made an appearance to offer me courage, and I worried about her appearance. Shame. Such a worrywart I am. I miss miracles blooming before my eyes: I concentrate on a fading star and miss the constellation. I overlook dazzling thunderstorms worrying whether I have laundry hanging.

The archipelago of liver spots on the back of my hand kept distracting me from her face. I jerked it back, covered it with my left, and held both like a bouquet of prayers before my heart. She ignored me and walked toward the lieutenant, her husband-to-be, her husband-who-never-was. He was much younger than she in my dream. She kissed him, which couldn't possibly have happened while she was alive, and he returned her kiss, matching passions. She undressed him with uncommon verve, her kisses deeper, her lust brazen.

An observer would receive the wrong impression from this salacious tableau. Their ages were wrong, I thought. Incompatible. Insidious Nabokov insinuated himself into my dreams once more, not allowing me to lose myself in watching what was before me, not allowing me to engage life. Hannah was Humbert, the lieutenant the ingénue. Fire of my loins. They fucked, no other term can be used. Hannah and her lieutenant fucked and fucked.

Why Hannah? Why now?

There was a time when nary a minute passed without my thinking of her, without my wondering about her last days, her consummate loneliness and how well she masked it, her insatiable longing. She'd come into my thoughts unsought, uninvited. Maybe Hannah and her ghost stayed away before this morning's dream because they felt sorry for me in my old age, for me and my weary remembrance, maybe they felt it necessary, if only to relieve me of one of my grotesque obsessions. You have to move forward, try to live.

But life isn't necessarily as considerate as its ghosts, or as compassionate.

Nor is it fair.

"She was Lo, plain Lo, in the morning, standing four feet ten in one sock. She was Lola in slacks. She was Dolly at school. She was Dolores on the dotted line." I won't translate *Lolita* even though I've always wanted to. It's against the rules. Nabokov's earlier work in rowdy Russian I could. "But in my arms she was always Lolita."

"Lo. Lee. Ta."

My memory has aged into an unruly child but is still quite precocious.

It is the loneliness, the abject isolation. Hannah reappears in my memories to remind me of how alone I am, how utterly inconsequential my life has become, how sad.

I have reached the age where life has become a series of accepted defeats — age and defeat, blood brothers faithful to the end. I struggle to get out of bed, as I do every morning. Still night outside, no light trickles through the short slats of the bedroom's wood shutters. I've been awake for over an hour, probably more. I move my feet toward the edge of the bed and lower them to the carpet, which helps me sit up with less effort. Ouch. I extend a sleepy arm and turn on the bedside lamp, a fifty-year-old relic that barely functions, one of the first possessions I bought on my own.

Barely functions, like me: swollen limbs, arthritis, insomnia, both constipation and incontinence, the low and high tides of aging nether regions. In my morning veins, blood has slowed to the speed of molasses. My body is failing me, my mind as well. When my body functions, it seems to do so independently of my desires, and my mind regularly forgets what those desires are, not to mention where I've left my keys or my reading glasses. One could say that every day is an adventure.

I sit up tentatively, rest my feet on the night carpet next to the bed, the first of many offerings from Hannah. It is a peculiar prayer rug, small and handwoven, Persian or Afghan, with a miniature qibla compass at the top so I can spread it to the east. The compass still points eastward, but the rug does not. It does prevent my feet from facing the cold floor every winter morning.

I stand up carefully, lean and twist to stretch my back. The lower back pain isn't necessarily age related — I've lived with mild back pain for years. What has changed is the complexity of the knots: in my younger years the back muscles felt like a simple bowline knot, whereas this morning they feel more like a couple of angler's loops and a sheepshank. I'm able to name a few knots used by sailors, but I have never been on a boat. Joseph Conrad's novels planted the seeds of love for sea stories. Annie Proulx's *The Shipping News* led me to read *The Ashley Book of Knots*.

I am a reader. Yes, I am that, a reader with nagging back pain.

When my bones ache or my back rebels, I consider the hurt punishment for the years of alienating my body, even dismissing it with some disdain. I deplored my physicality when I was younger, and now it deplores me right back. As I age, my body demands its rightful place in the scheme of my attentions. It stakes its claims.

The mind over body then, but no longer.

Aaliya, above it all. Aaliya, the separated.

Aaliya, Aaliya, über alles.

Sad, sad, sad.

I walk gingerly toward the door, probably looking like a waddling gnome. My bedroom is one of the safe spaces in the apartment from which I've banished mirrors. In one of her books, Helen Garner says that all women over sixty instinctively learn to pass by a mirror without looking. Why risk it is what I say.

Of course, by avoiding my reflection, I end up ignoring Rilke's exquisite admonishment:

*Though the reflection in the pool*
*Often swims before our eyes:*
*Know the image.*

How lovely that is!

I'll move more gracefully, or less awkwardly, in a few minutes, once my muscles and joints have warmed up.

I flick on the ceiling lights in the kitchen, boil water for my tea. As the stovetop flame wavers livid and blue, the bulbs in the ceiling hiccup once, twice, and die, as does the one streetlight outside. The government electricity is down again. The building's generator won't be turned on until at least six A.M., until someone else wakes up, most likely Marie-Thérèse, who calls for one of her roaming cats every morning, which wakes Fadia, who'll turn on the generator.

I'll wait in the dark for the lights to come on. I'm used to it.

Without power, night is night once more, not the cheap imitation that passes for night in a modern city. Without electricity, night is the deep world of darkness once more, the mystery we dread.

Darkness visible.

My city seems to be regressing to an earlier age. Barely functions.

A hospital in town recently had one of its wings remodeled to what they call "super ultra deluxe," which means that you have to hock your jewelry just to breathe the air inside.

The floors are parquet, the pillows down, and all the technology is the latest, including bathrooms with toilets that use motion detectors to flush. What no one took into account is that the detectors go berserk and have to be recalibrated every time the electricity cuts off and the generators take over. Since it's Beirut, this has to be done twice a day if not more. The hospital had to hire an in-house toilet calibrator.

Darkness risible.

As I sit in the dark kitchen sipping darker tea, I think in a flash of an evening long ago, when I was still a child — must have been winter as it is now; it was dark early. The meal, simple and barely enough to feed the family, waited impatiently on a big brass tray sitting atop a round burlap ottoman. The apartment wasn't large enough for a dining table and six children. My mother refused to feed us until the return of her husband, a tailor's assistant in a downtown shop, as he remained until he passed away. The moment my mother heard him turn the key, she stood up. The electricity went out, plunging the room into blackness and causing my mother unspeakable distress, for her husband might injure himself entering a dark room. As she ran to greet him, warn him, and guide him, her leg knocked the tray, which flipped and banged my half brother the eldest on the head; he'd used that instant cover of darkness to sneak a slice of white cheese. Food landed all about us like shrapnel.

"Don't move," warned my mother, "don't you dare move."

She tottered blindly into the kitchen, returned with a fluttering kerosene lamp. We remained stock-still, but entering the apartment, her husband stepped in the spilled olive oil. When he moved his shoe away, we could see a footprint stain in the carpet. All of us knelt and began to pick up food — cheese, black olives, radishes, sliced tomatoes, white onions — only the olive oil was unsalvageable. We sat around the tray and ate our dinner silently. All evening, my mother's cheeks blushed a deep red that could be noticed even in the low light of the lamp.

My books show me what it's like to live in a reliable country where you flick on a switch and a bulb is guaranteed to shine and remain on, where you know that cars will stop at red lights and those traffic lights will not cease working a couple of times a day. How does it feel when a plumber shows up at the designated time, when he shows up at all? How does it feel to assume that when someone says she'll do something by a certain date, she in fact does it?

Compared to the Middle East, William Burroughs's world or Gabriel García Márquez's Macondo is more predictable. Dickens's Londoners are more trustworthy than the Lebanese. Beirut and its denizens are famously and infamously unpredictable. Every day is an adventure. This unsteadiness makes us feel a shudder of excitement, of danger, as well as a deadweight of frustration. The spine tingles momentarily and the heart sinks.

When trains run on time (when trains run, period), when a dial tone sounds as soon as you pick up a receiver, does life become too predictable? With this essential reliability, are Germans bored? Does that explain *The Magic Mountain*?

Is life less thrilling if your neighbors are rational, if they don't bomb your power stations whenever they feel you need to be admonished? Is it less rousing if they don't rattle your windows and nerves with indiscriminate sonic booms just because they can?

When things turn out as you expect more often than not, do you feel more in control of your destiny? Do you take more responsibility for your life? If that's the case, why do Americans always behave as if they're victims?

Hear me on this for a moment. I wake up every morning not knowing whether I'll be able to switch on the lights. When my toilet broke down last year, I had to set up three appointments with three plumbers because the first two didn't show and the third appeared four hours late. Rarely can I walk the same path from point A to point B, say from apartment to supermarket, for more than a month. I constantly have to adjust my walking maps; any of a multitude of minor politicians will block off entire neighborhoods because one day they decide they're important enough to feel threatened. Life in Beirut is much too random. I can't force myself to believe I'm in charge of much of my life.

Does reliability reinforce your illusion of control? If so, I wonder if in developed countries (I won't use the hateful term *civilized*), the treacherous, illusion-crushing process of aging is more difficult to bear.

Am I having an easier time than women my age in London?

Marie-Thérèse calls for her cat to come home, the daily aubade. The uncaring, intricate world begins to rouse. In time the curtain edges will grow light.

"Maysoura!" Marie-Thérèse's voice has risen in volume since her husband passed away. "Maysoura!"

I don't understand why she allows her two cats to roam the streets of our neighborhood. Beirut isn't a pet-friendly city. Like my mother, Marie-Thérèse loves cats. However, my mother never owned a cat; she showered her love on the city's ferals.

The generator comes on with its soft hum. Fadia must have awakened. I don't turn the light on, remain in the not-quite-as-dark.

I think of Brodsky:

*I sit by the window. The dishes are done.*
*I was happy here. But I won't be again.*

The sun rises, and the kitchen takes shape, revealing its details. The awakening of my city is more beautiful to my eyes, and to my ears, than the breaking of dawn in some bucolic valley or sparsely populated island paradise, not that I've actually been to a bucolic valley or an island paradise. In my city, the sun multiplies its effects on the myriad of windows and glass in colorful reflections that make each morning distinct. The faint light creeps through the window, curious to see what is happening in my kitchen. It falls across my face and falters. I make myself stand up. I sway a little, lean on the wine-red and urine-yellow abomination of a breakfast table that my husband brought with him when we were married and left when he left. I shake the loose folds of my robe de chambre. Dust motes hang thick in the air. The kitchen has two windows on adjacent walls. A spider with shockingly long front legs busies herself with prey caught in her web. All that remains is a wisp of gossamer with striated veins. The spider chose the wrong window; her home will be washed away with the first rains. I stretch on my toes, draw back the short drapes of the second window, and unveil more morning light. I allow brightness to flood the kitchen from both sides. I slide open the pane for the first time in a couple of days. This window looks onto the outdoor stairwell, and my neighbors are able to quench their curiosity as they *click-clack* up and down. A slight breath of air makes the stagnant motes waver; a handful of sunlight kindles them golden and luminous.

Apollo, ever the alchemist, still sails his chariot in the skies of Beirut, wielding a philosopher's stone. Into gold I transmute the very air.

*You must change your life.*

The surprising sound of Marie-Thérèse's strapless sandals floats through the window — surprising since my downstairs neighbor hasn't made the trek upstairs in a long while. After she passes the window, I lean over to observe. She doesn't seem to be dragging her shadow and isn't wearing a mourning dress. It takes me a moment to remember that this is the day after the one-year anniversary of her husband's death. As my heels return to the floor, I realize my neck has stiffened.

Fadia's voice descends from above. "Well done, my love, well done. I'm proud of you." The voice sounds invigorated, as if its owner has been dunked in an Italian fountain of joy.

The coffee klatsch is reuniting this morning. Good for them.

The three witches have been having syrupy coffee
together every morning for almost thirty years. On the
third-floor landing, in front of Joumana's apartment, my
neighbors gather around the round brass tray, smoking,
gossiping, and getting ready for the day. Marie-Thérèse
hasn't sat on her stool at all in the last year—a bit too much
mourning, if you ask me, but understandable. That she's
making the trek upstairs is a grand occasion.

"You light up the day," Joumana calls down. Her voice
rings out along the stairwell and drops right into my kitchen.

It's a glorious, gilded Levantine morning.

The acoustics in the building are such that in my kitchen
I hear every word spoken on the landing. Every morning,
I hover intimately among my neighbors. I hear the clink of
cups on their saucers, the clank of saucers on the brass tray,
the pouring of the coffee, their sacred ritual—"irrigating the
Garden," Joumana calls it. I hear them chatter and gossip:
Have you heard this? Can you believe that? They curse enemies and laud friends. I hear every sigh and giggle. I listen
to them make plans, compare notes, exchange recipes, and
exhibit every newly purchased inessential.

Years of conversation.

So many mornings: Fadia unleashing her frightening
trademark laugh, a crackling falsetto exhalation that makes
her elongated throat swell and undulate like a baker's bel-
lows, a wild and epidemically infectious laugh, and she's
prodigal with it. Joumana's husband putting his head out
the door; he good-mornings the women, jokes with them,
and shouts down to Mr. Hayek, Marie-Thérèse's husband
and tormentor, in the apartment below mine to make sure
he's ready for their walk to the American University, where

they both teach. Joumana teaches at the university as well, but she drives her car and never rushes her coffee. She pokes fun at the men because most days they walk in a dawdling mosey and she picks them up along the way. "They want exercise," she says, "but not perspiration."

Poor Mr. Hayek no longer makes that walk.

I pick a fragrant mandarin out of the bowl, poke a hole in its bottom with my finger, and begin to peel. I pour myself a second cup of tea.

"I'm so happy you're out of mourning," Fadia says. "A year is too much."

I concur, of course. A year is too much if you loved your husband. It is much too much for Mr. Hayek.

"I understand why you chose to do it," Fadia goes on. "I'm with you, my love. But I say six months — six months is more than enough. I loved my husband, everyone will vouch for that, but I couldn't keep wearing black."

"I didn't mind the black," Marie-Thérèse says. A loud car horn from the street obscures her next sentence.

"It's better that you took it off," Joumana says. "He'd have wanted you to. Your husband hated black."

"And don't wear those black nylons anymore," Fadia says. No car horn, no backfiring truck or rumbling motorcycle, is able obscure her voice. "Although they do cover a lot."

"Fadia!" Joumana admonishes.

"What? Don't look at me like that. Fadia tells the truth. You know that. I think we could all use a little depilation. That's all I'm saying. Am I lying? Tell me. No, I most certainly am not. We all need a good pedicure as well. Am I right? Am I right? This evening we'll all go to the salon. Just

the essentials, that's all. Top to bottom. And you know, my
love, unshaved legs are contagious. If we don't do something
about yours, who knows what will happen to mine? It's even
worse with unpedicured nails. Look, look." Fadia's voice
hoots and shrieks. "The color is chipping as we speak. We
need an emergency intervention." Fadia, who always enjoys
her own joke, laughs, the crackling falsetto.

"Girls' night out," Joumana says.

"We can be young again," Fadia adds.

At sixty-two, Fadia is the eldest of the three. I, of
course, am much further along. She isn't aging gracefully;
she fights every slight sign of decay with vigor and bitterness. Her makeup keeps getting thicker and her fashions
more adolescent, a late desperate grasp at a fondly recalled
youth. Even so, she looks younger and fresher than Marie-
Thérèse, ten years her junior, who is aging without bitterness
and with obvious resignation. Her elbows have collected as
many furrows as a walnut, as many furrows as mine. She's
become a paltry imitation of what she once was. Her eyes
settled into incuriosity a long time ago.

Marie-Thérèse has an inscrutable face, a life-is-but-
a-dream look giving the impression that she wishes not to
be disturbed by disturbing realities — a mask, really, for the
impression is not true, the facade doesn't match the house it
conceals. For some reason she reminds me of the girl Fernando Pessoa tried to befriend, the single romantic liaison
in his life. I can't tell you why. I don't know what that girl
looked like. I'm not sure anybody does. I can't even remember her name — Blanca, Maria, Francesca? My memory
wishes to frustrate me this morning. The girl worked in the
same import-export office as my poet, and he considered

asking her out, or whatever hopeful twosomes did back in 1929 Lisbon.

I must say, I imagine that Marie-Thérèse looks like that girl as she aged, not as she was when the genius considered her.

Of course, Pessoa didn't go out with that girl, didn't do whatever they did back in 1929 Lisbon. Her name was Ophelia Queiroz. I am growing senile. Forgetting an Ophelia? The liaison's brevity was due to the malicious interference of none other than Álvaro de Campos, Pessoa's own creation, one of the seventy-two literary identities he used, the bisexual dandy who loathed Ophelia and believed her to be a distraction to Pessoa's literary ambition. He wrote the poor girl and told her to flush any ideas she had about a relationship with Fernando down the toilet.

There is no evidence, at least none that I know of, that Ophelia had any idea who Fernando was, let alone that he spent his time inventing literary personas that wrote some of the great masterpieces of the twentieth century. She worked in the same clerical office, but I can't imagine that they ever exchanged words. I can't imagine him exchanging words with anybody.

Fernando died in relative obscurity, a virgin and a recluse.

I thought I'd be reading a new book today, but it doesn't feel right, or I don't feel like it. Some days are not new-book days.

After reading Sebald yesterday, I realized that translating *Austerlitz* was an easier project than *The Emigrants*, possibly because the latter laid the bitumen, smoothed the ride, for *Austerlitz*. A troublesome issue arises in translating Sebald into Arabic. His style, drawn-out and elongated sentences that wrap around the page and their reader, seems at first glance to be an ideal fit for Arabic, where use of punctuation is less formal. (Translating Saramago's *The Year of the Death of Ricardo Reis* was a relative breeze.) However, Sebald's ubiquitous insertion of Jacques Austerlitz's tongue into the unnamed narrator's first-person narrative was difficult to convey precisely, since Arabic, like Spanish, drops pronouns more often than English or German. Sebald's *I* spoke for at least two people.

The above problem has invaded my thoughts like algae this morning. I'll reread my translation of *The Emigrants*, which I haven't looked at in years. I must examine how I solved the problem then. But first I must bring it forth out of storage.

I don't wait to finish my tea before searching for a flashlight — from the dark I come and into the dark I return. I have two flashlights, but can't find either. Both are in the kitchen, I'm certain of that. I count to ten before searching once more, repeating every step in case I missed something the first go-around, returning to where I've been before. In vain. I down my tea, place the cup in the sink, and wax two candles onto the saucer. The rim of the saucer's depression is lightly discolored — a dusting of rust and red and brown, remnants of teas gone by that did not wish to be washed away, refused to be forgotten, the age rings of a small plate. The maid's room, barely larger than the boxes stored in it, is in the back of the kitchen behind the maid's bathroom. I live in an ambitious building: all four apartments have identical layouts, with midget maid's quarters, yet no resident has ever had a live-in maid that I know of. The room has no light; its ceiling bulb expired years ago. I am tall, but I'm uncomfortable with heights. I depend on a handyman to change high lightbulbs, hence the need for a flashlight or candles.

I begin the march toward the room, saucer and candles in hand, a breath of smoke and sulfur in my nostrils.

Crates fill the maid's bathroom. No need for candles in here. No shower, no bathtub, just a low metal spigot and a drain, toward which the tiled floor is slightly angled. A street-facing lofty window, a wedge of early northern light, illuminates the cartons of manuscripts. The toilet has three boxes stacked atop one another. These aren't what I'm looking for; these are boxes from the last ten years, overflow from the maid's room.

The windowless maid's room devours light and messes up my circulation. It has been more than a few years since I've opened the door — since the room overflowed into the bathroom, I no longer enter as often. The room induces an irrational heart. Sometimes upon entering, my heart works so hard it reaches the point of seizing. Other times, it thumps so joyfully it approaches the point of bursting. On still other occasions, it slows to the beat of torpor and dies out. This morning the veins in my temples throb with a big, blooming, buzzing confusion.

"Irrational heart" — I love the phrase, read it in *Murphy* years ago, and it carved itself a prominent place in my memory. I could also have written that my heart behaved "like a rocket set off," from Welty's "Death of a Traveling Salesman."

I'm unable to translate Beckett because he wrote in the two languages that I don't allow myself to work from.

Early on, I decided that since some Lebanese can read English or French, I wouldn't translate writers who wrote in those languages; might be a somewhat arbitrary decision, but a necessary one I felt. Restricting choices is not always a bad thing. I have never translated a French writer, an English writer, or an American one. No Camus, no Duras, no Faulkner, no Welty, no Hemingway (thank the Lord), and not the young writers I admire, Junot Díaz (wonderfully macaronic language) or Aleksandar Hemon (macaronic in a single language). My self-imposed rules meant that I couldn't translate some African writers, say J. M. Coetzee, Nadine Gordimer, or Nuruddin Farah, since they wrote — write — in English. No Australians, not Patrick White, whom I adore, not David Malouf. I can't translate Milan Kundera, the Czech, because he wrote and rewrote the French versions of his books, nor can I work on Ismail Kadare, because the English versions of his novels were translated from the French, not the original Albanian.

However, I'm fluent in only three languages: Arabic, English, and French. So I invented my own special system: to achieve the most accurate representation of a work, I use a French and an English translation to create an Arabic one. It is a functional and well-planned system that allows me to enjoy what I do. I know this makes my translation one step further removed from the original, like Kadare's English novels, but it is the method I continue to use. Those are the rules I chose. I became a servant, albeit voluntarily, of a discipline, a specific ritual. I am my system, and my system is me.

I wouldn't translate Beckett's *Murphy* even if it were written in another language, say Serbo-Croatian, because I dislike the novel. I've read *Waiting for Godot* three times and I still can't tell you what it is about. If, as some critics claim, it is about being bored while waiting for God to return, then it's even duller than I thought.

Crates, crates, boxes, and crates. The translated manuscripts have the two books, French and English, affixed to the side of the box for identification. Tolstoy, Gogol, and Hamsun; Calvino, Borges, Schulz, Nádas, Nooteboom; Kiš, Karasu, and Kafka; books of memory, disquiet, but not of laughter and forgetting. Years of books, books of years. A waste of time, a waste of a life.

Sebald's box lies atop Nooteboom's, under three other translations. I place the saucer of candles on a pile. I take the top boxes down, making sure they don't fall on me. Sebald is weighty, as if it added heft during its perfectly sedentary lifestyle all these years. I can barely carry it, so the saucer is out of the question. I blow out the candles, throwing the maid's room into darkness, just the smell of smoke and must and dust.

After one of the Palestinian fighters defecated on the floor of this bathroom, a hand's width south of the drain, I spent hours on my knees cleaning the soil of the soldier, the silt and dregs. I used a coarse wire scrubbing brush, like a blackboard eraser, most innocuous of instruments. Out, out. Even though no trace remains, I always step over the spot as if it were an Israeli landmine —*upborne with indefatigable wings over the vast abrupt*. The passel of Palestinians didn't steal much, there wasn't much to steal — there was never much of a market for books.

I place the heavy box on the floor next to the reading armchair. With a slightly damp cloth, I wipe off the dust. I tear open the masking tape and remove the lid. The reams of paper are there, of course, just as I left them so many years ago. I remove a short stack from the top. The first page has the title of the book in Arabic written in indelible ink, Sebald's full name, and mine, Aaliya Saleh, below it, a bit smaller. The sheet is slightly brittle at the edges, nothing too worrisome. I stretch my back and consider whether I want another cup of tea before delving into Sebald's world of melancholy.

I shouldn't have opened the door, should have looked through the peephole, but I certainly wasn't expecting my half brother the eldest to appear. I haven't seen any of my half brothers in years, and none has been to my home in a decade or more. Yet I should have known it was he. I'd heard Fadia's voice say, "Trouble," when my doorbell rang. From the landing, she has an unobstructed view of my door, my comings and goings. He rang the bell, and because my movements have slowed and it took me a few extra seconds to get to the door, he rang the bell once more, a longer, more persistent ring. My half brothers, like so many men and boys, have the impatience of the entitled.

He bristles with fury in the doorway, carrying two old-fashioned suitcases, aged but not worn. His wrinkled face is deformed by unchecked emotion and fat, his body by the weight of the suitcases. He huffs and puffs, displays the anger of Achilles and the countenance of the little pig. His square head, his face, and his neck flush and blotch with red — a bloated, color-saturated Cubist figure. He storms in, drops the suitcases, slams them onto my floor.

Even under nonhostile circumstances, each of my half brothers has the ability to induce jitters in me. This is more than simply hostile. I can feel the room's temperature rise. My tongue tastes of copper, which means I'm overbreathing, getting ready for fight or flight, ready to pick up my sword or jump on my horse. I slow my inhalation. I focus on calming myself.

I gently ask him what he's doing.

"Dropping off your mother," he replies. "It's your turn. We shouldn't be taking care of her. She's your responsibility. You're her daughter and you don't have a family. You were supposed to be taking care of her for all these years. It's time, it's your turn. We can't do it anymore." He doesn't yell, but waits for me to contradict. He wants a reason to shout.

I don't give him one.

He takes a cigarette from a pack in his shirt pocket, holds it between his dry lips, dangling weakly, but he doesn't light it. He's a once-strong man reduced to mere rough and vulgar: doughy neck, broad shoulders, soft chin, eyes ringed with fatigue, distracted comb-over. His brown polyester pants, from a different suit than the jacket and vest, flap and squeal as he paces the foyer. He stares me down, waiting for me to cower. I do.

I cower because even though he looks like a parody of a tough guy — always did — I knew him once to be dangerous and menacing. At the beginning of the civil war in 1975, he put on the cheap camouflage outfit of one of the militias, a tragicomic dress rehearsal. Don't ask me which militia. I didn't care then and I don't now. He looked like a caricature, his spindly torso (not fat then, just slightly convex) decorated with medals and his shoulders with betassled epaulettes, triumphantly imitating Napoleon, the Corsican Comet.

Bluster and hubris, that's what he was, what he is, but that's what makes him more dangerous in some ways.

Think Bush—that indecent amalgam of banality and perdition.

*How nations sink . . .*
*When Vengeance listens to the Fool's request.*

An unpleasant thought.

Whenever I think of Bush, I think of an image: a shattered visage in the desert sand.

*My name is Ozymandias, King of Kings:*
*Look on my Works, ye Mighty, and despair!*

A more pleasant thought.


My half brother the eldest frightens me. He didn't while we were growing up; then, he only irritated me. We shared a mattress and I regarded him as nothing more than a space eater. He was obtuse, careless, and, according to my mother, infallible. He found inordinate pleasure in practical jokes and all manner of horseplay. He cultivated an obscene satisfaction in bullying his younger siblings.

After my husband left me, my mother did her best to convince me to follow him out the door and leave my home. She suggested that I exchange apartments with my half brother the eldest—his was small, fit for a lonely one; mine was larger, fit for a still-growing family, which included her, of course.

"Look at how many rooms you have," she used to say. "How greedy do you have to be? How selfish?"

At first, I argued with her, but then I noted that it was more effective to ignore her, to allow her tongue unlimited flapping until it flagged. When it became obvious that her words weren't having the desired effect, my half brothers jockeyed into the conversation. Each began to involve himself when his family increased its numbers—irresponsible reproduction being the family's ennui annihilator.

My half brother the eldest first appeared at my door after the birth of child number two or three—I should know which because I was there at the hospital for the birth (I was still not ready to abandon the family completely). Bluster and hubris. He wasn't able to talk then, to converse or negotiate, but simply began shouting, demanding that I do the right thing. I stopped opening my door when I knew it was he. My half brother the eldest banged his simian chest and cursed outside. He terrified me, an incontinent terror.

He returned and returned, again and again, the big bad wolf scaring me with his obstreperous threats, but you know, that worked against him. You not only inure yourself against the fear, finding it bearable after a while and coming to terms with it, you also absorb it. I absorbed it. It belonged to me and I to it; faithful companions, sisters, my fear and I.

I remained afraid, but I was no longer scared. Children get scared. With every return, with each bang on my door, my fear and I matured a little.

Before the AK-47, I waited with a sharp chef's knife next to me (I wasn't much of a cook, but I found a chef's knife the most versatile). I waited, walked in circles, ovals, and squares, moved from room to room in my spacious apartment carrying the knife. Just in case. I don't doubt that had he ever broken into my home, I would have stabbed him. I was that afraid. The imbecile.

My half brother the eldest's first job was as a doorman at a three-star hotel. He loved it because of the uniform, felt it gave him some class, some cachet. The peasantry, when it wishes to escape peasantry, has always, for centuries, across all borders, escaped into a uniform. That was the only paying job he's ever had, he loved it that much, but in the early days, he had a lot of problems with one of the managers, who mistreated him, he felt. Unfortunately, I may have unintentionally added to those problems. It seems the manager didn't trust some of the employees, my half brother in particular. He'd wait at the employee exit and search certain people as they left, probably looking for towels, linens, or miniature toiletries. My half brother the eldest felt humiliated, and to his horror, one day as I was walking home from the bookstore, I saw him standing outside the hotel's back exit, his arms and legs spread, the hotel manager kneeling before him patting him down.

Rage veined his face when he saw me.

Sad, because in that moment I felt sympathy, compassion even; in his vulnerability I identified with him, I saw him as family.

By the time the war started in 1975, I'd stopped inviting my mother to my apartment. I'd call her and she'd join me in one of the cafés on Hamra Street. One day her son and a group of his friends dropped her off. They were wearing imitation military outfits, driving a beat-up convertible and not a Jeep.

When the car stopped, my half brother the eldest looked my way and whispered something to his friends, who sniggered. They looked less like militiamen than like a group of fraternity brothers out on the town, naive hooligans, ill-mannered boys trying to look suave. I could see them in bright red suede windbreakers and flower-patterned silk shirts with wide lapels. My half brother looked to be the eldest of the group, a man playing at being a boy. He had already begun to collect medals.

"He sleeps with them on," my mother told me as we ordered our coffee.

I couldn't tell from her straightforward tone whether she was proud or dismayed that her son kept the intimate company of fake medals in bed.

Sleeping with the medals was not what horrified me. She informed me that he had captured an Israeli spy and they'd dealt with him. She used the innocuous word *dealt*. I tried to extract more information but she knew nothing. Boys' dreams are mothers' nightmares, but in my mother's case, her boy's dreams were her oblivions. I couldn't imagine my half brother being able to deal with anything more complicated than opening car doors for his betters.

In the newspaper a few days later, there was a small item saying that the hotel manager had been found dead on a side street, bound and tortured. I couldn't imagine my half brother killing the man. He was too much of a coward. I could, however, imagine that he lied, that he informed others about his nemesis, that he poured pestilence into the ears of a future politician, that he witnessed the elimination of his humiliator.

Do no harm to your fellow man unless he's your boss.

I tried to imagine that I was mistaken, or, if not, then to justify his actions in my mind. This was during a civil war when innumerable crimes were committed — crimes that made my half brother the eldest's seem like lunch-recess pranks in comparison. Vengeance was in the very air then. To quote the poet Czesław Miłosz, during the Lebanese civil war, "causing someone's death was dissociated from the reek of demonism, pangs of conscience, and similar accessories of Shakespearean drama." Young men in perfectly clean uniforms were able to shoot people while gnawing on a kebab sandwich and sipping Pepsi.

I tried to justify but I couldn't.

I don't know what to think.

He may be my half brother, but we're not related. A chasm of incommunicable worlds lies between us.

When my stepfather died, my half brother the eldest magically morphed into the man of the house that he had never moved out of. My mother went on living with him. She wouldn't have considered living with me, nor would I have wished it. My mother loves her sons only and never cares to be discreet about it. She treats her youngest daughter as a second-class citizen, a second-gender offspring. I, her eldest, hardly register in her consciousness. Once I stopped trying to impress myself into her life, she forgot about me. If she considers her youngest daughter Fanny Price, I'm her Quasimodo, to be confined in the bell tower.

For my half brother the eldest to bring her to my home means that every one of his brothers has adamantly refused to take her off his hands.

I tell him, calmly, that I don't think it's feasible. I'm about to suggest that she won't be happy when I see her standing in my open doorway, held erect by my sister-in-law. My mother, alarmingly fragile in all black, is hunched over, as if she has walked out of Goya's *A Pilgrimage to San Isidro*. The face has the paleness seen in skin long hidden from the sun. Hair is still dyed black, fading, with a thumb's-width vein of white at the roots. She barely keeps her head up; breathing is an effort, as is living. The lines of her body, of her form, seem to have melted; for a moment, incongruously, as light streams through the door behind her, it seems that I can see both the front and the back of her. My mouth drops, my shoulders droop. My mind becomes congested, jammed with feelings and thoughts that I can't formulate nimbly enough. I haven't been in her presence in so long. I've forgotten how scrambled my brain becomes when she's around. My sister-in-law walks my mother gingerly into the foyer, holds her tightly like an overboard sailor clutching a piece of driftwood, but also delicately, as if she's gossamer. My sister-in-law's wedding band glimmers as her fingers wrap around my mother's elbow.

I receive a whiff of the musty, sour odor of my mother's age.

"She belongs to you now," my half brother says. The wormlike vein in his temple throbs and thickens.

"She's yours now," my sister-in-law says, spitting the words out of tightly pressed, raggedly crimsoned lips. Her mousy face reddens, like a wet shirt brightens on a laundry line.

My mother, a modern-day succubus, has the ability to drain my soul and my voice without having to resort to something as rudimentary as a kiss. But I can't allow this charade to go on much longer. I take a long motivational breath.

"No," I say, in a low, sticky tone. "She is not mine."

My mother raises her wraithlike head and looks at me. Her furrowed face contorts, shrinking the wrinkles and multiplying them tenfold. Her mouth draws open in toothless horror. Her gnarled hands rise, her palms face me, warding off evil. My mother tries to pull back from her daughter-in-law's arms. The black shawl drops from her bony left shoulder, but doesn't fall off completely. Her eyes display strident, unspeakable dread. She screams, a surprisingly loud and shrill shriek. From such a frail body, a defiant skirl of terror that does not slow or tire.

None of us budge; in a well-lit 1950s foyer we stand like Italian terra-cotta sculptures, Renaissance, all of us terrified, my mother screaming and screaming. The normally invisible dust in the foyer dances and prances in the light, mocking the immobility of the humans.

Her body exudes a cold of ancient winters. The chill rises up from my feet. I shiver and tremble.

My half brother the eldest finally turns to me, his hand palming his right chin; his body, his face, the age-old universal pose of the horror-struck. "What have you done?" he asks, while my mother screams some more.

Nothing. I'm still in my nightgown and robe de chambre, for crying out loud.

Nothing. I've done nothing.


Fadia storm-troops across the foyer, her clogs loud enough to be heard alongside the scream, but not till she is almost upon me does she ask, "What is happening here?" Her eyes are questioning, more surprised than anything. Eyelids already hued with blue eye shadow, azure—not fully made up yet, but on the way. Her lips are outlined with black eyebrow pencil, but not filled in with color. Girlish golden hoops adorn her ears.

"She doesn't recognize you," shouts my sister-in-law, still holding my mother. "That's all. She doesn't recognize me most of the time either. It's nothing. She'll get used to you. I know she will. She has to."

"Can someone shut her up?" yells Fadia, her open mouth showing teeth stained by nicotine. "My nerves can't handle this."

I can't tell whether Fadia means the screamer or the speaker. No one is asking about my nerves.

I notice that my upstairs neighbor Joumana has entered my apartment as well. Marie-Thérèse remains in the doorway, curious but considerate, too many people in my small foyer. Joumana, in a winter dress with scalloped neckline, positions herself next to Fadia, holding a long-handled broom bottom side up, other hand on hip, looking less like a menacing sentinel than a burlesque of a Pontormo painting. Why did she rush down with a broom? Did she expect a swordfight? Dumas, Marías, Conan the Barbarian?

Joumana and a broom, a university professor and a housecleaning implement, an incongruous vision.

My mother tires suddenly, looks hopeless and threadbare. The decibels drop; her screams are reduced to mewls and whimpers.

"Tell her she must keep her mother." My sister-in-law nudges her husband, who appears the most shaken. His white comb-over stands on end. "She must. I'll not take her back. I cannot bear it. You tell her."

"I will do no such thing," I say.

"You tell her," yells my sister-in-law.

My mother begins lowing softly, like a sick cow. She drops her head as if she wants to fold into herself. She is tiny, making it difficult to imagine that I, the tallest person in the room, am related to her in any way, let alone that I'm her offshoot.

"You want to leave her here?" asks Fadia. "Are you insane?"

"This doesn't concern you," my sister-in-law says. Her teeth crowd together as if trying to jump out of her mouth.

"Of course it does." Fadia's eyebrows fly up toward her hairline. "Everything in my building concerns me. Leave now. I've had all I can take from your family for fifty years. No more. Get out."

My sister-in-law tries to move my lowing mother forward, and the scream returns. I cover my ears.

"Take her back," shouts Fadia. "Leave and take her with you. Take her back."

I lean against the glazed door separating the crowded foyer from the rest of my apartment. I wish to be transported to another dimension. Nothing makes sense. I watch the proceedings as if I were at a screening of an Antonioni movie without subtitles. My hands, usually so calm, tremble slightly, and my left eye moves restlessly, independently. In my head, and only in my head, I hear a fast rendition of one of Liszt's transcendental études, played by Sviatoslav Richter on 78 rpm.

There is a remoteness to the air about me. I am off kilter. Take her back.

I am slowly beginning to regain my composure, to collect its dispersed shards, when I realize that my neighbors and I are emphatically forcing my mother out of the house — my own mother. How rude it is.

Kicking your mother out—your dying mother.

Now, describing my mother as dying doesn't mean much, signifies almost nothing. All of us are dying; all days are numbered. My mother has been at death's door for quite a while, but has willfully managed to keep from opening it, or knocking for that matter. Yet that body, that vessel, can't withstand life much longer.

Above her head a ticktocking alarm clock should be floating, one of the old ones with a metal dome on top.

At the end of every summer, my mother cooked lamb fat in salt to store for winter, and kept up this ritual even with the advent of refrigeration and the availability of meats year-round. She shouldn't cook lamb fat this year. No green bananas. She'll soon be departing this building, my life, and this world. But not soon enough.

"Take her back," Fadia keeps repeating, "take her back," in an unrelenting tone that brooks no discussion, no disagreement, a tone that grows stronger and more insistent with each repetition. "Take her back."

*Let me go; take back thy gift.*

Of all the lovely phrases and images, the bright jewels embedded in Tennyson's "Tithonus," this sentence, *"take back thy gift,"* is my favorite. Lodged in my memory from the moment I first read it, it quickens my essence.

*I wither slowly in thine arms,*
*Here at the quiet limit of the world.*

Joumana and her broom remain silent as Fadia talks and talks. How she, a university professor, can be so close to Fadia, who was unable to pass her baccalaureate, is difficult to understand, a most odd pairing. They're conjoined like an orange and its navel.

Fadia, arms wide like wings, guides the invaders out the door. Her offensively bright housedress, *Yellow Submarine* palette, is long enough to sweep the floor as she moves. My sister-in-law seems dispirited, like a weary actress in a failed play.

Take her back.

Here at the quiet limit of the world it isn't so quiet.

Untangling my feelings toward Fadia is as challenging as any of Psyche's tasks, and more difficult still is trying to understand hers toward me. The child looked up to me as a young bride; she despised me as a divorcée. Yet as we aged, after she married and had her own family, she seemed to soften. She became civil; she may not like me, but she doesn't loathe me either, and from time to time she exhibits a kindness and generosity so profound as to confound me.

The war forced us to be strangers no more. We helped and supported each other during the battles, though that didn't transform our relationship into any recognizable kind of friendship. Other than uttering polite meaningless words, we hardly spoke. A word here, a phrase there.

The longest exchange we ever had was on a cold morning in 1995 as I was heading to work. Coming out my door, I surprised her, cheeks ruddy with cold and good health as she ascended the stairs to the daily gathering of the witches, having bought a warm tray of kenafeh, its smell hunger inducing even wrapped in waxy paper. Good morning, good morning, and Fadia suggested I wear an overcoat on such a cold day. I told her I was warm-blooded, but she insisted that once I was out on the street the wind was freezing cold.

"Once you're out there," she said as her hands stroked her camelhair coat, "you'll thank Fadia."

She was right that day.

I stopped dismissing her as inconsequential early on. Fadia was outrageously frivolous as a child, and remains so as an adult, yet she possesses a courage, a gumption, that few of her generation have. One night years ago—she was nineteen, possibly twenty, definitely no longer a student— the sky was inky, India ink, and she was outside her door fuming much too loudly. Sartre wrote, "Hell is the Other," which I agree with, of course, but I also agree with Fernando Vallejo: "the torment of Hell is noise." That night Fadia was the inferno of my soul.

At the time, Fadia was causing her father, Hajj Wardeh, great concern, and concerned he should have been, as it turned out. The favorite and the youngest, she was the only one of his three daughters who was still unmarried. Worse yet, her delight in Egyptian romantic movies, her obsession with them, banished sleep from his nights. He correctly worried that she not only watched them with her girlfriends but was also sneaking into theaters by herself when she had the chance. Having watched a few of these films himself, he understood that they were breeding grounds of illusion, planting misbegotten seeds in the minds of impressionable young Arab girls and sowing unhappiness and discontent when life turned out to be less ideal than it appeared on those cursed screens.

He tried to forbid her from going with her girlfriends, but the truth was, and he was fully aware of it, that his family had reached the point where his daughter ruled the realm. She could inveigle her father to agree to whatever she wanted, within reason, of course. She considered his demands mere suggestions. She possessed a potent weapon: her pout. He loved her so deeply that all it took was for her to curl her lips and push them out, squint her eyes and stare at him, and he would hastily rescind whatever it was that he had merely suggested.

Hajj Wardeh arrived at the most expected of solutions: it was high time she was married. He found the perfect suitor, a son of a good friend of his. The husband-to-be's name was Abdallah, a handsome twenty-six-year-old, educated, intelligent, decent, a good Muslim, an engineer who had graduated from the American University of Beirut with high honors. When Hajj Wardeh invited his good friend's family for dinner, he noticed with great glee that Abdallah practically fell over every time Fadia looked at him. He kept expecting the poor young man's eyes to jump out of their sockets as in the popular cartoons. Nothing was said during the dinner, of course, but he foresaw a full proposal by the next day.

Joy caressed his heart, if only briefly.

That night, after she figured out the purpose of the dinner, Fadia the noisemaker threw her infamous tantrum, which the entire neighborhood heard. She would not marry just anybody, and certainly not this son of her father's good friend. She would marry for love, and only for love. She would not reenter the apartment until her father promised he wouldn't give her to that man. She didn't care who heard her night cries. She'd sleep on the landing. All of Beirut would know her father was an indecent man for forcing her to marry against her will. She didn't care how he was to tell his best friend that she wasn't interested. She wouldn't set foot inside her home unless her father relented. The poor man did, and a suddenly meek Fadia was smart enough not to gloat in her triumph.

What Hajj Wardeh didn't know at the time, although he was wise enough to understand it later, was that Fadia already had her eyes set on a future husband. Yes, she would marry for love. She and her girlfriends had noticed a young man at the theaters, attending the same movies they were. They approached him the third or fourth time they saw him. They found him charming and delightful, as enamored of Egyptian movies as they were. He was a gentleman from a good family and treated them with the utmost respect. All of Fadia's girlfriends wanted him as a husband, this well-mannered, considerate man with a good job who had the same interests they did. What girl would want anything more?

I should have slipped them a copy of *Giovanni's Room* or, had they been more intelligent, *Corydon*.

Fadia worked on him for two years before he understood that he was supposed to propose, and propose he did, asking for her hand officially from her father. Their marriage worked in its way. In time she lost her infatuation with Egyptian films, but he never did. He was kind to his family and supported them. He was amiable to me, for which I was grateful. He passed away with no one who could say a bad thing about him. At the same time, he passed away with no one outside his immediate family who could remember much about him. Most people weren't able to recognize him from one sighting to the next; he had to constantly reintroduce himself. And then he died.

I myself can't recall what his face looked like — the metaphorical cataracts, once more.

He was a dutiful husband who never cheated on Fadia or strayed. She, of course, did, as I had expected. What I hadn't expected, and neither did Fadia, was the choice of whom she strayed with. She encountered Abdallah at some gathering, and apparently, as a married woman, she found his interest in her more intriguing. She claimed he seduced her while sitting next to his wife; he removed the red rose in his boutonniere, plucked it, and ever so inconspicuously allowed the petals to drop from his hand along her path as she passed him. She was his faithful mistress for twenty-three years. They were somewhat discreet in order not to hurt their families, but the whole city knew of their affair — knew of it discreetly, of course. I heard her talk about him regularly to Joumana and Marie-Thérèse up there on the landing. It is noteworthy that only Fadia's eldest child takes after her husband. The rest of them do not take after Abdallah, but they certainly don't look like their father, whatever he looked like.

Had it not been for Abdallah's untimely death by sudden cardiac arrest while in an unsober condition, the lovers would probably still be together. She mourned him more than anyone in his family; she mourned him more than she did her husband, of course. After her lover's death, she discreetly accepted condolences. She was considerate enough not to attend his funeral. However, she was inordinately pleased to hear that at the obsequies an old lady made the egregious blunder of addressing her lover's wife as Fadia.

She was certainly pretty all those years ago, and as she shoos my mother, half brother, and sister-in-law out of the apartment, I can still see who she once was, how she was. Framed by the light crossing the threshold, Fadia's old face seems to be dismantling, and the face I remember breaks through like a newborn chick out of its shell. I sometimes see her as impervious to time.

"Out, out!" Fadia says, even though my interloping relatives have already left the apartment. Fadia wants them out of her building. "Don't make me call the gendarmes," she says as they slowly lead my mother down the stairs. "I never want to see you here again. I don't like you."

My feet feel as if they're swelling in their slippers, my knees unable to bear my weight. My robe hangs heavily upon my shoulders. I wonder if I can simply lock the door against Fadia, but Joumana is still in the foyer, joined now by Marie-Thérèse, both regarding me quizzically, wanting to know, looking like characters out of a bad Lebanese soap opera.

"I must sit," I announce as I take slow steps, tread softly across the worn kilim, and retreat to my reading room. "I must sit." As I fall back into my trusty fauteuil, I realize it's a mistake, a grievous error. My throat constricts. I shut my eyes. I haven't allowed anyone in this room in decades.

My breath shudders within my body's unyielding limits, my heart seems to be walking about inside.

Joumana and Marie-Thérèse, my neighbors above and below, follow me into my sanctuary. Joumana crouches before the chair. She wants to know if I'm all right. That must have been traumatic. Am I okay? Is there anything they can do? Joumana has a strong face, with features more Slavic than Semitic, more Israeli than Lebanese, slightly rough but not unattractive, broad brow above shrewd eyes that make me uncomfortable. Do I know why my mother screamed?

No, it felt like an aberration. I can't tell what scared my mother. I'll never know. What was it that was unleashed from the chambers of her memory? How can I know?

Delicately and discreetly, Joumana examines my hair, then shakes her head. Does that mean she doesn't think the blue dye is what caused the screaming? I say nothing.

A mistake, a lapse. They shouldn't be in the room. I try to catch my breath, try to concentrate on the vase of hothouse flowers on the stand next to me: red dahlias, white delphiniums, glass vase, sweetish smell. Perishable flowers, they cost more money than I can afford, but once I saw them in the shop, I couldn't return home without them.

Like most Lebanese, Joumana speaks rapidly, one sentence dovetailing into another, producing guttural words and phrases as if gargling with mouthwash. I prefer slow conversations where words are counted like pearls, conversations with many pauses, pauses replacing words. I prefer my visitors elsewhere. She's looking slightly above my chair. Her eyes, the color of quince jam, reinforce her easy demeanor, her loquacity.

"I need to rest," I say. "The air feels humid." Pause. "I might be getting a headache."

Joumana's eyes suddenly dart from one side to the other, gathering information at high speed. The crow's feet around them tighten. I shut mine in despair. "Oh my Lord," exclaims Joumana, "what is all this?" She twirls unhurriedly in place, looking up and down. Her face lights up and glows. "What have you been hiding in here?"

"It's only books," I say. "Only books."

I imagine looking at the room through a stranger's eyes. Books everywhere, stacks and stacks, shelves and bookcases, stacks atop each shelf, I in the creaky chair that hasn't been reupholstered since I bought it in the early sixties. I have been its only occupant; years ago its foam molded into the shape of my posterior. The accompanying ottoman holds two stacks of books that haven't been disturbed in years, except for semiweekly dusting. How many hours have I moved around this room, from nook to nook, making sure that everything is in its proper place, every book in its proper pile, every dust mote annihilated? An unframed circular mirror—when did I put that up and why had I kept it?—hangs by a nail on the door. I'd completely forgotten about it. Every surface in the room shines with dedicated cleanliness except for the mirror, of course. I've trained my eyes to avoid my reflection so admirably that I forgot it was there. Helen Garner is right. The vegetable-dyed Kazakh rug with noticeable rips was once a boisterous pomegranate, but the vacuum cleaner, after hundreds of passes, has sucked the fresh life out of it. I found the tortoiseshell floor lamp during the war, lonely and abandoned, outside a building that had just been looted—the pilferers had no use for a reading lamp. I spent an entire week restoring its luster. From one of its elegant metal loops, I hang a pair of reading glasses for easy access. The vase sits on seven books, liver-spotted paperbacks of the Muallaqat; each contains one of the poems with its annotations and essays. My favorite poems, four versions of them scattered, though not haphazardly, around the room.

The Suspended Odes, the Hanging Poems, seven poems from seven poets before Islam. The myth tells us that these poems were once written in gold on Coptic linen and hung on the drapes of the Kaaba in the sixth century. Erroneous, of course, since poems were memorized, rarely written, but a beautiful story nonetheless. I love the idea of a place of worship with hanging poetry, gilded no less.

In Joumana's apartment upstairs, my reading room, this room, was her daughter's bedroom. I know that because I heard her music through the years, her dancing with her boyfriend, her walking, her stomping, and, every so often, her yelling and door slamming. She's now studying for a graduate degree in art or art history in France—quietly, one would hope. In Marie-Thérèse's downstairs apartment, this was her son's room, the no-longer-there boy. He was much quieter. I have no idea what Fadia uses hers for. I have never been in their rooms. Why do they feel it's their right to be in mine?

A draft originating from the still-open front door, an unseemly breeze, brazenly ruffles the hairs at the back of my neck and peeps into a stack of papers on the desk.

"I knew you worked in a bookstore," Joumana says, "but I had no idea you had so many . . . so many . . . this is a stockroom of books." She moves cautiously and reverently, tiptoes almost, occasionally craning her neck to read titles.

I want to tell her to stop, to let me be; no, I want her to stop, she must stop. I open my mouth but the sound gets stuck. Her fingers, her profane fingers, drum — the index, middle, and ring finger of her right hand drum a commotion, they drum on my chairback, on a shelf, on the spines of my books, the torturous *tap-tap-tock* clattering over everything.

A greater commotion makes a grand entrance.

"They're gone," Fadia announces. "I waited till I saw the car leave. They'd better not come back if they know what's best for them." Her forehead is damp and pearly, the hair above it flat against her skull. The flush of her cheeks is exaggerated, and naughtiness twinkles in her eyes. She too is surprised at the sight of so many books.

"So this is what you do indoors," Fadia exclaims. A lit cigarette sizzles close to her fingertips. The sunlight filtering through the windowpanes wreathes her right hand in blue smoke. "I always wondered how you spent so much time all by yourself during the war. Oh, wait. While the Lebanese were experiencing bloodlust, yours was booklust." She emits a bubbling brook of laughter. When she realizes I'm not laughing, she adds, "You have to admit that was clever."

"Yes." I nod patiently.

"And funny, right?"

"Thank you for your help," I say. "That was very kind of you. I'm not sure how I'd have handled the situation had you not arrived when you did."

"Think nothing of it," Fadia replies. "Someday you should come up and see my library."

"Your library?" Marie-Thérèse asks.

Joumana shakes her head as if to say, "I can't believe you didn't see that one coming."

"My library has two books," Fadia says, "and I have yet to finish coloring the second one." She brightens, and her laughter grows louder when she realizes I've cracked a smile. "Fadia can be funny sometimes."

I rake my hair of blue and wait for them to leave.

Such a messy morning. I need to get out of the house, clear the ant farm out of my brain. I intend to breathe some city fumes. My nightgown, crinkly and wrinkled from dried perspiration, I discard on the impeccably made bed. Fresh talcum powder under my arms, clean underwear. I put on my gray dress, which has gone in and out of style a number of times while I wasn't paying attention, and a blue cardigan. My time of bracelets, perfumes, and frivolous adornments has long since passed. I clasp my locks into a makeshift bun and cover my head with a scarf, making sure I show enough neck skin. I don't want anyone to think I'm covering up for asinine religious reasons.

I lock the door and try to hurry down the steps, afraid the witches might return. Past Marie-Thérèse's apartment, I forget about the stone that has worked itself loose on the third step from the top. I land on it. The hollow thud it emits beneath my low heels reminds me to slow. I can relax for a bit.

The stairwell is no longer exposed and friendly. Fifteen years ago, in 1995, half-walls were constructed to protect the building from flying bullets that were no longer around. They look unattractive and unnatural. Part of the post–civil war renovation, they were supposed to serve their defensive purpose while maintaining the building's older Beiruti character and keeping the common stairwell relatively open-aired. Like most things Lebanese, they arrived after the time when they were most needed had passed.

As soon as I leave the last step and try to cross the street, battered taxis begin to blow their high-pitched beeps, clumsily inquiring about my willingness to use them. The bleating cars comfort me. My pace is quicker than it should be.

No car will slow down for me to cross — none ever has, none ever will. I zip in between vehicles, dancing the Beiruti Hustle to the other side. What will happen when I'm too slow to do this? Will I someday lose the ability to get all the way across the street before the light changes?

Will I live long enough to see a fully functional traffic light in Beirut?

I pass what used to be Mr. Azari's grocery, now a strange store selling unnecessary electrical widgets: old-fashioned irons, neon tubes, light fixtures that are supposed to look like candles, the stems dripping permanent plastic wax, vibrating filaments within tapered flame-shaped bulbs. The store stands next to a Starbucks filled with youngsters, future married couples, preening and chatting and flirting, all of them lounging in seemingly uncomfortable and unsustainable positions, all drinking lactescent swill. A street cleaner in a green jumpsuit picks up cigarette butts off the pavement. Across the street is another one. These street cleaners of Beirut, the Sisyphuses of our age. The one before me is an East African, a young man with an old demeanor.

The city belongs to the young and their apathy. That is no country for old men. Or old women for that matter. Byzantium seems so distant.

Beirut is the Elizabeth Taylor of cities: insane, beautiful, tacky, falling apart, aging, and forever drama laden. She'll also marry any infatuated suitor who promises to make her life more comfortable, no matter how inappropriate he is.

In the early pages of his gorgeous novel *Sepharad*, Antonio Muñoz Molina writes: "Only those of us who have left know what the city used to be like and are aware of how much it has changed; it's the people who stayed who can't remember, who seeing it day after day have been losing that memory, allowing it to be distorted, although they think they're the ones who remained faithful, and that we, in a sense, are deserters."

Certainly a beautiful sentence, and a lovely sentiment, but I respectfully yet strenuously disagree. There may be much I can't remember, and my memory may have become distorted along the way, but Beirut and how she was, how she has changed through the years—her, I never forgot. I never forget, and I have never left her.

Why did my mother scream? Why did she do that?

I can't allow myself to dwell on it. Unfettered perambulation isn't permitted on the ant farm today.

I feel a little dizzy. I press my hand against the Starbucks window to steady myself. White dots and grayish striations flitter and quiver across my eyes, so I rest my forehead against the glass, as I used to do when I was a

child, rest my skull against the wall whenever my boisterous half brothers grew too irksome, whenever my mother
reminded me over and over to stop at the bakery on my way
back from school. "Don't forget the bread," she used to harp.
"Remember bread, bread," and my head would need a rest.

A taxi driver leans forward and yells out his window,
"Taxi?"

I take a deep breath, pull my head back. Sisyphus pretends not to notice me as he collects butts with a pair of
extra-long tongs. Two youngsters behind the clean glass, a
boy and a girl with Bakelite thighs, interrupt their duel of
saliva to regard me quizzically, suspiciously. Their hands
and bodies touch along many points, a languorous contact
that speaks of desperation.

Touching, so alive, so bright, these teenagers. Before
them, on the glass, my pale, silvery reflection superimposes
itself. I recoil. Immortal age beside immortal youth.

*But thy strong Hours indignant work'd their wills,*
*And beat me down and marr'd and wasted me.*

A Diored woman sporting noteworthy high hair and
wasp-stung lips slows her steps, hesitates near me, lifts up
her sunglasses, concern showing on her face. I smile, grimace
really, my ever-nervous gesture. I shake my head, indicat-
ing that I'm all right. Mild geriatric disorder is what this
is, nothing more. No one needs to stop. She acknowledges
my silent communication and moves on. I follow suit in the
opposite direction. Air breathes up the back of my scarf. In
front of a building grows—no, not grows, stands—a hewn
rusty-hued bush of indecipherable leaves, of which only a

few remain greenish. But of course, I — I would notice such a thing.

*The woods decay, the woods decay and fall.*

Have I grown too old for Beirut?

Beirut, my Beirut.

Around the corner from the building I live in is a Pizza Hut outlet that proudly identifies itself as DELIVERY ONLY. If you happen to walk in, maybe to ask for directions, or possibly to inquire whether anyone knows what happened to the owner of the store they've just replaced, the young men regard you condescendingly before announcing that they only take phone orders.

The store these smug, ill-mannered boys replaced was an idiosyncratic record shop that opened its doors two days before the civil war broke out, and surprisingly kept open throughout the fighting. The owner — a portly, mustached Beiruti of indeterminate age and sect — rarely bothered to hoist his ample behind out of his chair. He always seemed oblivious to anything occurring outside the expansive world of his store. Come to think of it, he barely noticed anything outside his own mind, so content was he, so self-sufficient and complete. Nongarrulous Beirutis are as rare as vivid primary colors in the snowy Arctic, yet here we were, two of us, patient sufferers of verbal sclerosis, not more than a hundred meters apart.

Ever the autodidact, I used his store to teach myself. When he opened for business, I knew little about music. I kept track of mentions in the novels I read. For example,

I first heard of Mozart's Sinfonia Concertante in Styron's book *Sophie's Choice* — a beautiful if somewhat soppy novel, and an unbearable film. I heard of Kathleen Ferrier when Thomas Bernhard mentioned her uplifting rendition of Mahler's *Das Lied von der Erde* in *Old Masters*.

In my thirties all I understood was Chopin, glorious Frédéric. To thank me for finding a rare book, a college student offered me an invaluable gift, a double album of Artur Rubinstein playing Chopin. I didn't have a record player at the time and had to save up before I was able to listen to it. Once I did, Artur's spirit wafted through my home. I played my record over and over and over and over. I bought a cleaning and care kit for albums. Once a week I delicately wiped the damp cloth across the disc to ensure it remained playable for eternity. It was the only album I had for years, and the only music I listened to. To this day, I can probably whistle the melody of Ballade no. 1 in G Minor without having to think about it. I became a Chopinophile.

Even now, I think that if I'd never listened to anything else, I'd still consider myself a lucky human being. This was Rubinstein. This was Chopin. Pole playing Pole. But I had a yearning. Sometime in the early eighties, while my city was self-immolating, while everyone around me was either killing or making sure he wasn't going to be killed, I decided it was time I taught myself how to listen to music.

I visited the fat man's store and looked through his stacks of records. I didn't buy anything until the fifth visit. By that time, my fingers, imitating Olympic short-distance racers, could sift through a stack of albums in seconds. I couldn't tell where to begin, which pianist was better than the other. I knew to begin with the famous composers (Bach,

Beethoven, Mozart) but couldn't settle on which versions. I
made a somewhat arbitrary choice. I decided I would select
albums from the Deutsche Grammophon label.

You might ask why, which is a good question.

Don't laugh.

The way I looked at it at the time was that the composers were German (or German-speaking), so Deutsche
Grammophon just seemed logical. Don't you think?

But also, I just thought the design was classy; the yellow
rectangle label added a touch of panache. I always wished
for a touch of panache in my life.

It turned out to be a good decision, a great decision,
though limiting at first. I didn't know about Gould's *Goldberg
Variations* for ages. Someone could have saved me a lot of
time by explaining things, or by pointing out that I should
have listened to the bourrée from Bach's English Suite
no. 2 (Englische Suiten!) much earlier, instead of finding
it by accident on a Pogorelić disc. What if I had missed it?
The hours of pleasure I wouldn't have known.

If only I had someone to tell me every now and then,
"Aaliya, you must listen to Scarlatti's sonatas, fils, not père."

If only I had someone to guide me, the pillar of cloud going
before me on my wanderings, to lead me and show me the
way. If I had someone to offer me the benefit of her attentions.

The queen calls to her worker ants. Come back, come
back, don't go there.

I bought my Deutsche Grammaphon albums from
the fat man—two a month, one with each paycheck, which
was all I could reasonably afford. Beethoven came first, of
course, piano works followed by the violin sonatas (Kreutzer
still delivers shivers), and so on.

On the weekday my paycheck was to be deposited, I would sneak a peek out my living room window, through a tiny vertical crack between the louvered wood, and gauge whether Azari's green shutters were up, which would mean that the bank branch in my neighborhood might be open and I had to unlock the bookshop's doors. More likely than not, the record store would be open regardless of fighting. On my way to work, I'd stop at the bank for cash, and on the way home, I'd stop at the store for an album, one of the few rituals I looked forward to in those days. I'd plan in advance the next five or six albums I was going to purchase, the early, the middle, and then the late quartets. I would agonize over deciding whether a double album was one purchase or two.

The portly owner sat on a high toothpick of a barstool and still had to look up to me. He rarely spoke, yet as we began to know each other and feel comfortable, he'd grunt approval with every purchase. When I first bought *The Sofia Recital* by Richter, he of the pink plastic lobster, the shop owner's smile floated toward me like a leaf on a river. With Martha Argerich's *Début Recital*, his face wore the three-foot grin of an alligator. After such high praise, walking the three-building distance home was torture; I couldn't wait to listen. And when I bought my first Gould, his eyebrows climbed up his forehead, his eyes shot up to the ceiling. Finally.

On new album days, while a war raged around me and chaos ruled, I felt triumphant.

Buying music was almost my sole expense but not, of course, my sole luxury. I have far more books than I have albums, far more, but I didn't buy most of them. Do not judge too harshly. I've had to live on a minuscule salary. No one was making any money on my bookstore's sales. The owner kept it open because he was proud of its reputation among Beirut's pseudointellectuals and high priests of literature as the only place in the city where one could find obscure books, which none of them read. These literary dilettantes know books about as well as an airline passenger knows the landscape he overflies; they talk about novels in highlights as if they're reading a fashion magazine. I ordered books, and if no one bought them, I carried them home. I'll admit that sometimes I ordered two of each just to make sure — all right, sometimes three.

I would never have been able to buy them otherwise. Once I paid my rent, I could afford little, and because I had to put something away for retirement, the days of ago-nizing leisure, I had even less. I began to cook vegetarian fare early because any kind of meat was way beyond my meager means. I survived — still do — on fruits, vegetables, grains, and rice. I haven't had lamb on Id al-Adha in years. Luckily, I never smoked, because I certainly couldn't have managed to pay for that. During the lean years of the war, Fadia upstairs, who smokes as much as a French philoso-pher, and who could certainly afford more than I ever could, used to break her cigarettes in half for economy's sake and stuff them in an elegant gold-plated holder. She halted the practice after the war ended.

I like to consider my little thefts a public service. Some-one had to read Eliot's *The Waste Land* as the glow of Sabra burning illuminated Beirut's skyline. No, seriously, had I not ordered some of these books, they would have never landed on Lebanese soil. For crying out loud, do you think anyone else in Lebanon has a copy of Djuna Barnes's *Nightwood*? And I am picking just one book off the top of my head.

Lampedusa's *The Leopard*? I don't think anyone else in this country has a book by Novalis.

Why did my mother scream? I wish I knew. What I do know is that I shouldn't have stopped seeing her. As crazy as she was becoming, I shouldn't have abandoned her. When was the last time I'd contacted her? Not since I stopped working, probably earlier than that. Once I'd decided not to have her to my apartment all those years ago, I began to call her from work and ask her to meet me at a café or restaurant. But when she crossed into her eighties, she grew more difficult to bear, less civil, more ornery. Trouble was all I received from interacting with her, toil and trouble. I'd call her and the first thing she might ask was why I was calling. I'd invite her to lunch and she'd tell me I was being silly since she had a serviceable lunch at home. She leached out sanity and equanimity from my head. I stopped calling. I understood she was getting old and cranky, but it wasn't as if she didn't remember who I was. She was lucid, just difficult.

I don't think she knew who I was today. I don't recall her ever being so terrified, not even during the war years. The only time I'd seen her scared, though not as deeply as this morning, was when my half brother the eldest, eight years old then, was kicked in the head by a mule. He was playing an imaginary war game with other boys in the neighborhood. He was retreating, machine-gunning anything that moved, when he backed into the mule's behind, irritating the beast. My mother rushed out of the house, and when she saw my half brother the eldest lying prone with blood seeping from his head, she wailed as if it were Judgment Day and she had been judged wanting. We, she and I alone, waited outside the hospital while the doctors fixed my brother. They wouldn't let us in the waiting room because it was too crowded and we certainly looked like we didn't belong. My mother, small and wilting, leaned on the hood of a doctor's car. When I leaned on the car beside her, she said, "Don't," in a low voice. She added, "Don't do what I do."

I remember that an intern came out to talk to us after a few hours. He explained that my half brother the eldest was going to be all right. The intern interspersed French phrases into his Lebanese sentences, which only scared my mother more.

If this were a novel, you would be able to figure out why my mother screamed. Alain Robbe-Grillet once wrote that the worst thing to happen to the novel was the arrival of psychology. You can assume he meant that now we all expect to understand the motivation behind each character's actions, as if that's possible, as if life works that way. I've read so many recent novels, particularly those published in the Anglo world, that are dull and trite because I'm always supposed to infer causality. For example, the reason a protagonist can't experience love is that she was physically abused, or the hero constantly searches for validation because his father paid little attention to him as a child. This, of course, ignores the fact that many others have experienced the same things but do not behave in the same manner, though that's a minor point compared to the real loss in fulfilling the desire for explanation: the loss of mystery.

Causation extraction makes Jack a dull reader.

I do understand the desire, though, for I too wish to live in a rational world. I do wish to understand why my mother screamed. My life would be simpler if I could rationalize. Unfortunately, I don't understand.

While a traffic war rages around me and chaos rules (lest you forget this is Beirut), I flash to a theory about why we desperately wish to live in an ordered world, in an explainable world.

No, wait. I don't mean to imply that I thought about it just this instant, or that it's some sort of philosophical treatise. Neither French nor German am I.

Let me rephrase: I'd like to consider a possibility concerning our incessant need for causation, whether in books or in life. I've trained myself not to keep inferring or expecting causality in literature—the phrase "Correlation does not imply causation" keeps ringing in my head (think Hume)—but I constantly see it, inject it, in life. I, like everyone, want explanations. In other words, I extract explanations where none exist.

Imre Kertész says it well in *Kaddish for an Unborn Child*. Here you go:

> But, it would seem, there is no getting around explanations, we are constantly explaining and excusing ourselves; life itself, that inexplicable complex of being and feeling, demands explanations of us, those around us demand explanations, and in the end we ourselves demand explanations of ourselves, until in the end we succeed in annihilating everything around us, ourselves included, or in other words explain ourselves to death.

I want to know why my mother screamed. I do. I will probably not be rewarded with an explanation, but I need one.

Let me elaborate.

So many people died during the war. The woman who lived above me was one of the first. A different family lived in that apartment before Joumana and her husband (I don't remember his name, but no matter). In the early months, fall of 1975 or thereabouts, the wife, the mother from upstairs, was shot in the head while driving home from work. Within two weeks the family cleared out and immigrated to Dubai, where every day is the same bright.

The rumors and false stories that circulated in those two weeks were astoundingly vivid, all attempts at explanations. She was a spy, she worked for a bank and was carrying large amounts of cash, she was sporting a flashy diamond necklace, she didn't see a checkpoint until it was too late. All untrue, all drawn with soft pencil, easily erasable, all attempts to explain the unexplainable.

It turned out she was simply unlucky. A stray bullet killed her.

We needed an explanation because we couldn't deal with the fact that it could have been any one of us. Assuming causation—she was killed because she couldn't hear anything since the radio was too loud—lets us believe that it can't happen to us because we wouldn't do such a thing. We are different. They are the other.

None of us knows how to deal with the aleatory nature of pain.

I was lucky. I knew that what happened to the woman upstairs couldn't happen to me because I never had a car. I walked or used public transportation.

I wasn't like her.

That's my theory anyway. I'm sure more erudite minds have dealt with this. Sartre I'm not, but then neither am I ponderous and portentous. One reason we desire explanations is that they separate us and make us feel safe.

In a silly essay on *Crime and Punishment*, a critic suggests that Raskolnikov is the epitome of the Russian soul, that to understand him is to understand Russia. Tfeh! Not that the proposition isn't true; it may or may not be. I've yet to meet Russia's soul. What the reviewer is doing is distancing himself from the idea that he too is capable of killing a pawnbroker. We're supposed to infer that only someone with a Russian soul could.

If you think that Marcello of *The Conformist* becomes a porcine fascist because he killed lizards when he was a boy, then you assure yourself that you can never be so. If you think Madame Bovary commits adultery because she's trying to escape the banality of Pleistocene morals, then her betrayals are not yours. If you read about hunger in Ethiopia or violence in Kazakhstan, it isn't about you.

We all try to explain away the Holocaust, Abu Ghraib, or the Sabra Massacre by denying that we could ever do anything so horrible. The committers of those crimes are evil, other, bad apples; something in the German or American psyche makes their people susceptible to following orders, drinking the grape Kool-Aid, killing indiscriminately. You believe that you're the one person who wouldn't have delivered the electric shocks in the Milgram experiment because those who did must have been emotionally abused by their parents, or had domineering fathers, or were dumped by their spouses. Anything that makes them different from you.

When I read a book, I try my best, not always success-
fully, to let the wall crumble just a bit, the barricade that
separates me from the book. I try to be involved.

I am Raskolnikov. I am K. I am Humbert and Lolita.
I am you.

If you read these pages and think I'm the way I am
because I lived through a civil war, you can't feel my pain.
If you believe you're not like me because one woman, and
only one, Hannah, chose to be my friend, then you're unable to empathize.

Like the bullet, I too stray.

Forgive me.

I stray but not too far. I circle the streets around the building, avoiding home, but go no farther than a prescribed
distance that I instinctively cling to, like a pigeon flying
above its coop.

Next to the street that parallels mine is a small plot
of land that is still undeveloped and used as a car park.
Toward the northwest corner, where cars can't reach, tiny
red carnations miraculously flourish in a small patch of
earth. When I saw them a week ago I assumed they were
confused red poppies — Lebanon's flower, and Proust's,
the wondrous wildflower with its color-saturated tissue-
paper petals. I'd never seen carnations blossom naturally
in the city before, and certainly hadn't expected them to
last until winter.

The winter air smells metallic, of bronze. In fading
tawny light, the city glimmers, except for one large box
of a building, concrete hued, that absorbs and swallows

surrounding color. It has a name; in human-sized letters it calls itself THE GARDEN CENTER, yet not a sprig of green can be found anywhere in its vicinity.

I am a blob in a photorealistic painter's cityscape canvas. I stay out until evening, until my bladder begins to scream.

Before the final turn to my home, I see one of the neighborhood's teenage boys holding court, leaning against a wall that already needs a coat of paint even though it received one in spring. Two beer cans — one squashed, the other only dimpled — loiter at his feet. I often notice this fifteen-year-old around this grand realm of his when school is out. He disappeared for a few weeks this summer after his mother chased him about the neighborhood with a rattan, but he seems to have returned to his full form and splendor. His mother must have woken him from an afternoon nap and kicked him out of the house before he had a chance to comb his haystack hair. His court, three younger boys, probably eleven or twelve, throw respectful — no, worshipful — eyes at him while desperately pretending nonchalance. Slim, wired, and cocky, he must have practiced his how-to-smoke pose before many a mirror. He appears the celebrated philosopher enduring the intellectual infirmities of his inferiors, an appearance that belies preening and nervous self-consciousness — in other words, he looks like a typical Beiruti teenager.

"First you wet the filter with your spit," I hear him say as I approach. He sticks out his long, overly moist tongue and impresses the end of the cigarette onto it. "Then you inhale deeply, which you can't do until you're old enough to know how to smoke without coughing, and the filter will darken to show an alphabet. See?"

The court of boys oohs and aahs as he continues. "That will be the first letter of the name of the next girl who'll sleep with you. It always works that way."

"It's a *T*," says one of the boys.

"I see an *M*," says another.

I don't slow down, but I hear myself say, "It's a *C* for *Cancer*."

*What words are these have fallen from me?*

Have I just channeled Fadia or, worse, my demented mother before she went completely insane? I feel my face flush and my pulse quicken.

But the court doesn't seem to have heard me, doesn't catch my small, disembodied retort. The boys and their world persist without me.

"It's an *S*, of course," the kinglet now says. "Can't you tell that it's an *S*?"

On the way home, a scarf veiling my blue-tinted hair, I remain invisible.


Allow me to stray once more—briefly, I assure you.

Raskolnikov was the catalyst for my obsessive translating. *Crime and Punishment,* the vehicle, was one of the first books I picked up at the bookstore—well, *Crime et Châtiment,* because at the time my French was more seasoned than my English. I loved the novel. (I'm not sure I still do, but that's another subject. I promised you I wouldn't stray too far.) I remember it as the first adult novel I read, or the first with a fully developed theme. Dostoyevsky's St. Petersburg burst into such splendor around me that it became more real than my life, which I found more incomprehensible with every passing day. I belonged in his book, not mine.

So thoroughly impressed by the novel, I read the English translation, and was less so. It was the Constance Garnett translation, and it would be years before I came across the controversies surrounding her work. At the time I hadn't even heard of Nabokov, let alone his vitriolic rants against her. It was so long ago that I'm not certain he'd even published *Lolita* yet.

The Garnett version was by no means awful. Had I not encountered the French one first, I would have considered it a spectacular book. Only in comparison did I find it lacking. I thought the Garnett version was less charming, more matter-of-fact. I didn't know which version was the more accurate one, more Dostoyevskian. I thought that if I translated the book into Arabic, I could combine both. I did.

Constance Garnett taught herself to translate. She began with small steps, with Tolstoy's *The Kingdom of God Is Within You*. Richard Pevear and Larissa Volokhonsky began with the most difficult Russian bear of all, *The Brothers Karamazov*. I began with *Crime*, the right novel for me. Call me Goldilocks.

I still admire Garnett, once aptly described as a woman of Victorian energies and Edwardian prose. I do appreciate all the criticisms leveled against her and her poor translations. As Joseph Brodsky said, "The reason English-speaking readers can barely tell the difference between Tolstoy and Dostoevsky is that they aren't reading the prose of either one. They're reading Constance Garnett."

Who reads translations anymore? Mr. Brodsky misdi-
rected his Russian anger. Instead of attacking Garnett, he
should have bashed people who don't read Russian authors,
or German, or Arabic, or Chinese, but choose Westernized
imitations instead.

Before she began her missionary work, only the rare
English speaker who knew Russian could read those writers. She introduced so many of us, those who can read
English but not the original language, to Heaven's passions. So Joseph and Vladimir can rant, and they do, ever
so elegantly and eloquently, but Constance's zeal has been
a blessing.

I can't tell you how good my translations are since I
can't look at them dispassionately. I am intimately involved.
Mine are translations of translations, which by definition
means that they are less faithful to the original. Like Constance, I try my best. However, unlike her, I don't skip over
words I don't know, nor do I cut long passages short. I didn't
and don't have the intention of translating an entire canon —
my ambitions are neither expansive nor comprehensive. I
translate for the pleasure it engenders, and I certainly don't
possess Victorian energies. I am an Arab, after all.

Garnett wasn't the most prolific translator by any means.
The Renaissance Venetian Lodovico Dolce translated more
than 350 books (Homer, Virgil, Ovid, Dante, Castiglione, to
name a few), and I'm not sure he was the most prolific either.
Earnestness is a common trait among translators.

If you ask me, though, Garnett's biggest problem was
that she was of her time and place. Her work is a reflection
of that; it appealed to the English of her generation, which is
as it should be — completely understandable. Unfortunately

for everyone, her time and place were maddeningly dull. Old chap and cheap port, that sort of thing.

Using Edwardian prose for Dostoyevsky is like adding milk to good tea. Tfeh! The English like that sort of thing.

She also wasn't a genius. Now, you know, Marguerite Yourcenar did much worse things when she translated Cavafy's poems into French. She didn't simply skip over words she didn't understand, she invented words. She didn't speak the language, and used Greek speakers to help her. She changed the poems completely, made them French, made them hers. Brodsky would have said that you weren't reading Cavafy, you were reading Yourcenar, and he would have been absolutely right. Except that Yourcenar's translations are interesting on their own. She did a disservice to Cavafy, but I can forgive her. Her poems became something different and new, like champagne.

My translations aren't champagne, and they're not milky tea either.

I'm thinking arak.

But wait. Walter Benjamin has something to say about all this. In "The Task of the Translator" he wrote: "No translation would be possible if in its ultimate essence it strove for likeness to the original. For in its afterlife—which could not be called that if it were not a transformation and renewal of something living—the original undergoes a change."

In his own confounding style, Benjamin is saying that if you translate a work of art by sticking close to the original, you can show the surface content of the original and explain the information contained within, but you miss the ineffable essence of the work. In other words, you're dealing with inessentials.

Take that, Mr. Brodsky and Mr. Nabokov. A right hook and a sucker punch from good old Mr. Benjamin. Had Constance translated Russian works more faithfully, she would have missed the essential.

All right, all right, Constance may have missed both the essential and the inessential, but we should applaud her effort.


Yourcenar also translated Virginia Woolf's *The Waves*. I can't bring myself to read her translation, though. In Woolf's case, unlike Cavafy's, Yourcenar could read the language. Proust couldn't read anything but French, and before he wrote his masterpiece he translated the apostle of the aesthetic John Ruskin, an incomparable stylist. Read Ruskin, then read Proust, and compare the influence — compare the incomparable stylists.

Walter Benjamin translated Proust into German. In one of his letters, Benjamin wrote that he refused to read more Proust than was absolutely necessary to finish the translation because he was terrified that the translatee's exquisitely delicate style would forever seep into the translator's.

I hope that the lepidopterist Nabokov would have approved of my work, but I'm not certain. I'll never know.

Let me come out and state this, in case you haven't deduced it yet: I have never published. Once I finish a project, once the rituals of the end are completed, I inter the papers in a box and the box in the bathroom. Putting the project away has become part of the ritual. When I finish my final edit, I lay the manuscript aside for a few days, then read the whole thing one last time. If it is acceptable, I place it in its box, which I tape shut, hoping the seal is airtight, and attach the original books to the outside for easy reference. I store the box in the maid's room, or now in the maid's bathroom since the former is filled. After that I'm done with it and hardly think of my translation again. I move on to the next project.

I create and crate!

Jacques Austerlitz awaits burial. It is that time of year.

I understood from the beginning that what I do isn't publishable. There's never been a market for it, and I doubt there ever will be. Literature in the Arab world, in and of itself, isn't sought after. Literature in translation? Translation of a translation? Why bother?

Actually, I should say that when I started I may have deluded myself into believing that my translations might find a home. That didn't last long. After all, the dozen or so who wish to read *Anna Karenina* are usually educated enough to do so in English or French. The two or three who might wish to read it in Arabic would choose a translation from the original Russian, not one done through my chosen system. Translating, not publishing, is what I bet my life on.

Now, you may ask why I am so committed to my translations if I don't care much about them once they're crated. Well, I'm committed to the process and not the final product. I know this sounds esoteric, and I dislike sounding so, but it's the act that inspires me, the work itself. Once the book is done, the wonder dissolves and the mystery is solved. It holds little interest after.

That's not all, though. In *The Book of Disquiet*, Pessoa writes: "The only attitude worthy of a superior man is to persist in an activity he recognizes is useless, to observe a discipline he knows is sterile, and to apply certain norms of philosophical and metaphysical thought that he considers utterly inconsequential."

Although I can't say that I understand all the implications of such a stance, I have recognized that my translation activity is useless. Yet I persist. The world goes on whether I do what I do. Whether we find Walter Benjamin's lost suitcase, civilization will march forward and backward, people will trot the globe, wars will rage, lunches will be served. Whether anyone reads Pessoa. None of this art business is of any consequence. It is mere folly.

Vanitas vanitatum, omnia vanitas.

I didn't believe that when I first started. I wanted my work to matter. Early on, I hoped that someday in the future an enthusiastic Mendelssohn would initiate an Aaliya revival. That hope fed this vanity of human wishes, my blameworthy vanity. Luckily, the dream didn't last long — it sounds so silly and naive now.

If I tell the truth — and I should, shouldn't I? — I translate books with my invented system because it makes time flow more gently. That's the primary reason, I think. As Camus said in *The Fall*: "Ah, mon cher, for anyone who is alone, without God and without a master, the weight of days is dreadful."

I made translation my master. I made translation my master and my days were no longer alarmingly dreadful. My projects distract me. I work and the days pass.

But then I wonder if that's the emphatic truth. I have to consider that I do what I do because it makes me happy sometimes. I don't suffer from anhedonia, after all; I am able to experience pleasure. I read a poem about happiness by Edward Hirsch that ends with these lines:

*My head is like skylight.*
*My heart is like dawn.*

I think that at times, not all times, when I'm translating, my head is like skylight. Through no effort of my own,
I'm visited by bliss. It isn't often, yet I can be happy when
I commune with translation, my master. Sometimes I think
that's enough, a few moments of ecstasy in a life of Beckett
dullness. Peaks cannot exist without valleys. My translating is a Wagner opera. The narrative sets up, the tension
builds, the music ebbs and flows, the strings, the horns, more
tension, and suddenly a moment of pure pleasure. Gabriel
blows his golden trumpet, ambrosial fragrance fills the air
sublime, and gods descend from Olympus to dance — most
heavenly this peak of ecstasy.

During these moments, I am no longer my usual self,
yet I am wholeheartedly myself, body and spirit. During
these moments, I am healed of all wounds.

I'll be sitting at my desk and suddenly I don't wish my
life to be any different. I am where I need to be. My heart
distends with delight. I feel sacred.

Dante describes these moments best in the final lines
of his masterpiece:

> *But already my desire and my will*
> *Were being turned like a wheel, all at one speed,*
> *By the Love which moves the sun and the other stars.*

Sometimes I think that's enough, that I'm grateful.

Most often I think I'm delusional. Vanitas vanitatum,
omnia vanitas.

*    *    *

By the way, when the war was winding down in 1988, I think, a publisher called and asked if I would be willing to "try my hand" at translating a book. Not one of the translators he normally used was left in our violent city. He'd heard from his distributor that my English was rather good, so why not try? For a brief moment, a frisson tickled my heart. I could be someone. I could matter. While talking on the phone, I began to rebuild this house of cards called ego.

A huff and a puff.

The book he wished me to consider was *Lana: The Lady, the Legend, the Truth*.

Before my door, before the threshold, lies a silver salver under an oval platter of fine porcelain, covered in crinkly aluminum foil. Without having to look, I can tell; I can smell the okra and lamb stew, still warm. My stomach serenades it, but my bladder is more insistent. I scrape the soles of my shoes on the doormat before I enter my apartment. I place the tray on the kitchen counter and rush to the bathroom. I suffer strange tingling in my fingertips whenever I relieve myself these days. I consider, not for the first time, that I should rearrange the crates in the maid's bathroom so I can use that toilet in emergencies. I doubt I will. I am in large measure a creature of habit, years of habits.

The platter could probably sate four starving Ethiopians into a crapulous state. Fadia is nothing if not over-the-top generous. It has been a while since she's blessed me with one of her gifts. She doesn't cook as often these days since she lives alone, her husband dead, her children married.

Fadia's children may be the most well-mannered people in the Middle East (which isn't saying much), but they're also the most ridiculously boring humans on earth. Fadia implanted good breeding in their cells, insisted on correct etiquette throughout their childhood. She showered them with so many sermons that Joumana once called her the professor of homiletics. The children grew up embarrassed, if not horrified, by their mother. She was so desperate for each of them to have a better life that she raised them not to have a place for her in it. She shows up at all their events and gatherings, incredibly proud of them, and they ashamed of her. Fadia's offspring would cross her off their list if she didn't frighten them. None of her almost middle-aged children has ever dared criticize her or point out a faux pas, because they're probably afraid she'll shoot them, literally.

Every now and then — more then, for sure — I wonder what my life would have been like if I'd had children. But then I think of Fadia's, and I think of the children downstairs, and I feel grateful. When I think of the once-loud daughter upstairs, I rejoice, pop open a bottle of champagne to celebrate my progenyless existence.

I hear no noises in the apartment above. Joumana and the witches must have gone to the hair salon. I don't have to climb the two flights of stairs to thank Fadia this evening.

I take the bottle of red wine out of the pantry cabinet, pour a glass, and recork the bottle with the vacuum stopper, a wonderful invention for single people. I set out my dinner at the red-and-yellow kitchen table as the streetlight goes on outside my window. From the vase in the middle of the table,

I remove the dead flowers, twisted flags of dried irises, and throw them into the garbage. Irises in late December? Who'd have thought such a thing was possible forty years ago?

I draw the curtains in the house, pull the window shades down to the sill.

The first bite of the stew makes my eyes water. Delicately, delectably divine.

This is art.


I bet you believe in the redemptive power of art.

I'm sure you do. I did. Such a romantic notion. Art will rescue the world, lift humanity above the horrible quagmire it's stuck in. Art will save you.

I used to think that art would make me a better human being. I believed in the foolish idea that listening to Kiri Te Kanawa or Victoria de Los Ángeles purified my soul. "Vissi d'arte" and all that.

*I lived for art, I lived for love,*
*I never did harm to a living soul!*

Well, no, non vissi d'amore. I wasn't that lucky. I also can't say that I haven't harmed a living soul. I sold books, after all.

I did live for art, though. It wasn't a conscious decision, I don't think. I didn't sit down one day and plan on a life devoted to aesthetic beauty. I'm not berating myself for that. I slipped into art to escape life. I sneaked off into literature.

The forbidden aspects of this life may have seduced me. I don't think anyone approved of my reading when I was a child. My mother certainly didn't, and my stepfather made sure to criticize when he noticed: "Reading is bad for your eyes. You'll soon need glasses, which will make you even less attractive." My family would have been incontrovertibly hostile to art had they known that such a thing existed—if you showed them a grand piano, they probably wouldn't have known what manner of beast it was. Of course I received various permutations of the "Who will want to marry you if you read so much?" lecture, but I also had to endure the chilly "Don't try to be so different from normal people."

Different from normal people? When I first heard that, I was sorely offended. I thought every person should live for art, not just me, and furthermore, why would I want to be normal? Why would I want to be stupid like everyone else?

May I admit that being different from normal people was what I desperately sought? I wanted to be special. I was already different: tall, not attractive and all. Mine is a face that would have trouble launching a canoe. I knew that no one would love me, so I strove to be respected, to be looked up to. I wanted people to think I was better than they were. I wanted to be Miss Jean Brodie's crème de la crème.

I thought art would make me a better human being, but I also thought it would make me better than you.

Better? Yo, la peor de todas.

*Oh, the sad vanity of flesh and blood called mankind,*
*Can't you see, you're not the slightest bit important?*

Poetry brought me great pleasure, music immense solace, but I had to train myself to appreciate, train and train. It didn't come naturally to me. When I first heard Wagner, Messiaen, or Ligeti, the noise was unbearable, but like a child with her first sip of wine, I recognized something that I could love with practice, and practice I most certainly did.

It's not as if you're born with the ability to love António Lobo Antunes.

I know. You think you love art because you have a sensitive soul.

Isn't a sensitive soul simply a means of transforming a deficiency into proud disdain?

You think art has meaning. You think you're not like me.

You think that art can save the world. I used to.

Why didn't I train myself to be a better cook?

What was it all for? What good did it do me?

What good is a personal skylight if I'm the only one who sees its light?

How special!

*The sun-comprehending glass,*
*And beyond it, the deep blue air, that shows*
*Nothing, and is nowhere, and is endless.*

I can relate to Marguerite Duras even though I'm not French, nor have I been consumed by love for an East Asian man. I can live inside Alice Munro's skin. But I can't relate to my own mother. My body is full of sentences and moments, my heart resplendent with lovely turns of phrases, but neither is able to be touched by another.

I have my writers' neuroses but not their talents.

In *The French Lieutenant's Woman,* John Fowles describes his character as possessing Byronic ennui. Let me paraphrase:

I am filled with Byronic loneliness but have neither of the poet's outlets: genius and adultery.

All I am is lonely.

Before I go to bed, I must put away Sebald, both *The Emigrants* and *Austerlitz*. I can't read him now, not in this state. He's much too honest. I will read something else.

I must prepare for my next project. January first arrives soon.

In the wire rack next to the sink, the dishes dry, slowly dripping water upon the gray stone countertop. A winter wind starts a low moan outside my kitchen window. Rain comes.

I must sleep. Forget the Aaliya revival. I need the Aaliya asleep.


Of course, my mother's visit delivers a night of anguish. I am unable to sleep. Tumbling thoughts of why, how, and what occupy my mind. I raise myself out of bed rather quickly, hoping to banish the worries from the mists of my head. The cool early temperature is a feathery hand tickling my spine. I put on my robe. My nightgown, darkened with moisture, sticks to my torso like the skin of an onion. I glance back, notice that I've left two damp bulbs on the sheet.

As I boil water for my tea in the unlit kitchen, I try to clear my thoughts, to sift out the dark morning dregs. It's drizzling outside my window, and the street's one functioning lamp, my familiar, emits weak light, lonely light, a diffuse conical beam to the asphalt. I'm weary. I don't wish to think about my mother this morning. I don't wish to think about my life. I want to be lost in someone else's. An easy, effortless morning is what I need.

I walk myself back to my bedroom, back to the stack of books on my mirrorless vanity, unread books that I intend

to read, a large stack. Choosing which book isn't difficult.
The choice is typically the last one I brought home. I acquire
books constantly and place them in the to-read pile. When I
finish with whatever book I'm reading, I begin the last book
I bought, the one that caught my attention last. Of course,
the pile grows and grows until I decide that I'm not going
to buy a single book until I read my stack. Sometimes that
works.

The top book on the pile is *Microcosms* by Claudio
Magris. I've only read one other book of his, *Danube*, from
which, among his many impeccable sentences, one wrapped
its octopus arms around my frenetically feeble mind for
months. It goes like this: "Kafka and Pessoa journey not
to the end of a dark night, but of a night of a colourless
mediocrity that is even more disturbing, and in which one
becomes aware of being only a peg to hang life on, and that
at the bottom of that life, thanks to this awareness, there
may be sought some last-ditch residue of truth."

If Kafka, if Gregor Samsa, can resign himself to being
a cockroach, if he can accept being the blade of grass upon
which the stormtrooper's boot stomps, is it immoral for
someone like me to want to be more?

Ah, splendid *Microcosms*, the deliciousness of discovering
a masterwork. The beauty of the first sentences, the "what is
this?," the "how can this be?," the first crush all over again,
the smile of the soul. My heart begins to lift. I can see myself sitting all day in my chair, immersed in lives, plots, and
sentences, intoxicated by words and chimeras, paralyzed by
satisfaction and contentment, reading until the deepening twi-
light, until I can no longer make out the words, until my mind
begins to wander, until my aching muscles are no longer able

to keep the book aloft. Joy is the anticipation of joy. Reading a fine book for the first time is as sumptuous as the first sip of orange juice that breaks the fast in Ramadan.

Now, I haven't fasted since I was forced to as a child. I just remember what it was like.

I adjust myself in the reading chair, pull my legs up. It's going to be a long, voluptuous ride.

I flip delicate pages with an unhurried and measured beat, a lazy metronome timing. I lose myself in the book's languorous territories. I'm transported to a café in Trieste, become intimately acquainted with its idiosyncratic patrons. I travel along the book's meandering paths — breakfast with a young man in one village, lunch with a crone in another — salivate over beautiful sentences, celebrate holidays I'd never heard of. I read and read until I am abruptly bashed over the head by the full weight of Esperia's story, a throwaway of no more than four pages in a three-hundred-page tome. Esperia, an incidental character indelibly rendered in a few phrases, a bit player in life, mirrors Hannah.

I'm not allowed an escape.

The story induces a state of disequilibrium: dizziness and a slight nausea. In my ear a ringing commences, a small hyperactive church bell. I'm no longer able to see what is before me, I'm no longer able to hear what is around me, I'm no longer able to recall who I am. I lay the book facedown upon my chest, steal a long breath. Shudders course through my body, electric shocks through my vertebrae. I feel cold. Steady breathing can't warm me.

First my mother barges back into my life, then Hannah. What is this?

I don't believe in coincidence.

❋   ❋   ❋

"Hunger is what I remember of my childhood — hunger, insatiable, voracious, devouring." Hannah wrote that sentence in one of her middle-years journals. She began registering her thoughts in diaries at an early age; the first recorded birthday was her tenth. I inherited all of them, of course. She gave them to me — well, left them to me, my name on a little piece of paper.

The early diaries are barely legible, childish script in pencil in spiral-bound notebooks. The wires have rusted and stiffened. The fold-around orange cover has faded, the manufacturer's logo (Clairefontaine, I believe) is almost unrecognizable. The paper is aged and warped and frayed and discolored, or not discolored but multihued — aging births new colors, variations of yellow and burnt orange in this case, the colors of a dying fire. Reading the childhood diaries is like deciphering ancient papyrus. The post-teen journals are better preserved, in indelible ink on pristine white paper, her handwriting flawless and arabesque formal.

Immaculately committed to the process, she wrote every night, and some days, until a couple of months before her death. Those months, those weeks, are the ones I'm most interested in. I have a general idea of what happened to her, or at least I've formed a plausible theory, but if I had her writings of the last few weeks, I might be able to understand fully what induced the Ovidian metamorphosis, what she was thinking, to understand her pain, or possibly humiliation, the second transformation of her life, from butterfly to self-conscious housefly. Those months were lost to me.

Hannah wasn't only speaking of physical hunger. The year of her birth, 1922, fifteen years before mine, was after the Lebanese famine had ended for the most part — Ottoman soldiers and a plague of locusts, the interchangeable pests, had feasted on all our food during the Great War. She arrived into a lower-middle-class family, though by no means poor, the fifth child, the only daughter.

It was said that her mother was in labor for a whole week because Hannah was much too shy to make an appearance in our world. It was said that when she was finally forced out, she was too embarrassed to cry, or even whimper. Her face, her bottom, her entire newborn body, was as red as a dry-farmed tomato. All this was told as if it were fact, without a trace of irony. She did have fox-red hair.

As a child, her parents loved her, her brothers adored her, doted on her. She was the family's baby. She was fed. She did not sleep on an empty stomach.

She was born with two deformities: a slight clubfoot and that excessive shyness. The latter was healed in her twenties, the former never completely so. Treatments for her left foot began when she was still an infant.

Three buildings to the right of her father's home, the house where she joined our world, stood an azadirachta tree and a faux Ottoman three-story building in which an Arabic healer lived. Out of respect, many Beirutis called him an Arabic doctor; ungullible people called him a quack. The azadirachta, also called a neem, or zanzalacht in our beautiful language, was his bread and butter, or bread and sap. The alleged medical benefits of the tree's resin brought the ill to his doorstep from all over Lebanon. (In the 1990s, years after our pretender ungracefully expired, years after

Arabic doctors ceased to practice, a resourceful Sri Lankan laborer struck the rich tree and sold ampoules of the resin to the thousands of Ceylonese maids in Beirut. The neem's curative powers were known in their homeland as well.) The sap seeped into every medicine the Arabic healer prescribed. He even mixed it in with the plaster he used to set bones.

Hannah wrote of the pains she endured at that charlatan's hands, some remembered, some reimagined. Hoping that it would reset correctly, he broke her foot twice before she was four. She couldn't possibly remember what the first time was like, she wrote, for she was barely six months old. Yet when she was informed of the incident, she began having nightmares about wailing infants that lasted into her early twenties. She wasn't anesthetized for any of the breaks. She couldn't recall the procedure itself, whether any implements were used — unfettered minds might imagine anvils and mallets and blacksmith's aprons — but she recalled the resulting agony.

I'm intrigued by the details she remembered, what she wrote in her journal — details recorded in her late teens, more than ten years after her visits to the quack. She remembered a clean white waiting room; the Arabic doctor's Jordanian wife mopping a constantly wet floor and dusting every nook but unable to reach one corner of the ceiling, from which dropped a bunch of plastic grapes and their dusty, insincere leaves. Hannah's father, not her mother, at her side. The second room, the torture chamber, outwardly clean but suffused with a subtle purulent scent. Light air, subtle air, shallow breathing. The man himself: lanky, emaciated, with bright, clear eyes and a malevolent smile. Was it all reconstructed? He wore frayed moccasins with no socks.

Her father's courtesy that bordered on the extravagant. On a shelf, jars of powders, herbs, and viscous liquids. The pain.

Hannah didn't think her shyness had much to do with the inflicted pain — no causality, at least not according to her. Her barely perceptible hobble didn't explain her shyness, but she thought that it certainly didn't help matters. You and I might not have noticed much of a limp, but she did (she described her walk as that of a non-alpha gorilla). It was difficult for her. She was also right in suggesting that any prospective suitor, and his keen-eyed family, would notice.

There were no suitors, except for the lieutenant, and he wasn't exactly one either. I'll get to him in a minute.

Nothing could explain the hunger, however.

Hannah ate and ate, anything and everything that was before her. She couldn't stop, nor did it occur to her to. As a child, she had a fondness for fruit. Apparently, her mother realized there was a problem when Hannah single-handedly ate an entire cluster of bananas that her father had brought home and placed on the kitchen table. That's about twenty-five bananas in one sitting. She was four.

Her family was slow to catch on because she wasn't fat, or, I should say, she wasn't obese. I knew her as well rounded, buxom and curvaceous, but not unattractively so. It seems she looked much the same as a child and teenager, robust and flush with good health. When her mother began to pay attention, she realized that Hannah was eating constantly. As in any Beiruti kitchen, rich or poor, food was always around, and Hannah partook.

Her mother began to put food away, offering it only at prescribed times. Hannah was confused at first, but adjusted. Since the meals were common plates that all shared, she still ate everything before her, except now that included everybody else's meal. Food landed on the table, food disappeared from the table. She swallowed food as if it were going to vanish, and, of course, it was going to. Dinners became a family race. A brother who hesitated for a second missed his meal. Her parents tried to talk to her, but she was too young to understand. She was hungry.

Her father tried a different tactic. He brought home a case of mandarins. He explained to Hannah that it was all for her, no one else was to touch it. She could store it in her room and eat at her leisure. The case of mandarins wasn't going to disappear.

It did, of course. By herself in the bedroom, she ate the whole case in one evening. At midnight she was wailing because of a major bellyache.

There were many drawings in her journals, mostly doodles and meaningless sketches. One, though, informed by hunger, as she called it, was striking, at least to me. Later, much later, as an adult woman, she wrote of her need to be loved, to be desired, as a ravenous monster with an exigent appetite living in a black hole within. Whatever love was thrown her way, the monster devoured it and left her with nothing. The drawing of the insistent beast was delicate and finely rendered. A dragonlike creature peeks its equine head out of the hole, a perfect circle—perfect ellipse because of the viewer's perspective—crosshatched unto death to show how dark it really was, how black the hole.

That was my Hannah.

Like all of us, she lived, she survived. Contrary to what you'd expect, or what I would, she wasn't teased or tortured in the neighborhood. A plump, freckle-faced redhead (not that rare in Beirut, but still) who had a limp and blushed bright blood at the appearance of any human of an unfamily variety?

How did she escape mockery for her awkwardness?

Her family was liked and respected. Her brothers, who watched over her, were popular. She wrote that if it hadn't been for her infirmities, she would have had suitors begging for her hand, and she was probably right, but that wasn't all there was to her being somewhat accepted. She had an insatiable desire to please, "an ignoble craving," as she described it in her journals. She had an uncanny ability to read what people wanted, even as a youngster, and was ever ready to offer what was needed. At home, she understood when her mother needed help around the house, when her father wanted a back rub. At school she always carried two of everything, pens, pencils, erasers. Just as a girl's pen ran out, Hannah's extra seemed to appear as if by magic. She was not disliked, was tolerated when not ignored. She was studious, of course, since that was what pleased her family and her teachers.

She wrote of what it felt like when a neighbor or teacher asked her a question or spoke to her, how fast her heart beat, how the skin of her hands flushed, how her lungs shrank, how her throat constricted, and how her jaw ached.

When she was seven, she moved back into her parents' bed. Their house had only two bedrooms, four boys, one girl. It seems that when one of the boys reached a certain age, her father decided Hannah shouldn't be in the same room with her brothers. Until her father built another two rooms when she was fourteen, she slept with her parents: father on the left, mother the middle mote, Hannah on the right. She wrote fondly of those days. She had no trouble sleeping at that age, a talent inherited from her mother. She would climb into bed behind her mother and disappear into the movie world of dreams. Her father lacked that aptitude, and since she also inherited her mother's snoring, his nightly insomnia became a long-running joke in the household.

"We breathed his air," she wrote.

She was socially inept, an affliction I am quite intimate with. In some ways, that's probably what brought us together, but I'm getting ahead of myself as usual. There was something else that classified us as quite different, at least in my book, and in her journal. Throughout her teenage years, she wrote her fantasies. They were detailed and intricate descriptions of romance, of marriage, never of sex, always of rescue. It was as if she was anticipating the sanitized romance novels that would hit the Beirut market a few years later. When she was older, she was addicted to Italian photo-romans (translated into French), mawkish love stories told in photographs and see-through talk balloons. However, those didn't appear in Beirut until the early fifties, so they couldn't possibly have inspired her elaborate adolescent fantasies. She was ahead of her time.

The fantasies were well drafted and delightfully drawn up. One impressive journal entry when she was fourteen described in minutest detail the future drawing room where she and her husband would entertain. The descriptions of her future beau tended to be more fugitive, changing from entry to entry: tall, medium height, hairy, smooth, mustached, clean-shaven. How they would meet—strolling on the corniche where eyes glance in passing, looking up from a schoolbook to encounter blue eyes filled with amorous and admiring desire—had more variations than the *Goldberg*.

One of the surprising things—it astounded me really—was that who she was varied as well. In over a hundred journal entries of romantic fantasies, not a single one included her. She wrote of a different Hannah. In some she was a blonde, in others a brunette. She was an Egyptian actress, an abandoned European princess, an exiled Russian countess. She kept her name but not herself. She was rich, she was penniless, she had long eyelashes, a small nose. She walked with the grace of a gazelle, of a poplar, of a girl without a limp. She wrote herself out of her fantasies.


What about my fantasies? I wouldn't consider them that— more like mild dreams or tame aspirations. I rarely dreamed of romance or adventure, never of love and husbands. I would be married, I knew that, but I treated that fact as a fact, an impeding fait accompli, not as something to look forward to. I didn't spend time considering whom I would marry or how. I wanted to be allowed to work. I hoped for a career as a secretary. In those days, I couldn't envision any other job. The only workingwomen I came across at the time were in the service business: maids, cooks, store clerks, secretaries, schoolteachers. By temperament, I couldn't be around a lot of people. Secretary seemed like an idyllic job— an assistant to an intelligent, honest, and decent man, of course. I spent more time dreaming of my ideal boss than of a husband.

How does the old cliché go? When every Arab girl stood in line waiting for God to hand out the desperate-to-get-married gene, I must have been somewhere else, probably lost in a book.

I do understand that it isn't just Arab girls who have that gene, but it is dominant in our part of the world. A force of nature and nurture, an epigenetic hurricane, herds us into marrying and breeding. Social cues, community rites, religious rituals, family events — all are meant to impress upon children the importance and inevitability of what Bruno Schulz calls the "excursion into matrimony." No girl of my generation could imagine rebelling, nor would she want to. A kernel of imagination begins to sprout in the minds of women younger than I. Fadia rebelled, yet her idea of rebellion was the same as that of every other girl of succeeding generations. She wanted the right to choose whom to marry. In time, the shackles of arranged marriage were dumped in the Mediterranean; families grew inured to exogamous marriages, be they interfaith, interclass, or interclan. Dating, premarital cohabitation, adultery, and promiscuity became ordinary painted scenes of the current Beiruti landscape.

Feminism in Lebanon hasn't reached espadrilles or running shoes yet; sensible heels are where it's at. The choice not to marry hasn't entered the picture. It may be entering now, but I wouldn't know. I don't associate much with the young.

As I write this I wonder if what I said about not dreaming of a husband is accurate. I'm not suggesting that I'm consciously dissembling. But to paraphrase the ever-paraphraseable Freud, who said something to the effect that when you speak about the past you lie with every breath you take, I will say this:

When you write about the past, you lie with each letter, with every grapheme, including the goddamn comma.
Memory, memoir, autobiography—lies, lies, all lies.
Is it true that I didn't think of a husband, wish for one,
or has the image I have of myself, the way I like to think of
myself, superimposed itself on what was happening then?
Does that question make sense?

Let me put it another way. It is quite possible that I, like
every Beiruti girl, dreamed of getting married, had fantasies
of what my future husband would look like, but that after
growing up, after having had a sad and incomplete matrimonial experience, I reinvented myself, convincing myself
that I hadn't dreamed of such trivial matters. It is possible.
I sincerely believe that I didn't, but I also don't see myself
having had that much courage as a young girl.

I keep the possibility open.


There are images that remain with me. I remember reading
an essay—I believe it was by Nuruddin Farah, but I can't
be sure—where the writer says that all we remember from
novels are scenes or, more precisely, images. I don't know
if that's the case, but a number of authors seem to write
their novels in one image after another—Michael Ondaatje
is probably the best practitioner of the form, as his novels
seem to me to be not so much plot as a series of discrete
divine images. I still can't remember who wrote that essay.
Maybe it was Ondaatje, but I doubt it.

I'm not a proponent of the above idea, because if all
we retain from a novel is an image, then the obvious conclusion is that photography, painting, or film would be a

better medium of communication and a higher art form.
Not a satisfying conclusion. Also, I loved *The English Patient*
as a novel, but the movie, with the exception of the lovely
Juliette Binoche, is much too syrupy.

I bring this up, however, to mention an image that is
seared into my memory—an image by the exquisitely disconsolate W. G. Sebald. He describes a great-uncle Alphonso in
the act of painting: "When he was thus engaged he generally
wore glasses with gray silk tissue instead of lenses in the
frames, so that the landscape appeared through a fine veil
that muted its colors, and the weight of the world dissolved
before your eyes."

Beautiful.

Sometimes I think I look back on my life wearing glasses
with gray silk tissue in the frames.

If I am to think of what image you'll retain from reading
these paltry pages, I assume it will be my mother's screaming,
the frail body, the position of her hands, the skirl of terror.

Am I right?

Most people say they feel nostalgia for their childhood,
or for a first love, or maybe for Beirut as it once was, or
for parents who have passed away. I don't, not in the sense
everyone means. I feel nostalgia for scenes. I don't recall the
years of my youth with affection; I don't my family either:
my dead uncle-father, or my mother still alive. However, I
do recall with a certain fondness the manner in which we
children slept on summer nights with their pitiless heat,
windows open and the smell of jasmine floating in, the colors and patterns of the sheets in the dark. What was most
irritating then—having to get out of bed when my little
half sister wet the mattress—I now remember with a tinge

of devotion, not for her or her predicament, but for how we always stood in the same spot around my mother as she examined the wet abstractions on the sheets, how we carried the mattress outside to air and sun-clean it. I feel a certain tenderness for the way the furniture was arranged in the main room, the way the large brass tray sitting atop the round burlap ottoman was set for dinner.

But then I feel nostalgia for the walks by Swann's Way, as well as by Guermantes Way, for how Charles Kinbote surprises John Shade while he's taking a bath, for how Anna Karenina sits in a train.


I met a secretary once, a classmate's mother. She walked her daughter to school one morning and delivered her to the gate, at which point the grizzled Armenian guard stepped briefly out of his kiosk to greet them, which he always did when a parent appeared.

Was Hercules the gatekeeper of Heaven? I wouldn't describe the aged Armenian as Hercules in any case. His job was to make sure that none of the students left before school was out and that none but students and teachers entered, which meant that even though he approached the mother obsequiously, he was in essence taking her child away and forbidding her entry. So no, not Hercules. As much as I loved it and felt at home within its cages, school is more Hades than Heaven — a ritual killing of childhood is performed in school, children are put to death. The guard was the ferryman.

As she handed him her daughter, the mother bathed him in a patrician smile. She wore a tailor-made dress that looked as if it belonged to someone else, as if she intended to grow into it though she carried it off. It was a gray dress of a shade quite different from the pewter gray of the menacing sky that day. Around her shoulders she had wrapped a bright blue shawl. Unlike the arriving teachers, all afflicted with a plague of inattentiveness, she seemed to be relating to the world around her, awake and participating. As I write this, I recall how wonderful I felt while watching her, how young she seemed as a mother, still retaining something organically girlish about her.

I watched the handoff from behind the school fence, looking out through the bars—yes, actual metal bars that my head could fit through only the year before. The bars were covered with lumpy layers of cheap yellow paint, caged-canary hue; it was peeling and chipping, the rust that peeked through complementing the yellow nicely. I was staring. My hands held on to the bars, my face squeezed in between, both cheekbones pressed to painted metal.

The daughter, my classmate, strolled to my side. She watched her mother exchanging unnecessary pleasantries with the ferryman. We, on the other hand, didn't exchange a word. Her mother noticed us and walked over. She politely inquired who I was, whether I was a friend to her daughter—a brief, kind question that only required me to nod yes or no.

"I wish you a most pleasant day, girls," she said.

She extended her arm through the bars. I can still see the shawl slip from her right shoulder as she ran her fingers through my hair—the one time, as far as I remember, that anyone ever did that—after which, she left.

"She can write shorthand," my classmate said.

❋   ❋   ❋

I've strayed too far once more. Sorry. Let me get back to
Hannah.

What brought Hannah and me together wasn't so much
our social ineptitude, as I've mentioned, but her meeting
my brother-in-law that fateful day, though that fateful day
occurred long before I was married, when I was still a child.

She was twenty-two when she met him, embarrassingly
single by the standards of the time, but not yet a certified
spinster. Her journal entries then were mostly meditations
on what her future life would look like, which girl in the
neighborhood had been proposed to, how her status in the
family was changing. By the time she harpooned the lieutenant, all her brothers had already married. Thirteen weeks
before that fateful day, one of her sisters-in-law had a baby
boy, the first grandson in the family, the fourth grandchild.

She described a telling incident. The newest sister-in-
law, Maryam, recently married and relocated to Hannah's
home (only two of the brothers were still in the small house
then), was deep in conversation with Hannah's father. The
discussion might have been beyond her depth, Hannah
wrote, but the girl, a few years younger than she, was happy,
peppy, and loud. Hannah wrote that her new sister-in-law
"couldn't understand stillness"—quite a wonderful phrase,
if you ask me.

The family was having afternoon coffee in the living
room. Hannah's father slurped his coffee as the girl went on
and on. When Hannah finished her cup, she picked up her
mother's empty one and carried both toward the kitchen.

As she approached, Maryam, still jabbering and hooting, eyes only on her father-in-law, held her own cup out, left arm extended straight in Hannah's way.

Hannah stopped, her toes curled, her shoes digging into the carpet. Of course, she was more embarrassed than furious at that point. She didn't know what to do. The girl hadn't even looked at her. Hannah tried to carry the extra cup but she wasn't as dexterous as her mother. Ticktock, the room's clock mocked her, but none paid attention.

"I'll bring the tray," Hannah told her sister-in-law. "Just one minute."

Maryam jumped up, horrified by her indiscretion and insensitivity. "Please forgive me, sister," she said, "I wasn't paying attention. I am shamed. Let me relieve you, please. I will take all."

"There is no need for forgiveness," Hannah said. "None."

Both girls took the cups to the kitchen.


Let me take a brief detour, very brief. Ticktock.

Pundits these days keep jabbering and hooting about the Internet being the greatest advancement. Web this, web that, and let the resident spider suck the life out of you. Being connected to the world doesn't appeal to me.

As someone living alone, as an aging woman, the technological discovery I love most is the electric clock, though with Beirut's electricity, I should say the battery-operated clock. Do you have any idea how much anxiety those old clocks induced? Ticktock, you're all alone in an empty apartment. Ticktock, the world outside is going to come and get

AN UNNECESSARY WOMAN          133

you. Ticktock, you're not getting any younger, are you?
Give me a tranquilizer, please.

The ticktock tattooing of the march of time.

The ticktock of the tiny object full of gears suffocating
all existence, wringing life out of life.

After that wonderful discovery, the clock's hands still
turned in the same direction — it's called clockwise, for all
you youngsters — time still marched forward, but miraculously, its heartbeat, its ominous announcement, was reduced to a meek buzz.


Hannah was being truthful when she told her sister-in-law
that there was no need for forgiveness. She didn't hold
the incident against her. It was inconsequential, Hannah
believed, a minor faux pas. It wasn't as if the insult was
intended. Maryam felt so guilty that she tried to appease
Hannah. As a matter of fact, the two women lived harmo-
niously in the same household until Hannah died, and to
this day Maryam is the one who brings fresh flowers to
Hannah's gravesite every week, placing them exactly two
hands' width in front of the tombstone.

The writing in the journals changed, though. For a
while after the incident the sentences shrank. The entries
grew terse and irritated — jerky, jittery jottings, even when
she wrote about the meals she had.

Toward the second half of 1944, with her nascent and
hopeful nation living through its first year of independence,
Hannah decided that she would not remain at home all the
time.

What could a young middle-class woman of her day do? One who was educated, fluent in two languages, Arabic and French, and "how do you do?" familiar with a third, English? One who had loved and excelled in philosophy in high school?

Not much.

To begin with, her father, as was to be expected, was opposed to his daughter working, opposed to her generating any kind of income. He was a good man. She adored him. His obstructionism was of its time.

She talked to him, pleaded and persuaded, until he relented on his first objection but not on his second. He gave her permission to work, but not to generate income. No girl of his was going to be allowed to ruin her reputation. She could help him at his grocery store. Hannah was ecstatic.

She began on a Monday morning and for three days she wrote of how much she enjoyed working. She did everything, from stacking to cleaning to helping customers to handling money. Her diary entries were longer, more florid, more detailed, and joyous. Her father was doubly ecstatic, for not only was he able to make his beloved daughter happy, but he began to notice that the women of the neighborhood were staying longer in the store and buying more. His daughter wasn't the most talkative of people, but women certainly talked to her more than they did to him or to his two sons who shared the work. Hannah was beginning to shed her shy skin. For a brief time she was the belle of the grocery store.

Three days, the perfection lasted three days. On Wednesday evening, at dinner, listening to her husband laud Hannah's salutary presence at the grocery store, Hannah's mother wondered if she too could help. After all, her children were grown, her household duties had long ago shrunk. Why not? All thought it was a grand idea, even the sons, and it most certainly was.

Father, mother, and child opened the store on Thursday morning. They worked together happily, and the business did well. It was a small store, though, and there wasn't enough work to go around. They shared, and since the income wasn't divided any differently, they managed. Everyone seemed content, though the situation was not as perfect as it had been in the first three days since she had less to do.

But as Hannah, a devout Muslim if there ever was one, always said, "God does provide."

One day about two weeks into her foray at the store, Hannah was standing around with nothing to do when a customer suggested that she volunteer her time where she would be most needed, the local hospital. Hannah thought it was a grand idea, her mother thought it was a grand idea, her father consented. For the next two months, until the day she met the lieutenant, Hannah was a hospital volunteer who never took any time off and worked as many hours as she was allowed.

Where would a hospital place a young middle-class woman who was educated, who was fluent in two languages and familiar with a third, who had loved and excelled in philosophy at school?

In the cafeteria, of course, serving food. Would you like a gloomy Wittgenstein with your rice, or a bitter Schopenhauer? A cup of Hegelian metaphors, perhaps?

Wearing a yellow front-buttoned uniform, a hairnet, a white bobby-pinned paper cap, beige tights, and low white patent leather heels, she waited for the doctors, nurses, and visitors to decide which of the stews they wished to eat that day before she ladled the choice onto a plate. Potato stew, plop, gone, next, cauliflower stew, plop, gone, next, lima beans, plop, gone, next, three hours a day. No one paid any attention to her.

She loved it.

Although by then her childish hunger had been somewhat sated, she also still loved to eat. She didn't write about it in her diary, but I can guarantee you that she partook more than just a little from every course she served. There we had an eater at an eatery.

She was happy, her mother was happy, her father was happy.

In the morning she put on her uniform—a uniform radiant with a supernatural cleanliness—went to work, and returned home after lunch still in that yellow getup.

How did she get to and from work? Therein lies the story.

Beirut at the time had a modest tram system, which of course disappeared when the city decided to modernize itself in the sixties and seventies. One line used to stop only two buildings away from her hospital. Unfortunately for Hannah, the line didn't reach her house. She would have had to walk for ten minutes to reach the tram stop, something she wouldn't do because she was much too self-conscious of her limp.

Beirut has another system for transporting its residents, a nonpublic one that has been around as long as the automobile. Beirutis call it a *service* (pronounced as in French, not

English). It is an organic jitney system. Customers stand at the side of the road, service cars slow down as they approach, the customer tells the driver where he wishes to go, and the driver decides whether to pick him up. For one cheap fare, you can go anywhere in the city as long as it's along the driver's route. Most cars can fit five passengers, two in front next to the driver, three in back.

In 1944 anyone with a car could pick up passengers, but sometime in the fifties you had to get a special license plate, a red one, to be able to do so.

In 1944 no respectable woman used a service. You had no idea who would share the car with you, or, worse, whether the driver would say something inappropriate. A respectable woman avoided a service. Hannah didn't.

The choice between being seen walking or being seen taking a service was a straightforward one. She always chose the latter, but she paid a double fare so she wouldn't have to sit next to a stranger. She wouldn't sit in front next to the driver. She sat in back and bought two places so that only one person could share the seat with her and would sit at the other window. She considered this a chaste and appropriate solution.

Her system worked. For two months she didn't have a single problem, not one. She girded herself against snide or salacious remarks from one of the drivers or passengers, but none was forthcoming. Beirutis, it seemed, were gentlemen, at least around her. She thought the crisp yellow hospital uniform and particularly the paper cap had a lot to do with the respect she received. Every morning she left home and waited briefly on the curb for the appropriate service. She wouldn't take a car that had more than one passenger in back. She arrived at the hospital not twenty minutes later. It was easy.

She had her first problem on November 21, 1944, a day she would consider the happiest of her life, the most felicitous.

God does provide.

It was the day before the country was to celebrate its first year of independence. Everyone seemed to be preparing for this joyous occasion. From their various inessential assignments around the country, soldiers poured into the city to prepare for a parade of grand pretensions.

Hannah had finished serving lunch and was returning home. The jitney that slowed down for her had two passengers in front and none in the back. Before entering the car, she made sure to tell the driver, a man advanced in age, with carefully trimmed white hair and mustache, that she was buying two seats. Not twenty meters ahead, my ex-husband's eldest brother, the lieutenant himself, joined her in the backseat, delivered to her by the iron chains of circumstance.

Providence! Destiny!

A man, just the right age, with carefully trimmed black hair and mustache; a handsome man wearing the national gray uniform — a uniform radiant with a supernatural cleanliness mirroring hers, a cap atop his head — sat next to her, less than a meter away. A man right out of her journals, out of her fantasies, a tenant of her dreams, shared the same car, shared her world.

The driver, impressed by having a Lebanese soldier in his car and by his own percolating patriotism, tried to chat up the newcomer, but received little in response. Hannah's lieutenant was just as shy as she was.

She blushed, as if she had just dipped into a tub of hot water, her skin turning tingly and red, the color of her hair. She couldn't help herself. She stared out her window but looked awry through the corner of her eye, trying to examine her possible future husband. She was sure he could hear the clamor of her insatiable heart. She tried to slow her breathing.

He was ever so quiet.

They'd been in the car together for only eight minutes when her panic erupted.

The car slowed for another soldier standing on the curb. She heard herself utter the word *no*, quite loudly. The service had four passengers already. This soldier would force her lieutenant next to her, into the seat she had paid for. "No," she said, before the driver could pick up the extra passenger.

The driver was genuinely polite at first, but sitting behind him, Hannah noticed that his hair wasn't carefully trimmed at all. A confetti of dandruff and a sprinkling of macassar oil held it together. "That won't be a problem, madam," he said, "I'll return the price of one fare."

"No," she said. "No." Her voice was louder and shriller than she would have wished. She wanted to insist that she had paid for two, insist once more and again. She wanted to explain that she had no wish to be squeezed next to a man, particularly this most endearing lieutenant, but her heart beat loudly, her lungs shrank like a deflated balloon, and she experienced verbal paralysis. The only word she could say was *no*.

"He's a soldier," the driver insisted. "We can't leave him standing on the side of the road. He's a Lebanese soldier."

"No," she said. "No."

The passengers in front glared at her with infinite disapproval. Incensed, the driver huffed like a fish out of water, lips pursed, cheeks puffed. "We must honor our soldiers," he said.

It was at this point that her knight came to the rescue and picked up her white handkerchief. "He can take another car," the lieutenant said, "since this one is obviously full."

Like most of us on many an occasion, he had vastly overestimated the power of reason. That sentence was the only one the chivalrous lieutenant was allowed to speak. The seething driver — the hottest smoke of Hell leaked out of his ears, the vilest words exploded out of his mouth — kicked both Hannah and the lieutenant out of his car, although he returned her double fare.

The princess and her knight, slightly shell-shocked, watched as their carriage sped away with the other soldier, leaving them behind in a fog of gray exhaust.

"I am sorry," said the lieutenant. "I probably made a minor matter worse."

"No," replied the princess, neither loud nor shrill, thankfully.

She wished to explain how much she appreciated his standing up for her, how helpless she'd felt before he intervened, how grateful she was, how long she'd waited for a man to come into her life, how happy she could make him and, most important, what a good wife she'd be.

"We can take another car," he said.

It was the use of that pronoun that sealed his fate. I can tell you that from the day she met him until the day he died, Hannah, in her journal entries, used the first person plural about five times as much as the singular.

Hannah was too overwhelmed to ride in another car. She couldn't. He asked if she wished to rest before they took another. She shook her head. He asked if she could walk home. That she could do. He walked her home. It was on his way. A Proustian promenade.

The comfortable autumnal temperatures still prevailed, the air crisp but not dry. A leisurely walk. She carried her handbag, while he carried a gun in his holster and a rifle strapped about his shoulder. She knew he noticed her minor limp with the first step because he slowed down to make her feel more at ease. He was almost as uncomfortable with the spoken word as she was. For the first twenty steps or so, each stuttered, trying to initiate a polite chat, a considerate conversation. Finally, Hannah was able to form a full, coherent, and grammatically correct sentence.

"Thank you for saving me," she said.

He begged her to think nothing of it.

"I am grateful," she said.

"I could do nothing else," he said, in a voice that cracked at the first syllable. "I was only doing my duty. No honest man could have lived with himself had he allowed that inconsiderate animal to treat a lady as he did."

In the journal, she underlined the word *lady* three times.

"You are from a good family, the driver isn't," he said. "He should know how to behave toward his betters."

She underlined the phrase "good family" only once.

"You bought that seat and he agreed to it," he said. "Only a scoundrel reneges on his agreements. A man's word is the only thing that separates him from beasts." The lovely lieutenant then looked into her eyes and finished the thought with, "I always keep my word."

If using the pronoun *we* had sealed his fate, that last sentence poured hot red wax over it and stamped it with his family insignia.

He may have been trying to be kind. He may have thought this was what a gentleman did. He may have thought that wearing the uniform, he was duty bound to present the national army in good light. No matter.

In Hannah's eyes, the gentleman lieutenant had proposed.

She wrote it down in her journal.

Her neighbors saw him accompany her. She walked with head held high, a proud woman, the tip of her nose pointing upward. She was certain everyone could tell that she had transformed into a woman betrothed; she undoubtedly walked like one.

Her neighbors saw him deliver her to her door, saw him take her hands in parting. They heard her say, "Please extend our invitation to your family for a visit." They saw Hannah's brother open the door, an expression of shock painted on his face, saw the men shake hands in greeting as Hannah demurely withdrew into her home. They saw the lieutenant leave the neighborhood, oblivious to the fact that he was being observed and measured.

Her family was stunned, of course. How unusual a proposal!

Her mother declaimed that she had never heard of such a thing. One of Hannah's brothers said that the lieutenant must have been smitten on the spot. Another brother thought God must have intervened and guided the lieutenant's will. How fortunate, her sister-in-law Maryam exclaimed, how propitious!

"Why didn't he come with his family and ask me for your hand," her father said, "like normal people?"

"I'm certain he will," Hannah replied.

An invitation to lunch was sent by hand to his family.


An invitation to lunch? I can't remember ever having any visitors over for lunch, other than my ex-husband and Hannah, neither of whom I'd consider guests, and both have passed away.

One of the things that concerns me is that I'm turning into the kind of old woman I've desperately tried to avoid becoming, the one always directing the conversation back to herself. Hannah's family invited my ex-husband's family to lunch. Oh, poor me, I've never had people over for lunch. I can't abide that. Well, I can't abide it in other people.

I used to find old people, men and women, terribly narcissistic. All they ever want to do is talk about themselves. But then, what are these pages if not an exercise in narcissism? What are these pages?

Yet I do talk about other people. I'm a failed narcissist. I haven't succeeded even though I've inherited the best genes. I'm not as good as my mother.

My mother didn't wait till she was older to reach her peak. She began circling the top of narcissistic Everest at an early age, and later, after her husband died and her children grew, she floated above the entire Himalayas. The subjects she specialized in, or was willing to engage in, were, in order: herself, her boys, her husband, and the inferiority of everyone else. I exaggerate only slightly.

As I write this, as the nib of my pen follows its shadow slowly from right to left, my mind floods with memories of the egregious things she's said. I feel my temperature rise. My cheeks and neck flush, my eyes seem to broil in their sockets, my tongue and palate become dry.

I feel physically ill. I should eat something this morning, maybe boil another cup of water for tea, but I can't move. I am listless and weary. I am lassitude. An amorphous anxiety smothers me.

The pelting rain on the windowpane soothes my wearied memories and me, but barely. My ears are damp from hearing its patter, my mind cools.

If, as a child, I returned home with some injury, say a bleeding knee from a fall, it was an opportunity for my mother to rattle off all the hurts she'd sustained in her life. How she'd bumped her knee on the coffee table just that morning, how she'd scalded her hand dropping a kettle when she was twelve, how much pain her delicate stomach caused her. Most times, she'd forget to tend to my cut.

My first period was a chance for her to elaborate on how awful hers were. I had to listen to her describe in detail the exact nature of the queasiness announcing that her period would commence two days hence.

She prepared me for my wedding night by regaling me with how unprepared she'd been for hers, how horrific it was, how negligent her own mother had been for not telling her anything. She sat me on her bed the night before my wedding while her husband was visiting my in-laws, finalizing contracts. The lights low, the summer heat suffocating, mosquitoes running interference, she explained about babies, then remembered that she'd already done that. She

AN UNNECESSARY WOMAN                    145

told me she'd experienced pain and lots of it. That was all she could think of to say. "It hurt so much and it went on and on until I was used to it."

You know, at least she did tell me. In her own way, she warned me of possibilities and explained the basic mechanics of sex by telling me how terrible her night was. Not that it helped me, of course, since I doubt she knew anything about male impotence. Neither one of us considered the possibility that I'd be a virgin for quite a while longer. She isn't a good mother, but she's better than her own.

While she is a narcissist and difficult to be around, at times I can forgive her. I don't believe you can reach your eighty-eighth year without being convinced that the world revolves around you.

At other times, I can't forgive.

You may think that the examples above show that my mother was more inconsiderate than nasty. Let me correct you.

I don't recall what took Hannah and me over to my mother's house all those years ago, probably just a visit. My husband hadn't left me yet, so it must have been in the mid-1950s. My mother, probably half the age I am now, answered the door. As soon as we entered, she led me away by my elbow and whispered in my ear, "Don't bring her here."

I was surprised. I wasn't yet inured to her admonishments at the time. I couldn't understand what the problem was.

"We're a good family," she said. "I don't want people to talk. You can keep company with her if you so wish, but not in my house."

I was confounded. "What's wrong with Hannah?"

"She has red hair," my mother said, as if that explained everything, even to someone as dense as I. Noticing that I was still confused, she snapped, "Bright red hair."

"Well, yes," I said, "I can see that."

She shook her head in frustration. "Her ancestors slept with Crusaders. Do I have to spell it out? That's how she has red hair. She has their blood."

It took me a few seconds to register this. "Wait," I said. "Are you blaming her for having red hair?"

"No, of course not, not me. Her mother also has red hair, though definitely not as bright. I don't blame her, but other people do. I can't help what the neighbors think. Personally, I don't judge. People can sleep with whomever they wish, but they shouldn't come in contact with my family."

What could I say? I was still a teenager.

I could have told her that her ancestors were raped by Crusaders as well, maybe the black Irish instead of the redheads, and by the English and Welsh Crusaders and the French ones. They were also raped by the Arabs when they conquered us, by the Ottomans, by the Romans, and by the Greeks and Macedonians. Hell, Beirut has survived for thousands and thousands of years by spreading her beautiful legs for every army within smelling distance.

You really think the whore was from Babylon?

That Babylonian was an amateur. Beirut, my dear Beirut.

How do you explain such things to my mother?

I keep trying to tell myself that she's an uneducated woman. She believes that if you look up at the stars, warts will sprout on your face. When I was a child, she admonished me whenever I glanced up, just a tap on the back of my head. She was never taught to read or write — I tried to teach her while I was still in school, but as usual, I failed. I can't keep blaming her. She hasn't had any opportunities, has had to make do. She's had a tough life. But I can't seem to stop criticizing her.

Whenever I gingerly remove my mother's noose from around my neck, it is with my own hands that I nearly strangle myself.

I don't like to complain, truly, I don't, but I do find that I am doing so often. To age is to whine.

Should I tell you about my bowel movements?

I'm joking, I'm joking. However, if you have the misfortune of reading Thomas Mann's journals, you'll notice that all he thinks about are his misbehaving bowels, and the perfumed boorish bore was not joking. He wouldn't have been able to joke if his Nobel Prize depended on it.

Most of the books published these days consist of a series of whines followed by an epiphany. I call these memoirs and confessional novels happy tragedies. We shall overcome and all that. I find them sentimental and boring. They are the modern version of *The Lives of the Saints*, with exemplary tales of suffering preceding redemption, only less interesting because we no longer have lecherous Roman centurions lusting after sultry virgin martyrs and smiting their perky, voluptuous, but eternally chaste breasts—less interesting because instead of rising into lush Heaven and His embrace all we get these days is a measly epiphany.

I feel shortchanged, don't you?

Blame Joyce and his *Dubliners*, which I adore, but do pity Mr. Joyce, because the only thing some writers ever understand from his masterpiece is epiphany, epiphany, and one more blasted epiphany. There should be a new literary resolution: no more epiphanies. Enough. Have pity on readers who reach the end of a real-life conflict in confusion and don't experience a false sense of temporary enlightenment.

Dear contemporary writers, you make me feel inadequate because my life isn't as clear and concise as your stories.

I should send out letters to writers, writing programs, and publishers. You're strangling the life out of literature, sentence by well-constructed sentence, book by bland book.

Wasn't Herzog, that writer of cantankerous letters, around my age? That's probably the best Bellow novel. I can't remember whether *Herzog* ended with an epiphany, but somehow I doubt it. I must check.

One day I made a resolution not to complain. As you can see, I failed, but I did make that resolution once. I resolved never to complain again after witnessing a horrific incident years ago.

It was a day early in the civil war, August 1978. Beirut was racked with convulsions under the double weight of oppressive summer heat and three years of fighting; a bleak city, a wearied city. There had been a lull in the engagements, one of that multitude of brief cease-fires. I was walking home from the bookstore, rushing home in point of fact, toward the safety of my reading room with its brocade-patterned cream wallpaper that was faded in many a spot, my reading room with all the furniture in its appropriate place.

About fifteen minutes away from my building, I noticed a man on the other side of the street, a sinister-looking old man wearing multiple layers of coats in that groaning heat, obviously not well, probably insane. I remember that the topmost coat was a green loden. His dark eyes seemed to bore right into me across the distance. He leaned against a charred wall, immobile, next to an open doorway—a double door that had been closed every time I'd passed it—and through that doorway was nothing but darkness, an impenetrable darkness, or a darkness not yet penetrated. I realized even then that I was tired and stressed, that I might be daydreaming, hallucinating a scene, but I hastened my steps and refused to look back. The problem, dream or not, and as terrifying as the chimerical darkness seemed, was that I, or at least a part of me, wanted to walk through that doorway.

I realize now that it must have been a hallucination for it really was too obvious a foreshadowing, a touch of death foretold. Only a few minutes later, several steps on, I saw the corpse.

A man on the side of the road, thrown there, discarded, probably recently, blocked my path—not just a little in my way, but "thou shalt have to step over me" in my way. There was a smell to him, tart and a tad musky, like that of a carpet left in the attic too long. Underneath dried, flaky clots of blood the color of coffee grounds, his face had a bluish pallor. His head lay at an unnatural angle; his forehead wrinkles gathered around the promenade above his nose. Curly hair, a premature white that seemed almost dyed (no blue tint, no Bel Argent), thin and sparse at the edges, gave his head a spectral effect. I thought he was well and sensibly dressed, in a light-colored summer linen suit and a nice tie, also at a bizarre angle.

I was calm at first, placid and tranquil, transcendently serene. I considered the Pessoa quote "Whenever I see a dead body, death seems to me a departure. The corpse looks to me like a suit that was left behind. Someone went away and didn't need to take the one and only outfit he'd worn."

As bloodied and bruised as his face was, his clothes were spotless and dirt free, as if his murderer was someone of refined taste who dressed him up after killing him, waiting until the blood stopped running. I remember thinking, *Yes, it's quite possible that Ahmad, my Ahmad, would do such a thoughtful thing.* It was at that point, I believe, after that notion crossed my mind, that I panicked and ran home as fast as my skinny legs could manage.

I won't bore you with the how-to-calm-yourself-after-seeing-a-dead-body techniques at which all Lebanese become experts, although we are each adherents of different schools of practice. After reaching my apartment, I made a solemn vow that I would never complain about anything. I was alive — no matter what was happening, I was alive. The fact that I could breathe was a miracle. The fact that my eyes could see, the voluptuousness of seeing, that my heart beat, the joy of having a body. A miracle. I would not complain.

Let's get back to the lunch, shall we?

My ex-husband's family visited Hannah's house for lunch — not the entire family, just Papa Lieutenant, Mama Lieutenant, our knight, and his two younger brothers, including the listless mosquito with malfunctioning proboscis, who was eleven then — a most bothersome, sullen eleven, I'm sure. He worshipped his eldest brother and despised Hannah, so his version of events, which he never tired of telling when we were married, was completely different from what she recorded in her diary. He always swore that the lunch was just that, that his brother had not proposed, had no idea that she thought he had, that no one in his family figured out that it was an asking-of-the-hand lunch, neither before nor after.

In her diary entry of that day, Hannah reported that the lunch went swimmingly. "He shook my hand the minute he walked in and never left my side. *We* had delightful conversations, sometimes pleasant and fluffy, sometimes deep and serious. Everyone thought *we* looked good together, definitely well matched. *We* loved the appetizers, particularly the lentils and the cheeses; *we* didn't care for the fattoush, which was too lemony, and *we* couldn't have enough of the grilled meats. *We* ate at least a kilogram."

These passages were elaborately exuberant, the sentences overflowing, words leapfrogging one another, words jumping off the page into my lap. Each line ended with a loop that wanted to complete a full circle before flying off into the red-and-orange sunset at the other end of the room. "My soul was conquered by his right eye, praised and worshipped by his left." The writing sounded nothing like her before or after—a personality anomaly, a desperate infatuation. "He is my throne and I am his crown."

In comparison, Héloïse sounds reasonable and sane.

If, like me, you'd known Hannah before you came across this section of her journals, you'd have a hard time believing that this down-to-earth, sturdy, reliable woman could have written such absurdities. She always seemed to me like a woman who had studiously cut a clear path through the forest of life, but during this unfairly brief period she went off the path and into the thicket and its undergrowth.

Bless her. She was always braver than I, and more adventurous.

Yes, my ex-husband used to swear that his brother knew nothing, that had he proposed, he, my ex-husband, would have been the first to know, for he was the lieutenant's confidant. The last bit I doubt. Just the idea that the self-involved imbecile could have been anyone's confidant is too silly. The lieutenant didn't propose to Hannah, of course. I don't believe he could have. It wouldn't have made any sense. But I also don't believe that my ex-husband's family could have left that lunch still clueless. The self-involved imbecile said that his family believed the lunch was to thank his brother for his kindness in walking Hannah home. Laying down such a spread as a thank-you for walking their daughter home? My ex-husband was an idiot, but I doubt his family was equally unperceptive. I believe Papa and Mama Lieutenant were stunned and confused, were impeccably mannered during the entire lunch, and waited till they were at home alone with their son before grilling him for explanations. I believe the supposed groom was as stunned and confused as they were. Poor man.

The following day, Hannah's father paid her knight's father a visit. My ex-husband claimed that this was the first time anyone in his family had an inkling. Be that as it may, the meeting was friendly, each patriarch suggesting that a discussion with his progeny was in order before moving ahead.

Over the next two weeks, the lieutenant visited Hannah four times, twice each week. Each time, he was supposed to tell his damsel that he didn't intend to marry her. According to the imbecile, the lieutenant told her every time but she wouldn't listen, didn't know how to listen. I doubt that was the case. I think he tried to tell her but was too shy and the right opportunity didn't present itself. He couldn't bring himself to do it, didn't want to hurt her. Her parents left them alone in the living room so they could talk, and talk they did, but he didn't tell her.

There is a picture of them sitting next to each other in the living room, not too close, on two different couches, she beaming for the camera, he not looking too morose. She's in her best dress, her hair combed into a tight bun. He's in his uniform, sans rifle, of course, a filter cigarette in his hand. He is definitely better looking than his brother: wide mouth, fuller lips, and, most important, curious, inviting eyes. There is something so young about him, so vulnerable and kind, like a child about to offer his favorite toy to a less fortunate boy who's been eyeing it enviously.

He befriended two of her brothers and confessed. They, according to the imbecile, promised to help him. Once the lieutenant told Hannah the truth, they would be there to comfort her. After the fourth visit, he took her father aside and confessed to him too. He couldn't perpetuate the charade. He had been trying to tell Hannah but couldn't seem to manage. While Hannah was thinking that her father and her betrothed were finalizing the matrimonial arrangements, her father was promising that he would break the news to his daughter, he would break her heart.

Break her heart he would have. Need I tell you that she thought those two weeks were heavenly? Every detail was recorded, every imagined nuance. What he said, what he implied, what she inferred, what a future. His lips that spoke of love, his eyes that spoke volumes. She loved the shape of his fingers.

No longer as taciturn, she even teased him. He had a habit of stroking his cigarette lighter, of flicking the top open, striking a flame, and shutting it. She laughed and accused him of being a budding pyromaniac.

Break her heart her father would have, but he didn't have to.

It came to pass that on the day following their last meeting, a day that was to prove fateful but at the time was merely sorrowful, the lieutenant died not by himself in a car accident. The service he was in was hit by, or hit, a tram. Three people in the car died, including the driver. No one in the tram was hurt.


Hannah was miserable and anguished, of course. She wept the fervor of her trembling grief. Her parents, her brothers, even her sisters-in-law all gathered around her bed and comforted her prone, inconsolable form. She mourned the loss of her husband, the loss of his future, of their future. She wept like a child for the children who were dead before they were conceived. She eulogized the three of them, two boys and a girl, the middle child, that they would not raise; the flowers from the garden of the little mountain house that they would not build; the stone pine grove, the olive trees, the peach and cherry orchards, and the vegetable plots on the land that they would not cultivate. She felt the intimate loss of who she was meant to become.

*"Heard melodies are sweet, but those unheard are sweeter,"* wrote Keats.

No loss is felt more keenly than the loss of what might have been. No nostalgia hurts as much as nostalgia for things that never existed.

Hannah cried, moaned, wailed, and didn't care if her neighbors heard her—no, she wanted the neighbors, the world, to know her grief. She had finally discarded the last vestiges of her shyness, finally released the silt of immature youth. The Hannah I knew was born.

She wrote that she cried and cried until she suddenly woke up, alert and full of vigor. If she was feeling so terrible, her new family must be devastated, walking the grounds of Hell. Her new family needed her. Within hours of hearing of the death, she gathered all her loved ones—her parents, her brothers, her sisters-in-law—and brought them to her betrothed's house. They would help ease the lieutenant's family's pain in any way they could. Hannah would comfort his family and share their grief. She helped organize the funeral and the obsequies. She helped cook lunches and served coffee to the mourners. She did not return to the volunteer position at the hospital for more than six months, availing herself to the new family for whatever was needed.

Needed she apparently was. My imbecile of an ex-husband hated Hannah, but his family adored her. She made sure of it. She became the ideal daughter-in-law. I'm not just talking about the days of mourning. She was the dutiful daughter-in-law all her life until she fell into her final fog. After the sadness dissipated, after the family recovered from the lieutenant's passing, Hannah was still there. She visited at least three times a week, never refused an invitation, was present for all the holidays and important occasions. She never forgot a birthday, attended every new birth in the family. She knitted sweaters and baby blankets for nephews and nieces, and carefully considered which gift would be the most perfect for each relative.

Whatever my ex-husband may have thought, his parents came to consider Hannah an integral part of their family. They included her. When they arrived at my stepfather's house to ask for my hand, she came along. That was how we met, and by then I met a woman who would take me under her wing, who would become a friend and remain so after my husband left—I met a woman and not a shy girl. The transformation was complete.

The rattling of the radiator reminds me that I'm cold. The witches are awake. Turning on the building's heat for the first time this season may have been a group decision. Double, double, toil and trouble. One of them must have shivered, probably Marie-Thérèse. She feels the cold most. She's calling for her cat, who doesn't wish to return home this morning.

The *tock-tock* of the ancient radiator is irksome, forces me out of my comfort seat. I have to bleed the damn thing.

We had a warm autumn, but the season seems to have left us. Winter wheels in, picking up speed to make up for lost time.

I should get dressed, but right now dressing feels like one of Hercules's tasks. Over the nightgown of my abandoned sleep, over the robe of yesterday's embarrassment, I put on my burgundy mohair coat, my habitual resort through the years on these early winter mornings. Because of the age of my apartment and its inadequate insulation, the winter winds can be felt as well as heard indoors. This is your life, Aaliya. You pace your home in nightgown and flocculent overcoat, in comfy slippers so old that your left foot, like a pervert, flashes its five toes with each step. I hunch over the radiator, letting the air out. I place a small aluminum pan under the pipe, turn the knob, and wait for the flat note of a hiss to fizzle out, wait for it to die.

In one of the few Hemingway stories that I don't find wholly insufferable, "Hills Like White Elephants," a man and a woman in a café in Spain discuss the fact that she's pregnant. The man uses the phrase "let the air out" to mean get rid of the baby. When I first read it, I couldn't understand what Hemingway was saying. I kept wondering where the radiators were. I know the story is supposed to be clever, but it left me unmoved. I always wonder what the point is with Hemingway. Is the entire story about how difficult it is for the pair to communicate? I find that boring. I'm sure there is an epiphany at the end. Critics and college boys insist that the apparent text is just the tip of the iceberg. More like the tip of an ice cube, if you ask me.

I consider it a shame that most contemporary American writing seems informed more by Hemingway, the hero of adolescent boys of all ages and genders, than by the sui generis genius of letters, Faulkner. A phalanx of books about boredom in the Midwest is lauded (where the Midwest lies is a source of constant puzzlement to me, somewhere near Iowa, I presume), as are books about unexplored angst in New Jersey or couples unable to communicate in Connecticut. It was Camus who asserted that American novelists are the only ones who think they need not be intellectuals.

One of the things I have in common with the incredible Faulkner is that he didn't like having his reading interrupted. He was dismissed from his job as a post office clerk at a university (a position his father obtained for him) because professors complained that the only way they could get their letters was by rummaging through the garbage cans, where unopened mailbags all too often ended up. He is said to have told his father that he wasn't prepared to keep getting up to wait on customers at the window and to be beholden to "any son-of-a-bitch who had two cents to buy a stamp."

I didn't like having my reading interrupted when I worked either, but I was beholden to every son of a bitch and his mother who walked into the bookstore, whether or not they had two cents to buy a book. I couldn't afford any complaints. Most days I had few customers, and I spent my time sitting behind my desk reading. I was conscientious. I did earn my measly salary.

I fear I'm digressing again.

I try to get back to my reading, but my mind can't seem to concentrate. I lay *Microcosms* aside. I must listen to something, music to clear the cobwebs, rattle the ant farm. I turn on the record player. I own a CD player—I broke down and bought one eight years ago, only to discover that everyone had moved on to digital music players—but most of my music is still on old albums. I choose Bruckner's Symphony no. 3 conducted by Günter Wand, which I haven't heard in a long time, probably three years.

Here's a charming tale about Bruckner that I love, though I believe it must be apocryphal. When he conducted the premiere of this same third symphony, the audience abhorred it. Personally, I can't imagine why. Not only is

AN UNNECESSARY WOMAN                    159

it beautiful, but if it has a flaw, it may be that it's a little melodramatic and kitschy, two attributes that audiences tend to love. But who can account for tastes? The audience booed violently and stormed out of the hall. I imagine the composer looking back in abject sorrow at the honeycomb of heads in the theater before exiting and locking himself in the conductor's room, alone as he would always be. Forlorn and forsaken, Bruckner remained by himself until everyone had left the building, at which point he returned to the pit for a last farewell. He saw a young man still sitting in his seat, a young composer so overcome that he'd been unable to move a muscle since the symphony began, not a twitch. The young Mahler had been cemented in his seat for more than two hours, weeping.

I am not a young Mahler. Today, the music doesn't move me, and I do not find it soothing.

Wave after wave of anxiety batters the sandy beaches of my nerves. Oh, that's a bad metaphor if there ever was one. Just horrible.

Nothing is working. Nothing in my life is working.

Giants of literature, philosophy, and the arts have influenced my life, but what have I done with this life? I remain a speck in a tumultuous universe that has little concern for me. I am no more than dust, a mote—dust to dust. I am a blade of grass upon which the stormtrooper's boot stomps.

I had dreams, and they were not about ending up a speck. I didn't dream of becoming a star, but I thought I might have a small nonspeaking role in a grand epic, an epic with a touch of artistic credentials. I didn't dream of becoming a giant—I wasn't that delusional or arrogant—but I wanted to be more than a speck, maybe a midget.

I could have been a midget.

All our dreams of glory are but manure in the end.

I used to imagine that one day a writer would show up at my door, someone whose book I had translated, maybe the wonderful Danilo Kiš (*The Encyclopedia of the Dead*), before he died, of course. He the giant, me the speck with midget dreams, but he would come to thank me for caring about his work, or maybe Marguerite Yourcenar would knock on my door. I haven't translated her, of course, because she wrote in French. And what French. In 1981 she was the first woman inducted into L'Académie française because of her impeccable language. She would appear to encourage me, to show solidarity, us against the world. *I, like you, isolated myself. You in this apartment in this lovely but bitter city of Beirut, I on an island off the coast of Maine. You're a forsaken, penniless translator who's able to remain in your home by the grace of your landlord, Fadia, while I am an incredible writer whose girlfriend, heir to the Frick fortune, owns the entire island. I am respected by the world while you're mocked by it. Yet we have much in common.*

I had dreams. I would invite Danilo into my home. *Please, come in. Share a cup of tea. Smoke a cigarette.* He's always smoking in his photos. Maybe I'd offer him a comb for his eternally unruly hair.

But my dreams would shatter against my failures, if not my shabby furniture first. *Look around. Sit, Danilo, sit. I'm sure you can appreciate a navy chenille armchair with frayed fringes and tattered tassels. Yes, that's the shape of my derrière sculpted into the foam. Yes, that minisofa in the corner is real pleather, haha. A love seat, they call it. Marguerite and I often plop down on it together. Do sit and tell me about your work. Do you write in the morning?*

I'm such an idiot.

I used to dream that one day I'd have friends over for dinner and we'd spend the entire evening in sparkling conversation about literature and art. Laughing and cavorting and making merry, Wildean wit and sassy, delightful repartee parried back and forth across the room. My salon would be the envy of the world, if only the world knew about it.

In one of his poems, Brodsky suggested that "dreams spurn a skull that has been perforated." A spectacularly thick drill bit has punctured mine.

This morning will pass — at a sad and sluggish pace, but it will pass. Tomorrow and tomorrow and tomorrow creeps in this petty pace.

There's no urgency in Marie-Thérèse's cat call, which is growing louder but carries no trace of concern. Her cat has yet to return but she has made a habit of this. She disappears after she's fed dinner, to who knows where, and returns sometime after the sun rises, but that's an approximate schedule. She's a Mediterranean cat, after all. I think Marie-Thérèse loves her cats, particularly the wayward Maysoura, more than she loves her children, and definitely more than she loved her departed husband.

My mother had an unnatural fondness for cats as well, as I may have mentioned. Mind you, she had little tolerance for pampered pets. Once, during a dutiful visit to a distant family member when I was nine or ten, a fluffy cat sauntered into the living room. My mother pointed at it, scowling in disgust, and the hostess, my mother's second cousin, stood up in apologetic horror and scooted the cat out of the room. My mother would have hated Maysoura, so coddled and pretty. She cared only for the homeless and orphaned cats of the neighborhood.

I understand her obsession, and I did even as a child. Granted, I may have felt some envy, a sense that the cats had waylaid any maternal instinct and caretaking that should have gone to her daughter, but I'm writing about a time before animal care or control ever descended upon the Beiruti conscience. Feral cats were hounded, hunted, even tortured if caught by young boys. I witnessed a couple of atrocities as a child. If my mother, champion of the feral that she was, saw a boy trying to trap a cat, or the butcher kicking one that sniffed too close, she became a short bundle of wrathful frenzy, berating the heartlessness of the offender.

She chopped chicken into small pieces, fried them in salted lamb fat, and folded them in sheets of wax paper. As discreetly as she could, since she didn't wish to be known as the crazy lady—too late, one might think—she unwrapped these feasts on walls and Dumpsters, high enough so dogs couldn't reach them.

The aroma of fried lamb fat was a siren call for any feline within a two-street radius. That aroma, muted and less pungent, followed my mother even when food wasn't upon her person, a lingering faint smell that became hers. Her charges knew she was coming long before they could see her.

The mangier the cat, the bigger her portion. I remember one cat that was doing so poorly her fur was nothing more than discontiguous splotches of hair. My mother fed her every day until she transformed into a calico queen with a coat of unearthly sheen. The cat allowed me to pet her. My mother didn't try to touch her. Not one cat ever became my mother's companion. She never had one of her own.

When I asked my mother how she knew the queen was a female, she explained that males could be no more than two colors. Females had no such limitation.

During the winter of 1986, Beirut was passing through one of its many phases of shedding its humanity and its humans. A war raged—sects killing one another, militias strangling the population—and my mother was worried about a cat. I was imprisoned in my apartment for seventeen straight days. On a clear day, upon the first hint of a cease-fire, I left my hideout to forage for food and dropped in to check on her. She was unwilling to discuss anything but what had happened to this infernal feline. The fighting and shooting had forced the animal into a deserted apartment in the building next to my half brother the eldest's. My mother heard the mournful meowing night and day. She risked her life by taking food across the street, snipers be damned, to seduce the cat into returning with her to her building, where she could feed her regularly. As soon as my mother broke into the empty flat, the cat went mute. My mother searched the entire place and found the cat stuck atop a high dark walnut armoire, with barely enough space under the ceiling to crouch in. My mother pleaded and cajoled and the cat hissed and retreated. The ignorant cat wouldn't accept help, my mother said. She dragged a chair across the room and climbed on it, which drove the cat even more insane. My mother tried every trick she knew and a couple she made up.

"I even turned my face away from her," my mother said, "and put my hands on the ledge of the ugly armoire so she could use my arms to climb down and run away. Nothing worked. The stupid, stupid cat refused to be rescued. She couldn't understand that I was giving her an out. I was forced to leave the food on top of the armoire and go home."

For a few days, whenever there was a brief silence between bullets, missiles, and mortar shells, my mother heard the cat's calls, which went on and on, on and on, until they finally stopped altogether. When the break in the fighting arrived at last, right before I made my appearance to inquire about her, she rushed across the street and found the apartment ransacked—she'd assisted the militia boys who looted it by destroying the lock, advertising that the place was uninhabited—with furniture topsy-turvy and no cat.

The coffee klatsch has come to order. I must crane my head out the door and thank Fadia for last night's dinner before she climbs the stairs back to her apartment, before the three weird sisters end their matins. I must. I try to stand but I sway, beset by a vertiginous nausea.

Have you figured out yet that I dislike being around people? Can it be that I haven't mentioned it earlier?

Some believe that we are created in God's image. I don't. I am not religious by any means, though I'm not an atheist. I may not believe in the existence of God with a capital $G$, but I believe in gods. Like Ricardo Reis, aka Fernando Pessoa, I am a pantheist. I follow the lesser gospel, now deemed apocryphal. I worship—well, I worshipped, past tense, for this morning I don't have the stomach to believe in anything—at the shrines of my writers.

I am in large measure a Pessoan.

"Isolation has carved me in its image and likeness."
Pessoa said that. He also wrote: "Solitude devastates me;
company oppresses me."

In *A Short History of Decay*, Cioran wrote: "life in common thereby becomes intolerable, and life with oneself still
more so."

The presence of another person—of any person what-
soever—makes me feel awkward, as if I'm no longer me.
It wasn't always that way. Not that I was a social butterfly
flitting from acquaintance to delightful acquaintance, but I
didn't always have such a high level of discomfort around
people. I used to be able to spend time with my friend and
companion, Hannah, quite comfortably; my customers
didn't bother me at all. I talked to salesclerks in stores. I
got by. As I aged, as life isolated me more and more, I found
myself discomfited by others. "Isolation has carved me in
its image and likeness."

Merely thinking that I have to talk to Fadia, however
briefly, irritates me, makes me feel a bit edgy, maybe even
nervous. I can and do overcome those feelings, of course.
I'm not completely helpless. I am a functioning human being.
Mostly.

Just so you don't make too much fun of me, the *mostly*
above refers to *functioning*, not to *human being*.

The isolationists Fernando Pessoa and Bruno Schulz
had worse problems with people, much worse than mine.
Schulz was terrified in large groups, discombobulated
around people he didn't know, childishly timid. He behaved
like a two-year-old separated from his mother. He had a sad
habit of worrying the edge of his jacket, stroking the fabric.
Compared to them, I'm an extrovert.

I think it's safe to say that contact with other people has never been my strong suit, but lately, in the last eight or nine years, or ten, it has produced a mild anguish that's hard to define. These days the presence of other people derails my mind. I can't seem to think clearly, or behave naturally, or just be. These days I avoid people, and they in turn avoid me.

"The healthy flee from the ill," wrote Kafka in a letter to Milena Jesenská, his unrequited love, "but the ill also flee from the healthy."

Being around so many people yesterday unhinged me, unhinged my soul. The essential calm of habit and ritual was disturbed. Granted, being around my mother would unhinge most, and I wouldn't wish her screaming on anyone, not Benjamin Netanyahu, not even Ian McEwan. But being around all those people was not a pleasant experience. It never is these days.

Still, I must offer Fadia thanks for her generosity. I wouldn't forgive myself if I didn't.

Before putting my talking head out the door, I change out of my coat and nightgown. I can't face the witches in the same nightgown I was wearing yesterday morning. However, before I brave the firing squad I must look something up.

I don't think the Bruckner and Mahler story is accurate; something about it is off. I remember that someone else was there as well, some other composer. I did tell you that I thought it was apocryphal, but I want to check. I wrote down that particular story, copied it from a longer article. I know I read it in a magazine less than ten years ago, which means that the notes are in the box of miscellany in the maid's bathroom, not the oceanic darkness of the maid's room. I will not need candles or a flashlight to find it.

Find it I do, and right I am, or I am right that I was wrong. How my memory distorted this story.

The third's premiere was horribly received because it was horribly conducted, the original maestro having dropped quite dead right before the concert, an event not atypical considering Bruckner's ubiquitous misfortune. During the performance, Bruckner was understandably lost in his own score because he wasn't trained as a conductor. The audience, as lost as Bruckner, drifted, but didn't boo or storm out. The other musician in the audience, who was with Mahler and who was just as dumbfounded, was Hugo Wolf (I like his Italian serenade). There is no mention of weeping, I'm afraid. Mahler and Wolf went on to become Bruckner's students. For the rest of his life, Mahler spent the royalties he earned from his own music to publish Bruckner's scores.

My notes shed more light on the strangeness of the life of Anton Bruckner. He lusted after little girls but did not, could not, act upon his perversion because he was a devout Catholic. He was not a priest. Of his own accord, he checked himself into a local institution to treat his predilection—his pedophilia, not his Catholicism. He composed his Mass in C Minor to thank God for curing his ignoble illness. Of course, this minor mass is a mess of monumental orchestrated earwax, a religiously pubertal intoxication of sounds. Let's just say it's childish.

Anton Bruckner died a virgin at seventy-two.

Piet Mondrian also died a virgin a month before he turned seventy-two.

I am seventy-two, but I'm not a virgin and not dead yet.

Hannah, however, died a virgin.

✲   ✲   ✲

I will thank Fadia.

In the kitchen, I listen to what the witches are discussing on the landing. I don't wish to interrupt them at an inappropriate juncture. Joumana is dominating the conversation. She's announcing that her daughter, the once-loud one, has finally finished all her course requirements and all that's left is the dissertation. The ladies are ecstatic, happy for her and immensely proud. The sounds cascading from above have a feel of rampant euphoria.

I surprise myself by feeling happy for Joumana too. I've watched her daughter, heard her, grow up. Joumana moved into the building while pregnant with her. How can I not be happy for the girl, and for Joumana? Her daughter — that irritating, loud, obnoxious girl who sucks all the oxygen from any room she enters — will make something of her life. She will bowl over anyone in her way — or out of her way, above, below, on the side — and she will amount to something. She'll be happy. I'll be happy for her.

I wait for a second before I open my door, allowing them the privacy to be happy together. In my head, I practice. *I have something important I'm working on, urgent, that requires my attention, I only wanted to thank you for your wonderful okra stew. I will eat what I couldn't finish yesterday for lunch today.*

"Thank you," I call up to Fadia, but I intend it to be for the three of them. "That was a mouthwatering stew. I am grateful."

The three witches have a lot of hair atop their heads this morning, having obviously made it to the salon last evening. Even from below, I note the plucked eyebrows, the manicures, though I can't tell about the leg waxing — their legs are out of sight from the landing. Joumana, her hair rice brown with crisscrossing streaks of blond highlights, holds a coffee kettle, about to fill Marie-Thérèse's cup. Bad timing on my part.

"Let me pour you a cup of coffee," Joumana says. "Come join us."

The witches must have decided on a complete makeover. Fadia sports dark red hair. I'm trying to compare it to another color in order to give you an idea, but I can't. Like Faulkner, her hair color today is sui generis.

My white hair has little company in Beirut, my blue hair even less.

"Why, thank you," I say as I back just a tad into my doorway, "but I'm afraid I can't. I'm working on . . ."

Something. Just say the word *something*. You don't have to explain.

Rain falls behind the witches as if surrounding them; there is no wall at their backs. They regard me with some concern. I notice that their seating arrangement has changed recently — recently, meaning in the last two years, since that was the last time I saw the coffee klatsch. Witches should be heard and not seen. Fadia, not Marie-Thérèse, claims the middle position now, and moreover, she has given up on the wooden-legged soft-twine stool. Draped today in a palette more *Sgt. Pepper* than *Yellow Submarine,* she reclines sideways, reposes, on an outdoor chaise longue, a pre-impressionist odalisque, paying homage to the goddess of indolence, Greta Garbo (though Fadia doesn't want to be alone).

"Urgent," I say.

I am becoming incompetent, an aphasic stutterer.

So much hair, so many hair-care products. Short hair is rare in Lebanon; possibly one out of fifty women keeps

her hair above shoulder length, something to do with per-
ceptions of femininity, I assume. None of us wishes to look
different. My hair is up, clasped in a semi-bun right now,
as it is practically every day. Rarely is it loose or down, yet
I don't consider cutting it short.

I don't, even though I do look different. I can feel the
witches inspecting me. Our delightfully gawky neighbor, see
how wonderfully she straddles the border between woman
and giraffe.

This is ridiculous. I am playing the fool. I take a long,
calming breath.

"I'm sorry, Joumana," I say. "I can't have coffee right
now. I appreciate the invitation, truly do, but I'm working
on something, something I need to finish before leaving in
an hour. I can't spare the time at this moment. Thank you,
though."

Now I have to leave my shelter within an hour.

She should ask again, or at least suggest that I come up
another day—any one of the witches should. But they don't.

As I begin to withdraw—one step and I'm back in
the comfort of my apartment—Joumana announces loudly,
"My daughter finished all her course work for the Ph.D.
program. All she has left is to write the dissertation, and
defend it, of course."

"Dr. Mira," Fadia says, a bit too excitedly. "I like the
sound of it. Dr. Mira. We have a doctor in the house."

"That's wonderful news," I say, as if this is the first
I've heard of it. "I'm very happy for you. That'll be quite
an achievement."

"May I tell you the subject of her dissertation?" She
asks the question not forcefully but insistently.

She interrupts my head chatter. As if involuntarily, I feel a minuscule grin crease my face. I do in fact want to know.

Joumana's face brightens. "Tombstones," she says. "She's studying tombstones, particularly the relationship of the shape of the stones to the inscriptions and icons."

*The gravestone, upon its body, shall begin to consider where my name is to be inscribed.*

Why do such thoughts cross my mind?

"That's an awful subject," says Fadia. "It's so morose. Gravestones? Why would she be interested in something like that?"

"That's incredible," says Marie-Thérèse. "I think it could be very interesting."

"Have you told your daughter the truth, dearest?" Fadia says. "That she's adopted? She can't possibly be yours. Gravestones?"

Joumana seems to hear neither of her friends.

I say, "Non fui, fui, non sum, non curo."

"What was that?" says Fadia.

"Latin," says Marie-Thérèse.

"Do you know the language?" Joumana asks.

"Latin? Me?" I don't know why the question sounds preposterous. "No, I don't speak it."

"I do." Joumana looks elegant this morning, a cross between the society matron she isn't and the college professor she is. "What I mean is that I read it, of course, not speak it. Who speaks Latin anymore? I studied it in college."

Do I react slightly, or it is possible she's overly sensitive to her audience? In any case, she hesitates right after the last word.

"I wanted to read some of the classics in the original,"
she says.

Yes, I want to say. Yes. That would be so lovely. If only.

"Virgil," Joumana says.

"What's that?" Fadia says.

"Ovid," I hear myself say. I even hear a whispery wist-
fulness in my voice, a lilt of longing. Latin, or maybe Greek.
Almost everything that men have said best has been said
in Greek.

Then again, Latin.

"Tacitus," Joumana says. She places her hand on the
kettle, hesitates for a few seconds, then pulls it back to her
lap. "In the original. I thought it would be good."

You can also read a French translation of the original,
then an English translation, then work as hard as you can,
do your best, manage your frustrations, and translate it into
Arabic before you store it in a box in the maid's bathroom.

"Congratulations," I say as I withdraw. "You must be
so proud of your daughter. I wish you and her nothing but
the best."


If I am to leave my apartment soon, I must bathe first. I
should probably eat something as well. In my kitchen I
hear them being confrontational—not arguing, but challenging one another. Marie-Thérèse says something about
her two companions, suggests that they were the ones who
ignored something, the subject most probably being me. I
move away. I wish not to listen.

Non fui, fui, non sum, non curo.

I was not, I was, I am not, I don't care.

It is the most common text found on Roman graves.

The texts you find on Muslim stones are primarily ones extolling God and His prophets: "In the name of God, Most Gracious, Most Merciful. Praise be to God who created Heaven and Earth. Prayers and blessings to Gabriel, all the angels, Abraham, Ishmael, Muhammad, all the prophets, Muhammad's daughter, his wives, his cousin, his best friend in high school, his pharmacologist." I jest, of course. I have seen exquisite inscriptions on Muslim graves.

The stone upon my grave, what will its inscription say? So many possibilities, so much to choose from.

"Here lies Aaliya, never fully alive, now dead, still alone, still fearful."

"Death, be not proud, for here you have overthrown but a speck."

My favorite tombstone inscription is a writer's, of course:

*Malcolm Lowry*
*Late of the Bowery*
*His prose was flowery*
*And often glowery*
*He lived, nightly, and drank, daily,*
*And died playing the ukulele*

As a diehard Pessoan, my deathstone should be inscribed with his words, and there I have so much — so much to choose from.

What am I saying? An interesting tombstone? To quote Nabokov, "history . . . will limit my life story to the dash between two dates."

I'll probably be incinerated with my books.

❃   ❃   ❃

Since I must leave my apartment, I will visit the National Museum, my frequent escape from the world. I'll spend the day there. If I have time, I'll drop in on my mother. I have to know if she'll scream again, have to know whether it was a one-time quirk, an aberration. Only if I have time. I do not look forward to seeing her or my half brother the eldest.

I jump into the shower — well, wade into it. Hot water rolls down my body as I lather my hair with my regular baby shampoo, not Bel Argent. The blue will slowly dissipate, very slowly. Another shower, another day when I wish the building wasn't so old; I wish for hotter water, for more of it, a better pump, less noisy pipes. A Schoenberg symphony of glockenspiels erupts every time I turn the water knobs. The pipes and I have aged together.

Water glints like sprinkles of mica across my neck and shoulders. I towel it away. I twist excess water out of my hair — I have at least this in common with Titian's Venus rising from the sea and the Aphrodite of Cyrene. The Cyrene Aphrodite is headless, but she was supposed to be twisting her hair before being decapitated by time irreverent.

I dress quickly and haphazardly. My damp hair darkens the scarf in splotches. Walking shoes — I am walking, walking, walking. I stuff my handbag with the essentials, including a foldable umbrella and the most recent French translation of Rilke's *Duino Elegies* (never leave the house without a book of poetry), before rushing out the door.

Every Beiruti of a certain age has learned that on leaving for a walk you should never be too sure of returning home, not only because something might happen to you personally, but also because your home might cease to exist.

For youngsters today, the war years are an altogether different geological era.

At my request, the jitney stops before the steps of the National Museum. I had tried to walk, but the drizzle and breeze rendered the umbrella useless. I'd kept marching for a while even though I was wet, and I found that the strange smell of the sun-starved air, and its pearly color, added to my befuddlement. During the war, breezes were nauseatingly fragrant with the odors of bodies hastily and haphazardly discarded—odors of flesh, both fresh and decaying, a city's native perfumes. I flagged a car quickly, sanity being more necessary than calisthenics.

"Beirut Revisited (1982)" is not a poem I wish to recite today.

I made a healthy decision. The hour-long walk to the museum can be rejuvenating—I did it regularly on good days—but it has the subversive ability to unbalance a balanced Beiruti on occasion, since it is loaded with emotional land mines and unexploded ordnance. This road was the main Green Line that divided the city into east and west. There were probably more battles here, more snipers, more killings, more bodies, more decay and destruction, than anywhere else in the country—havoc and spoil and ruin. The area and the boulevard that knifes through it have been rebuilt. The bombed-out racetrack whose jutting beams and girders looked like skeletons of antediluvian animals has been refurbished, leaving nothing to remind us of the dozens of horses that burned alive in the stables—nothing but the breeze to remind us of the hundreds of pedestrians shot dead trying to reconnect with family or friends across a city at odds with itself.

I visit the museum to indulge in a much earlier history.

When the war started, the curators at the museum were rightfully fearful that it would be looted. No steel safe, no hiding place, would be able to stop a fully armed militia from getting its hands on the treasures within—in our war, we didn't have American marines to protect our museum (je m'amuse!). The curators and museum guards dug a crypt under the building, encased the valuables in wood and cement containers, and buried them, ancient sarcophagi within a contemporary one. The building was cratered, shelled, and shot, but no one knew, no one touched, what lay beneath.

The gentle chestnut-cheeked guard nods my way discreetly. A stranger to sorrow, he seems happy to see me as usual. I prefer to pay the entrance fee, but he feels insulted if I do. We've known each other superficially since the museum reopened. He's not a small man, but his excessively large head still makes him look like a dwarf afflicted with gigantism. He wears a short-sleeved cotton shirt—he is ununiformed—and I shiver for him. I once suggested that it wasn't ethical for me to enter for free, that the museum needed our support, but he countered that the price of one ticket wasn't going to bankrupt any coffer.

He calls me Tante. Bless him.

He sits at an old metal desk beside a metal detector that worked for a few years after the reopening. At first everyone was scanned, the X-ray machine swallowed and regurgitated purses, but then either the machines or the industriousness of museum employees broke down. As I walk through the arches of the detector, he bows his head and whispers in a conspiratorial tone, as if we were spies about to exchange supersensitive information, "It's macaroni today, Tante. Makes me hungry."

*Macaroni* is his secret spy code for Italians, which means that they account for most of the visitors in the museum today.

"I should call my wife," he whispers, taking out his mobile phone. "Maybe she can cook some for dinner. Do you like macaroni, Tante? Red or white?"

The reason I love the museum is that not many people visit it. For a long time, I was the only one strolling these halls. The Lebanese care little for history. Arab tourists reappeared in droves after the war, but they cared even less. They returned for the sun, the beach, the mountains, the clubs, the alcohol, the drugs, and, of course, the sex, orgies right on the pavement. The secret spy code for Arabs is *camels*. The guard is Shiite—he probably thinks I am as well and I've yet to correct him—so he dislikes Saudis, and on the rare occasion that they visit, he delights in hissing their code. Sometimes he puffs out his lips and chews on imaginary cud. He beams when Iranians visit; their secret spy code is *shahs*.

Lebanese emigrants visit the museum when they return home for vacation, to show their children, to recapture a sense of pride or what have you. The numbers of European tourists in the museum—Spanish are *paella*, Germans are *wurst*—keep increasing. The Italians now visit in larger numbers than the French, or so it appears since unlike the escargots, the macaroni always arrive in groups, rarely as individuals. They come to the National Museum because that's what cultured people are supposed to do, or so they're constantly told. Not that anyone is really interested in the art or the history. It is the exception who walks the museum; most visitors rush through it, hustling or hustled. They stay just long enough that once they return to Paris, Lyon, or Genoa, they can say without hesitation that they've been to the museum in Beirut. ("It's cute, small, and ever so quaint!") Nowadays, school buses from all over Lebanon can be seen parked on the streets outside the building. Children are brought to the museum because that's what is done. It doesn't matter what they do once they get there; it only matters that they're brought.

I come to the museum to be by myself in the world; I am out of the apartment but not in a crowd. It's one of the rare spaces left in Beirut that is not plagued by background music. In the supermarket, along the corniche, in hospitals, on the street, in stores, elevators, everywhere in the city, insipid music erupts from tiny nooks to scramble and deaden Beiruti brain waves—a catastrophe to rival the civil war, if you ask me. In the museum, I am able to think. In one of his novels, the rancorous and ever ornery Thomas Bernhard has a character who sits three mornings a week on a settee before the same painting, Tintoretto's *Portrait of a White-Bearded Man*, at the Kunsthistorisches Museum, because the room has the ideal temperature for thinking, a constant eighteen degrees centigrade maintained all year round to preserve the canvases. I don't know what the temperature in my museum is, but it's pleasant.

People, visitors, are beginning to crowd me out. I sincerely believe that I'm going to be crushed, mashed to a pulp, as if I am in a mortar and the crowd is the pestle. As you know, I avoid assemblages, eschew accumulations of people. I'm reaching the point when I'll no longer enjoy spending slow time in here.

The museum is all ocher limestone, protective glass, and ancient mosaics. It's built in Egyptian revival style, but I have no idea what that means. It looks French to me, if anything. The first thing that catches my attention every time I enter is the staircase. Even though I have walked up those stairs many times, I always feel that they're built for descent and not ascent, an effect probably due to them splitting at the top and circling toward the unseen mezzanine.

Macaroni aren't the only visitors today. Two five-year-old boys run around the halls as if in a playground. Unshackled from their mothers, they're loud and effervescent. The squeak of expensive sneakers reverberates in the air. I'll admit that I'm not fond of children. They stick to you like burrs, and tearing them off is cumbersome. I don't dislike them, I simply prefer them not to be around. I'm also not fond of Italians, who aren't noticeably quieter than children. But then, to be fair, I'm not fond of Arabs or Iranians either, or Americans, the loudest of them all. Well, most of the time I'm not fond of people.

I won't be able to stay here long, it's not a good day for the usual museum quiet. Maybe I'll just spend time with the ancient sarcophagi. Though they're of different periods, the tombs are so elderly that they seem bound together by sacred ties of centuries-old kinship. My favorite, close to the entrance and its nonfunctional metal detector, is the tomb of a noble. Its height is impressive, probably a meter and a half. All around the bottom of the sarcophagus, the most touching scene from the twenty-fourth book of the *Iliad* is carved into the old stone. Men, women, gods, and beasts surround Achilles as Priam genuflects to him and kisses his hand.

As I stand before the consummate story, the mother of one of the boys, the back of her skirt clinging to her bottom, perfunctorily admonishes the pair in broken American English. She tells one of them to tuck in his blue plaid shirt. They pay her absolutely no mind, as if she's as distant as the days of Homer. Their longish hair jumps up and down as much as they do. I'm not sure whether to blame their boisterous misbehavior on Lebanese upbringing or American environment.

My patience, like my time in this world, grows shorter.

A scion of a Lebanese immigrant wrote a novel retelling Priam's pleading with Achilles for Hector's body, David Malouf in *Ransom*, a masterful book. I've always been moved by the story, a historic king reduced to begging by his love for his son. Achilles drags Hector's body behind a chariot in triumph, revenge raging crimson in his veins, but is then able to forgive upon witnessing a father's grief, a parent's sorrow. Today, though, possibly because of my mother's reappearance, I find the sarcophagus a bit unnerving, and I move on.

I walk toward Eshmun's boys made of marble, but the real boys rush by me in the same direction. I turn and head the opposite way toward Astarte's thrones. Eshmun and Astarte, two Phoenician gods on either side of the museum — not the gods in person, but substitutes: statues of sons offered to Eshmun the healer in hopes of keeping the real ones healthy, and thrones of the divine Astarte.

*All hail to you, two thousand years too late.*

Or four thousand years.

I can't count the number of times I've stood before these empty thrones, broken-down relics of the once relevant, different sizes, none of them whole: the stone chipped, the sphinx on the side beheaded, a lion decapitated and de-tailed. My eyes want to see moss growing in the cracks as it does on statues in situ, but the thrones are scrubbed clean. The Phoenicians used to place betyls on the thrones, originally meteorites, sacred stones endowed with life, with the presence of the goddess. None of the betyls remains. The thrones are unoccupied. Astarte, Milton's "Queen of Heav'n, with crescent horns" — Ashtarout, Ishtar, Aphrodite, Venus — she reigns here no more.

When I am in the museum, my present is waylaid, my recent past forgotten; when I am before these thrones, my life in its entirety is set aside. I feel part of a larger history, of the grand waterwheel of time — delusional on my part, I'm sure. Still, it comforts me. I wonder at times what might have been had I lived in that other world instead of this. Would I sit on one of these thrones? No, I am not Astarte, not a goddess. Maybe a betyl.

When I'm in the museum I think often of Bruno Schulz, probably because of the brouhaha with his mural and the museum in Israel.

A writer and artist, Schulz was Polish, born and raised in a town called Drohobycz. By anybody's standards, Bruno was odd. He was sickly and shy, socially inept, full of idiosyncratic tics—an unusual child in a harsh world. Like Proust, the other puer aeternus to whom he is sometimes compared, he was immensely talented, and as with Proust, you can say that he was discreet about his desires—not a homosexual, mind you, but a sexual masochist; he liked his Venus in furs. For their eras, both had socially unacceptable desires, although Monsieur Marcel had the chance to indulge his. (Edmund White and others suggest that Proust also had a fetish for desecrating the sacred, particularly photographs of the Pope, though no one is sure how often he practiced it.) In Schulz's drawings, tall women with giraffe legs trample on dwarves with Schulzian faces. In one of my most cherished, a naked man kneels adoringly before a woman in a negligee as she sits on a bed or taboret, face in profile. Slim straps fall seductively from her shoulders, and we see her nude back as she looks dismissively down at her worshipper, who is wholly engrossed in her stiletto heel. The forefinger of his left hand seems to be tracing the shoe while the right arm encircles it as it would a lover. The man's cheek is on the floor, his face lost in adulation, as the heel of her right foot presses into his upper back—a supplicant bowing before the exalted Astarte and her shoe.

Schulz's literary oeuvre is tantalizingly tiny: some essays, a few articles, and two books of short stories—but what stories, what a brave new world he showed us. Unfortunately for us, and for him, his own story became more important than his stories. How he died, who he was, and what he was took center stage in the passion play. In 1941

Drohobycz fell to the Germans. When Schulz was forced to relocate to the ghetto, he hid his life's work with colleagues and acquaintances: drawings, paintings, and two unpublished manuscripts, which possibly included a novel called *Messiah*. They have all disappeared, like Walter Benjamin's suitcase.

The Gestapo officer in charge of the Jewish labor force, Felix Landau, decided that Bruno was no ordinary Jew, but a necessary one.

Think on the term for a moment.

What is a *necessary* human?

What saved Bruno's life, or, I should say, what delayed his death, was that Landau fancied himself a lover of art. He forced the necessary Jew to paint murals for his son's bedroom depicting scenes from beloved fairy tales. Landau kept Schulz alive until one day in November 1942, when Karl Günther, a rival Gestapo officer, killed Schulz to get back at Landau, who'd killed a dentist Günther favored — a necessary dentist, one presumes.

Günther said to Landau, "You killed my Jew — I killed yours."

Worse yet, a German filmmaker, with the help of the residents of Drohobycz, a Ukrainian city now, was recently able to trace the murals Schulz made for Landau's son. From beneath many a layer of whitewash emerged the kings and queens and fairies and dwarves of Bruno's imagination. The artist sprang to life once more, if only briefly, before being disappeared again. Three people from Yad Vashem, the Holocaust museum in Israel, pried fragments of the murals off the walls, stole them away in the middle of the night. The museum claimed moral rights to my hero's work. Tfeh!

Bruno Schulz was shot twice in the head by a Nazi.

Federico García Lorca was shot once in the head by a fascist and then twice in his behind, after he had fallen forward, to mark him as a homosexual.

When I read Schulz, I am baptized with Lorca's dark water.

In the museum, the Lebanese and not the Israeli, I contemplate an aged if not antediluvian throne. According to biblical historians, God caused the world to flood forty-five hundred years ago, so no, not quite antediluvian.

I hear the click of heels behind me, but I don't look back. The macaroni, at least seven, most of them women. The screeching sneakers of the two boys rush toward them. All this I hear, not see. The boys don't seem to be seeing either, since they both run straight into the pod of Italians. I hear bodies bumping, Italian cursing, but no falls or tumbles. I turn and watch chaos unfold. The Italians chide the boys in bad English, the mothers chide the Italians for hurting the boys' feelings, the Italians berate the mothers for their misbehaving children, which produces Lebanese cursing. No guard, referee, or anyone associated with the museum makes an appearance.

This culture clash does not concern me.

The groups separate. The Italians glare arrogantly at the Lebanese-cum-Americans and walk away. The mothers regard their nemeses suspiciously, as if they are a contagious caravan of the seven deadly sins. When she's sure the sinners aren't looking, one of the mothers backhands her son's head. He winces a few seconds after the fact. She flips her dark hair, which falls in sculpted waves to her shoulders, and leads her friend away from the boys. The slap wasn't hard, but the boy seems shocked, and neither boy is sure what to do. They face each other where the women have discarded them. It is the unhit child who begins, who inducts his friend. The hit boy seems bewildered. His friend's lips tremble, his breathing is jagged. Whether consciously or not, the hit boy follows suit in the exact order: lips, breath, welling eyes. They drop to the floor, sit on the stone, and cry—well, weep. As loud as their earlier ruckus was, this sorrow is practically noiseless. In the hall of the ancients the intermittent sniffling of young boys echoes.

The boys don't touch, don't hug, don't try to console each other. They simply sit on the floor and share a cry.

I too am inducted into a sea of feelings. I am witness to an innocence that has never been mine, to a childhood that I missed and miss. No nostalgia is felt as keenly as nostalgia for things that never existed.

I am able to control my lips that want to quiver, but my breathing betrays me.

I move quickly behind the stairs so no one can see me. Though I am still in the main museum hall, the tawny light turns grayish, and the hidden air feels damper with its taste of copper. Under the landing is an altogether different universe. Tears carve a couple of furrows in each cheek. Terror creeps from chest to limbs; I'm frightened because I seem to be losing all semblance of composure and can't figure out why. Sorrow settles on my heart like a vulture.

What's going on?

I inhale from deep in my belly. I can't allow sobs to escape these lips. Like the boys, I need to remain noiseless.

To my right an oblong of dense darkness attracts my attention. I sneak into the room, lean against the wall next to the door, and cry. I can discern walls but not their color. The room's temperature isn't a pleasant eighteen degrees centigrade—no, not pleasant. The febrile heat turns the room into humid summer, August in December. I expect to be attacked by mosquitoes at any moment. My throat is parched. I sweat. I'm overdressed for August, of course. I can't breathe as deeply because of a suffocating smell of paraffin and tobacco. I stroke the foldable umbrella for comfort. The fact that it's wet as well does comfort me, as does the room's atrocious odors.

I must hold on to my sanity. I must compose myself and leave this oppressive place.

I slap my head, once, twice—a habit to alleviate stress, or to make myself think when I'm acting stupid, just a slap on the top of my head. I run my fingernails through my hair, pull it back, and retie the scarf. I fan my face with the palm of my hand. The sweating, the wetness, seems to be contained in the triangle between my two armpits and my navel. I hold my handbag against it, take a breath of courage, and head out into the museum's light, which by contrast is now blinding. I wish I'd thought to bring sunglasses.

The hall is empty, no sign of the boys, their mothers, or their Italian nemeses. This is how I like my museum, empty and desolate and all mine, but I can't linger anymore.

The guard who always looks amused looks concerned. "Are you all right, Tante?" he asks.

I consider spouting the usual "I'm fine" refrain and continuing my rush through the exit, but I halt. He deserves better.

"I will be," I say, turning to face him. "I came here to escape some family problems, but wasn't able to." I hesitate, notice that I'm stuttering slightly. "Everything will be all right, though."

He nods slowly but assuringly, and relays the obligatory Lebanese homilies about family: its necessity, its insanity, its quandary, its mystery, and its comfort.

After the indoor heat, the cool air chills my bones; the drizzle has halted and is now hanging, damp in the air. I descend the outside stairs, cross the heavily trafficked street, and begin to walk. I don't care where or in what direction. I need to circulate my blood.

Why can't I be like my museum guard? Normal and imperturbably happy he seems — normal and belonging to the world he resides in.

Henri Matisse once said, "It has bothered me all my life that I do not paint like everybody else."

I love this quote, love the fact that the most incandescent painter of the twentieth century felt this way. Being different troubled him. Did he genuinely want to paint like everybody else, to be like everybody else? Did he truly wish to belong?

It has bothered me all my life that I am not like everybody else. For years, I was able to convince myself that I was special, that being different was a choice. As a matter of fact, I wanted to believe that I was superior, not an artist, not a genius like Matisse, but unlike the rabble. I am unique, an individual, not simply idiosyncratic, but extraordinary. I considered my individualism a virtue, protecting me from collective moods and insanities, helping me float above familial and societal riptides. That gave me comfort. Except it is failing me now. Not just now. For some time, I haven't been able to wall off my heart adequately.

"Every man guards in his heart a royal chamber," wrote Flaubert. "I have sealed mine."

I haven't done as good a job as Gustave. My sealant leaks. Jagged cracks have surfaced in my walls through the years. The weeping episode at the museum may have been unusual, but it certainly wasn't the first. They seem to occur more often these days. The walls are showing ineluctable signs of decay, cracks. I don't recall ever crying like this before I reached my midfifties.

I wonder at what age Flaubert wrote the line above. He died a couple of years before he turned sixty.

Pessoa, more a connoisseur of alienation than even Flaubert, wrote: "I've surrounded the garden of my being with high iron gratings—more imposing than any stone wall—in such a way that I can perfectly see others while perfectly excluding them, keeping them in their place as others."

What a way with words this poet has, what a grasp of images.

I am becoming one of the many things I despised when I was younger, a sentimental fool. These corroding walls can't even defend me against the predictable emotionalism of bad movies; bad Hollywood movies starring big heroes with bigger motivations now make me cry.

You want bad? *Imitation of Life* with Lana Turner. That manipulative film sank its sappy claws into my heart during a recent viewing. *Terms of Endearment*? I'm embarrassed to admit that it did too.

A few years ago, *The Color Purple* appeared on television after the news. I'd disliked the novel for its lack of subtlety, but it was a study in diaphanous nuance compared to the film, which aired on one of the tertiary Arab satellite stations, maybe Sudanese or Libyan, so even the television picture was mediocre. I couldn't stop watching. Yes, hating myself for it, I sat through *The Color Purple* in its fuzzily pixilated entirety. When the fallen woman — a former prostitute, once a lesbian, now a married blues singer who used to sing in the choir — leads the sinners back to the bosom of the church, whose pastor is none other than her strict, upright father who has disowned her for her wayward ways but now engulfs her in his forgiving embrace because she enters His demesne singing (wait for it) "Maybe God Is Trying to Tell You Something," while the gospel choir backs her up, and just in case you and I missed any of the portentous cues careening about the screen, she, the wandering daughter, tells her father, "Even sinners have soul" — when all that happened, every pretense of rationality abandoned me, and I bawled like — well, like a fallen child now redeemed.

Soppy stupid girl, that's me.

But it's not just movies. People make me cry as well.

Aaliya, the above, the bellower.

Fadia's lover, Abdallah, died about fifteen years ago; his heart gave up one evening. A mutual friend called her early the next morning. She had to force herself to listen to the news stoically, as if Abdallah were simply an acquaintance of not much import. Oh, his poor children, she must have been forced to say, his suffering family. She had to wait until she was out on the landing, after the men of the building had left. She had to wait till she was alone among her friends and their coffee.

Can you imagine how lonely she must have felt when she received that phone call? Your lover has just died, your companion has abandoned you, but don't you dare make an inappropriate sound, because your family is around. No one to touch you the way he did, no one to understand you, no one to hug you to sleep, but don't dare allow your face to show a glint of grief. The cutting pain of feeling alone amid loved ones.

I was waiting for the kettle to boil when I heard her break. She mentioned that Abdallah had passed away, mentioned it as if in passing, and at first I was shocked that she seemed so casual about it until I understood that she was waiting for Joumana's husband to leave with Marie-Thérèse's. The coffee klatsch didn't react, or at least I couldn't hear anything from my kitchen window. Then Joumana's husband and his prework commotion stumbled down the stairs, followed by more racket when Marie-Thérèse's husband joined him.

The women waited for a few seconds after the men's departure. Then Joumana and Marie-Thérèse began their comforting, and Fadia uncorked her grief. On the landing, Fadia couldn't wail, Joumana and Marie-Thérèse had to keep their voices low, but standing at the sink with yesterday's dishes drying in the wire rack, I heard every word, every whimper, every sob, every susurration. As you might anticipate Joumana and Marie-Thérèse deployed a litany of Lebanese condolences, still trite after so many generations: "God wants him close to His bosom," "Time heals all," "You still have your health," "God will help us." You'd think this would have been irritating. While crying together, they repeated the platitudes over and over—stupid, worthless, inconsequential, hollow words over and over, signifying nothing and definitely not full of sound and fury. It worked. They wept and grieved.

I wept and grieved in my kitchen, silently so as not to disturb them. I wasn't able to control my feelings. I'd never met Abdallah, I'd only heard his stories while listening to the women. I felt sorry for him. I felt sorry for Fadia. Like a sentimental teenager, I grieved for a love lost.

Now, I don't cry at the drop of a hat or at the drop of a bomb. What I'm saying is that I used to be stronger. I didn't cry when I was a child or a younger woman. The fact that I do now, rare as it is, the fact that I'm unable to control my weeping at these infrequent times, is disconcerting. That's all.

I'll have you know that it's not common.

I'll admit that I also lost control four years ago when Joumana's daughter announced to the coffee klatsch that she'd been accepted into a doctoral program at the Sorbonne. Amid the screeching congratulations and ululations on the upper landing, I shared their joy and wept over my gray stone countertop.

It is rare, however.


The mist of drizzle has lifted. The damp pavement and a quilt of tenuous low clouds—now comforting, now threatening—are the only evidence that rain passed this way. My legs, each trying to outpace the other, lead me along a side street. Unlike the main streets that cut the city with a butcher's cleaver, this ancient one wiggles its hips quite a bit. It negotiates with the neighborhood, it haggles, gives and takes; rarely is it straight, it is intrinsic. This street is more old-fashioned than the bigger boulevards, more settled. I walk on the asphalt, for the pavement—more discontinuous curbstones than an actual sidewalk—is covered with parked vehicles and the Vespas belonging to the many castes of delivery boys of the city. A film of drizzle residue makes the road feel like a sheaf of tar beneath my walking shoes, which squish ever so slightly. The buildings on this street are all four stories or higher, each floor with a balcony wearing long, wide outdoor drapes that were brightly colored once, a long time ago.

A small car passes, filled to the brim with smokers; it seems to be on fire with all the lit cigarettes and the smoke. In another car a bored boy presses his face into the back window. He notices me looking and extends his tongue into the smushed self-portrait. This brief exchange amuses me, as it does him, it seems. He pulls back, whether to admire my reaction or his handiwork on the window, I can't tell. A third car honks to make sure I don't jump in its way, then howls past me. I move to the curb, but only for one step, since a rack overflowing with bags of potato chips blocks my path. The owner of the grocery store sits outside on a stool, earphones plugging his senses, blithely unconcerned that he and his merchandise have overflowed his store and taken over the pavement. He seems happy in his world.

I pass a sign that says SALON AALIYA in Arabic lettering, though its Roman alphabet counterpart says SALON BEYONCÉ. I don't know whether to laugh or cry. There are no customers in the barber chairs.

It feels colder. The last traces of autumn are rising and disappearing. I clutch my handbag close. I'm no longer perspiring, of course, but moisture still clings to the valleys between my fingers.

A sandwich shop pumps the smell of garlic into the street. I'm hungry. I can't tell whether it's lunchtime yet or whether it has passed. I forgot my watch, not so unusual since my retirement.

This neighborhood is a rabbit warren, at least what I imagine a rabbit warren might be, but it doesn't compare with the ever-changing mazes of the Palestinian camps. It feels more solid. I probably see a chasm of difference because of familiarity. I haven't been to Sabra since I went looking for Ahmad all those years ago. I may not walk this neighborhood regularly, but I know it. It's changed some since I was here last, but it's recognizable, inherently so. The neighborhood I grew up in lies not far from here — not a stone's throw, a mortar's launch.

There were quite a few launches a couple of years ago. In 2008, the Shiites and Sunnis — *a plague o' both your houses* — clashed briefly and violently along these streets. Traces of the shooting can be seen on the buildings, a few bullet holes on one, two blotches on the second floor of another, a single beauty mark on a third, residues on edifices that can't afford plastic surgery. No trace of the psychological scars those battles caused can be found on any Beiruti, however. We suppress trauma so very well. We postpone the unbreathable darkness that weighs us down.

How do I talk about the betrayal we felt when Lebanese killed Lebanese once more? For years, since the end of the war in 1990, we deluded ourselves into thinking that we'd never fight each other again. We thought we'd buried our horror. Yet the Lebanese do not wish to examine that period of our history. We, like most humans, consider history a lesson on a blackboard that can be sponged off. We'd rather ostrich life's difficulties.

I can dig out the old chestnut from George Santayana, that "those who cannot remember the past are condemned to repeat it," but it serves no purpose. It's a hopelessly optimistic quote. We are condemned to repeat the past whether we remember it or not. It is inevitable; just ask Nietzsche (eternal return) or Hegel (history repeats itself) or James McCourt (history repeats itself like hiccups).

Beirutis are intricately woven into their city's wars.

I'm fond of Mark Twain's quote: "History doesn't repeat itself, but it does rhyme."

We're traumatized every time the Israelis go on one of their macho homicidal binges, but we explain it away. They are not us. It's the price we pay for living next to a neighbor who constantly has to prove how big his endowment is. It is big, trust me, nuclear even. The destruction our neighbors inflicted on us in 2006 was monumental—no, I shouldn't use that adjective, which implies raising instead of razing. The southern suburbs of our city were nearly wiped out, hundreds if not thousands were killed. They bombed every bridge in the country, every electric plant. I refused to leave my house even though my neighborhood was in no danger of being bombed. Yet as horrifying as that was, like most Beirutis, I dismissed all this as the insanity of the Israeli military and the lunatic fringe of Hezbollah meeting head-to-head. O Poseidon, grant that these sackers of cities both find troubles in their households.

Two years later, in 2008, when the clashes between Shiites and Sunnis erupted, I was no longer able to dismiss.

I'm sure you've noticed that I dislike Israel, that ridiculous pygmy state dripping with self-overestimation, yet many of the giants I respect are Jewish. There is no contradiction. I identify with outsiders, with the alienated or dispossessed. Like many nation-states, including its sister pygmy state Lebanon, Israel is an abomination.

Israelis are Jews who have misplaced their sense of humor.

I like men and women who don't fit well in the dominant culture, or, as Álvaro de Campos calls them, strangers in this place as in every other, accidental in life as in the soul. I like outsiders, phantoms wandering the cobwebbed halls of the doomed castle where life must be lived.

David Grossman may love Israel, but he wanders its cobwebbed halls, just as his namesake Vasily wandered Russia's. To write is to know that you are not home.

I stopped loving Odysseus as soon as he landed back in Ithaca.

I love the idea of homeland, but not the actual return to one.

A while back Czesław Miłosz wrote in an essay that in today's age of technology and mass mobility "the whole nostalgic rhetoric of patria fed by literature since Odysseus journeyed to Ithaca, has been weakened if not forgotten." Weakened, possibly, but I think not forgotten. It is that longing for a mythical homeland, not necessarily a physical one, that inspires art. Without that longing, patria is nothing more than the name of a Finnish company that produces armored vehicles used by Israel in its wars on Lebanon, or the name of an Argentine submachine gun.

I appreciate longing.

I also appreciate irony.

In the summer of 1982, while Israeli armored tanks and gunships imposed a siege of another age on rampartless Beirut, cutting off the water supply and food shipments, the modern catapults, the air force, leveled residential buildings, destroyed all infrastructure, and, amazingly, bombed the synagogue of Beirut's Jewish neighborhood.

There is no contradiction.

I notice a mother sitting on the pavement across the street, not Lebanese, as shows in her face, and not from this neighborhood, as shows in her haggard dress. A beggar by profession, she's surrounded by the tools of her trade: a baby in her arms; a girl of about five with dirty dress and knees, hovering in the world of her mother; the eldest, a girl of no more than ten, sitting on the ground, back against the building wall as she examines me from afar. The grim out-of-a-fairy-tale mother nudges her eldest, who jumps up and charges toward me in one smooth, experienced sweep. Brown hair, grimy face, and pink cheeks, she seems determined and overly earnest. Her eyes gleam with a heavy dose of resolve, a predator sighting her prey.

Except this quarry is prepared for her.

I wait until she comes around a parked car, until she's upon me, before I stop her by extending a demanding palm and saying, "Can you spare some change? I'm terribly hungry."

Her body reacts before her face, a lapse of a few seconds, recoiling. She practically lands on the blue Nissan to her left. The eyebrows lift, her lower jaw drops, her lips thin out, her cheeks flush puce. She uses the car as a support, leans on it with outstretched hand. It's then that I notice she's younger than she first appeared, a tall eight-year-old, probably.

I wonder if I went too far, but no, her recovery is quick. Her eyes smile first, bright girl. She breaks out giggling. Her laughter comes at me as if by catapult, and her gaze holds me transfixed. She examines me with mirth. I grin.

Her fidgeting mother across the dividing bitumen doesn't seem to be appreciating our peculiar scene and its urban charm. Her anxiety is palpable across this great distance. She pulls her five-year-old close, her right arm encircling the little girl's hips.

"You have blue hair," my girl says.

In an effusive gesture, I reach into my handbag and hand her all the paper money I have—everything I have except for what's in my pocket, where I keep my real money in case my purse gets stolen. I end up giving her just a little more than the price of museum admission. I'm not stupid, romantic, or a busy Russian novelist.

Beaming and preening, the girl counts the notes with the nimble fingers of a Beiruti moneychanger. She turns around, still counting, and begins walking back to her mother.

"Stay in school," I tell her.

"It's the holiday break," she replies without looking up or back, engrossed with her bounty.

I tuck in a strand of blue hair, adjust my scarf, and continue on my way.


In one of these side alleys, I can't remember exactly which, I had a humiliating experience that loiters in my memory, almost seventy years later. The recalled event no longer causes me much pain. I must have been a few months past four years old; my mother was second-trimester pregnant with my half brother the eldest. We were hurrying home, she dragging me by the hand. She walked with complete concentration and no little consternation. I couldn't understand then, nor would I for a long time, her terror of being a disappointment to her husband, to his family and hers. Like most of us, she was suckled on the milk of patriarchy (the courage of men, the fidelity of women). She sincerely believed that the world curdled if her husband held his breath, and if his every whim wasn't met, the universe itself turned to ash.

I still remember my hasty footsteps that day, their uncertainty, my sturdy brown-and-cream shoes of rubber and cloth, recently bought but long outdated. We traveled this path regularly, but that one time was different. Whether she was going to be tardy, wouldn't be on time to cook his dinner, finish cleaning, iron his nightshirt, or something else, I don't know. I know that it was still light, so he couldn't have reached home yet. I know that I could concentrate only on her calves, how they slid like tectonic plates with each step, and not on the familiar sights of my surroundings. She was running late, but not running because of her condition; passersby would have brooked none of that, would have felt obliged to protect my half brother the fetus from his irresponsible mother.

More people walked these streets then, many more.

In my mind, as I walk these streets now, I see her creamy calves as they were then, the calves of Hera or Athena in Rubens's *The Judgment of Paris*. I conjure up the sway of her black skirt's hem, its billowing below the saddle-shaped hollows of the backs of her knees.

As I walk these streets now, I note how much taller the buildings are today, most of them built in the fifties and sixties, how much taller I am now.

I remember I was panicking then. I needed to pee. I kept telling her that I couldn't wait until we reached home. I must have imagined that she, sorceress that she was, could conjure a toilet for me. Unlike Lot's wife, she wouldn't look back, kept her steady gaze forward, toward her Mecca. She needed to urinate as well, she told me as we kept moving. She always needed to in her condition, but she was going to wait until she reached our apartment. She always did. If she could, so could I.

I must have begun to cry. I must have stumbled. I must have done something, because other people showered us with worried glances, some with disdain. She stopped our forward progress. Must I always make demands, make a scene? Why couldn't I behave like normal children? My hand still in hers, she pulled me toward an alley between a couple of two-story ocher buildings. Severing our connection, she waved me away with a flapping hand. "There," she told me, "do it there, and do it quickly."

I may have been surprised or shocked at her pronouncement. I should have been one or the other, but I don't recall. I ran into the alley as she stood guard with her back to me. Fearing I would be noticed by a passerby, I sneaked through the gate of one of the buildings. Behind a large flowering bougainvillea, half obscured under its panoply of red, I crouched.

A woman in a dark dress and a dark, hair-covering scarf screamed at me and called me names. I had assumed no one could see me. I'd looked around before beginning my desecration, but I hadn't noticed the upper-floor balcony on which she stood. "Get out of here," she kept yelling, but I couldn't. I wasn't able to stop peeing. I wasn't able to meet her gaze either, or her fury. Her voice rose and her curses grew more vivid. My glance dawdled on the continental puddle forming in the soil below me.

By the time I was presentable enough to look up, my mother stood above me, looking more perplexed than angry, but only for an instant. When the balcony woman began cursing her and her parenting techniques, my mother unleashed a litany of imprecations so impressive that the woman turned red and speechless. The mute rude woman held on to the railing with a deathly grip, as if my mother had the power to blow her off the balcony. Below this balcony where the woman once reigned, an escutcheon depicting sheaves of wheat was carved into the stone, a make-believe crest that must have once been the same ocher color but had blackened, collecting the city's soot and grime in its grooves.

My mother prodded me back onto the street, grasped my hand once more, and continued her march back home. She ignored me the rest of the way, but she mumbled to the sky, to herself. She didn't hit me, she didn't backhand the top of my head, but she was furious. She was a one-handed gesticulating fury on the go.

I'm unsure which of the two added the most fuel to her fire: that I embarrassed her, the woman thinking she was an imperfect mother, or that I interrupted her speedy stride, her husband thinking she was an imperfect wife. I remember being horrified throughout the return, my eyes glued to two spots on my left shoe, two wet spots on the cream-colored cloth, not the brown rubber. How would I explain to my mother?

I am marching back to my mother's house. I can't say the march is fully unconscious. I'd considered the idea this morning, but I hadn't formulated a plan or made a firm decision. I'd been thinking about seeing my mother, and some muscle memory in my legs seems to have responded. My feet have been tortuously leading me with an uncertain pace in that general direction. As in many a fairy tale, I must end up there. Jung would have been unsurprised.

I'm not sharpening my knife, nor am I fluffing welcoming pillows. I should mention that I'm not fluffing pillows to kill her with either. I'm not planning anything. There will be no resolution, no epiphany; and most probably I won't understand more than I do now. I guess I don't want her skirl of terror to be my last memory of her. My intention — my goal — is simple.

I feel that I missed an opportunity at our last get-together, that I flubbed a pregnant moment. That was a pregnant moment, wasn't it? Should I have said something to her?

"It's me, Mamma, me."

Should I have quoted Milton, what the daughter, Sin, says to her father, Satan: *"Hast thou forgot me then, and do I seem / Now in thine eye so foul?"*

Should I have slapped her?

Everything seems sharp, slick, and shiny after the rain. Some rust collects on the dead leaves of a tree that I can't name. If she screams again when she sees me, I'll kill her.

Instead of seeing her, I should go home and put Sebald away in the maid's room.


I am proud that I finished the *Austerlitz* project. I consider it one of the best Holocaust novels. I have to say that much of what is being written about the Holocaust these days seems to be directed at the petite bourgeoisie. I find that when a subject has been heavily tilled, particularly something as horrifying as the Holocaust, anything new should force me to look with fresh eyes, to experience previously unexperienced feelings, to explore the hitherto unexplored. When I first read Primo Levi, my body shivered and spasmed at the oddest of moments for a week. I couldn't read Borowski's *This Way for the Gas, Ladies and Gentlemen* without clutching the edge of my desk. But then it took years, wading through mostly melodramatic books until I came across Kertész's *Fateless*, to feel challenged once more.

Kertész, like Levi and Borowski, escaped the gas chambers of Auschwitz, and he's the only one of the three who hasn't killed himself — not yet, at least. In 1951, Tadeusz Borowski, all of twenty-eight years old, opened a gas valve and put his head in the oven. The Gestapo had arrested him, a non-Jew, for surreptitiously printing his poetry.

Anyone who says the pen is mightier than the sword has never come face-to-face with a gun.

Two of my favorite books are *The Emigrants* and Ota Pavel's *How I Came to Know Fish*. What I love about them is that they deal with the Holocaust by looking at it indirectly; I don't recall the word being mentioned in either. Both refuse to soil grief with sentimentalism, and so they are devastating.

Grief is difficult to approach directly and must be courted obliquely. Very few of us are able to write about a tragedy without getting lost in the refractions of blinding tears. It seems to me that we must heed Bushy's advice in *Richard II*, and Slavoj Žižek's for that matter, and look awry.

Does grief make us lose short wavelength cones as well, make us less able to distinguish the color blue?

I wonder whether Hannah, in her last year, gazed directly at her life and was overwhelmed. Could she have saved herself had she looked awry?

From Rilke's *The Sonnets to Orpheus*:

*Even the trees you planted as children*
*Long since grew too heavy, you could not sustain them.*


The first time I saw Hannah was in my mother's apartment. When my ex-husband's family arrived to ask officially for my hand in marriage, she tagged along. I noticed her that day, though I didn't notice much; I was two months shy of my sixteenth birthday, too involved in books, schoolwork, and delusions.

I admit here that before that day I hadn't thought much of its possible consequences. I knew, was told, that this was a marriage proposal and my future husband's family was visiting to measure me, to judge me, that I must comport myself with some dignity, but I hadn't thought it through. I had no older sister who had gone through the procedure, no older cousins as models.

For example, I hadn't realized that marriage meant I'd be taken out of school. If I had, I would have asked quite a few more questions in class. I was a moth forcibly peeled from its chrysalis to face the world's harsh lights and frightening storms.

I didn't understand what my options were. If I had, I would have paid more attention, would have asked more questions of the nitwit.

I would have shoved his pretentious pipe down his throat while he puffed it.

My ex-husband had the first virtue of Stendhal's time, as Count Mosca explains to the delicious Duchess in *The Charterhouse of Parma*: "The first virtue of a young man today — that is, for the next fifty years perhaps, as long as we live in fear, and religion has regained its power — is to be incapable of enthusiasm and not to have much in the way of brains."

That's the fool I married, bless his rancid soul. In this case, you can also add, to lack implicitly a sense of either humor or honor; oh, and to be unable to earn an income, and to be content with his functional illiteracy, and to be a congenital coward. He was filled with virtues — overfilled, you might say.

When he and I were left alone to have a chat and get to know each other in the tiny living room, it took the impotent insect more than twenty minutes to have the courage to say anything ("You look nice"). Doused in uncomfortable silence, we sat there, our shifting eyes covering much ground but not meeting. I exaggerate little when I say that every conversation we ever had thereafter began with a silence that lasted a good twenty minutes.

Throughout our marriage, we would go for weeks without exchanging more than perfunctory communications, sharing little but the bewildered quiet.

And you think that I am lonely now? Heavens.

I wish I'd listened to Chekhov, or had read him then: "If you are afraid of loneliness, don't marry."

I'm not so self-centered as to believe that my marriage was the most horrific or that my ex-husband was the worst. He never laid a hand on me (he would have had to stand on a stepladder to do so) or caused me physical pain. I have come across worse men. I also know that my marriage was by no means unique, nor uniquely Beiruti. In the concise words of Madame du Deffand, who, like me, was married and almost immediately separated, "Feeling no love at all for one's husband is a fairly widespread misfortune."

But enough about him.

I noticed Hannah that day because of two things: she ate and she was happy. She devoured everything she was offered. My mother or I would bring out a tray of home-made sweets, chocolates, or candy-covered almonds, and she didn't hesitate, blink, or demur. The other guests would pretend to consider whether they should take more, hem and haw before helping themselves, but not Hannah. She thanked us profusely for every offering before gobbling it down. When I said, "Please, take two," she did.

My dear, dear Hannah.

Yes, and she was happy. She didn't talk much, but she seemed elated to be included, almost as if she were the groom. If not for conventions, mores, and manners, she would probably have jumped across the room and given me a hug, welcoming the new bride into her world. She lavished my ex-husband's family and mine with joy.

She was there for both the engagement and the evening that passed for my wedding. What endeared her to me was that two days after I moved into my apartment she was the first to pay me a visit. I say me, and not we, because my ex-husband hated her. She was oblivious to his loathing, and to tell the truth, she was mostly oblivious to him. Until her slip into the chasm at the end of her life, Hannah had an uncanny ability to simply ignore unpleasantness, and my ex-husband was nothing if not simply unpleasant. I don't know when she concluded that he was irrelevant, but it was early on, long before I did. She mentioned him only twice in her journals: the first time, she likened him to a porter at the airport, which in my opinion was an extraordinarily apt description; the last was when he left me and she called him a dog, a "scruffy, mangy mongrel" to be exact.

When she first came to the apartment that day, I went into the kitchen to make her a cup of coffee and she followed. As I ground the beans, she bent her head and I felt her brow ripple my hair in a caress. "He's such a cranky fellow, your little husband," she whispered, "but don't worry, I've known him since he was a child, and he's harmless." Her eyebrows, as was their wont whenever she thought she was being mischievous, flicked up and down a few times, begging for approval.

Of course she ended up teaching me how to brew a kettle of coffee, how many spoons of grounds, how much sugar, how much cardamom. We stumbled into friendship. She was the first person who wished to have me in her life, the first to choose me.

Hannah taught me many things. When I was married off, I was unprepared for life. Sometimes I think I'm still unprepared, but that's a different proposition now. She taught me how to cook, though she wasn't much better than I. How to knit, though I never cared to follow through on that. How to sew and how to mend buttons, which I grew quite adept at since losing buttons was a specialty of the impotent one. She slipped me books and magazines.

She also taught me how to pray, another discipline I didn't keep up with. In the beginning I was too busy, what with housework, cooking, and educating myself. I had little time for a god who had little time for me. As I matured, I had no use for one. Emmanuel Lévinas suggested that God left in 1941. Mine left in 1975. And in 1978, and in 1982, and in 1990.

Hannah, on the other hand, was dumbfounded that neither I nor the impotent insect had a prayer rug (he was not so much religious as superstitious), and further so when she realized that my mother hadn't sent one with me to my new matrimonial home (my mother didn't have one either). She bought me the prayer rug that became the first thing my feet touch when I get out of bed.

Hannah wasn't meticulous about her prayers. She did her best, but if she missed one or two a day, she took it in stride. She hardly ever performed the afternoon prayer since she arrived at the bookstore most days to help close, and then we'd walk home to my apartment together. Summer light or winter dark, she was there through the years, under umbrellas or beaming skies.

We'd chat as we muddled through the preparation and devouring of the evening meal. One of the images that I can't forget is of Hannah licking her forefinger and picking crumbs off the tablecloth. She'd sit with me in my reading room, which wasn't yet as packed with books as it is now, and like a newswire, she'd update me on the adventures of the families, hers and her fiancé's, my ex-husband's. Always knitting, she talked and talked while churning out sweaters for all the nieces and nephews of her two families — sweaters that helped her to be loved and to belong.

She visited me during working hours as well, although nowhere near as often, and there at the bookstore she wasn't chatty. Whether I had customers or not, she sat on a white plastic chair in the corner, knitting soundlessly except for the rhythmic *click-clack* of the bamboo needles. Sometimes she would write in her journal, her pen scratching faintly in the quiet store. I would be reading at my desk, something she deemed part and parcel of my job, and considerate as she was, she kept me company but left me undisturbed. We were two solitudes benefiting from a grace that was continuously reinvigorated in each other's presence, two solitudes who nourished each other.

I should say that at times we were three solitudes in the bookstore. She visited on occasion while Ahmad was there. Since neither spoke much while I was working, they got along rather well. I read at my desk, Hannah knitted in one corner, and Ahmad consumed books on the floor. He left me a couple of years before she killed herself.

Hannah taught me many things, but somewhere along the line, I'm not sure exactly when, probably when I was twenty-two or twenty-three, we commenced a new ritual: in the evening, as we sat together in my reading room after the meal, I began to read to her. She would sit on the love seat, quietly knitting, while I, on the navy chenille chair, became the babbling newswire. I read only books of philosophy to her—she always claimed to love the subject—and only in French since her English was weak (she used to say she got befuddled upon encountering the first subordinate clause). Both of us had trouble in the beginning, and frankly it was quite a long time before I understood much of what I was reading. I think it took two years of evenings, probably 1952 and 1953, to read, to leaf through, *Le monde comme volonté et comme représentation*, and I can't seriously claim I ever grasped much of Schopenhauer on that first reading, or the second, but I kept trying. In philosophy, I was a page-turner long before I was a reader. I worried the surface till I penetrated the essence.

As I write this, I realize that I can easily tell you how difficult learning was in those first few years, but it wasn't as easy to admit then. I wasn't able to share my fears with Hannah in the beginning; I couldn't tell her how foreign those philosophers sounded, how insurmountable the obstacles to my becoming a learned person felt. My only hope was to fake my way to an education. I assumed that she understood little of what I was reading either, that she listened because she enjoyed the sound of my voice. It took us one whole year to finish Spinoza's *Éthique*, the first volume only.

One day in the early history of my bookstore, when I was still unsure of so much, she was knitting on the white plastic

chair in the corner when a chic woman walked in trailing a
reek of lily perfume and petit bourgeois affectations. Something about her made me feel inadequate. She approached
my desk, lifted her sunglasses, and inquired about books by
Heidegger, the first time any customer had asked about a philosopher. When I directed her toward the books, she regarded
me roguishly and asked, "Which would you recommend?"

She was being mean, entertaining herself at my expense. I was a rube and I looked like one. I could have
answered; I'd read Hannah an essay about him, but I hadn't
yet read any of his work. I was embarrassed and about to
say the wrong thing.

Without lifting her eyes from the sweater she was working on, Hannah said, "We wouldn't recommend anything
by that proto-Nazi. He's a third-rate philosopher with a
ridiculous knit cap, and trust me, I know my knitting." I'd
shown her the picture that appeared with the critical essay.
She continued, sans façons, to embellish what I'd read to her.
"His only interest was in posturing, and only posturers are
interested in him. A woman of your intelligence shouldn't
waste time reading Heidegger. People who like him confuse
philosophy with cooking. Everything he's written is fried,
roasted, and completely baked. Try Schopenhauer — him
we can recommend."

Had we actually understood Heidegger then, we
wouldn't have dismissed him so readily. After all, anyone
who says that displacement is a fundamental way of being
in the world should have been considered a bit more seriously by the two of us.

We may not have comprehended much in the beginning, but we coped — she helped me cope.

❖    ❖    ❖

The philosopher I feel the most kinship with is Spinoza; I identify with his story and his life. The Jewish elders of Amsterdam issued a cherem — a fatwa, for you non-Hebrew speakers — against my kinsman when he was a mere twenty-three. He was excommunicated for his heresies. He didn't fight it, didn't rebel. He didn't even whine. He gave up his family inheritance and became a private scholar, a philosopher at home.

In paintings and drawings he is portrayed with big brown eyes (and a big Semitic nose like mine, of course), inquiring eyes that penetrate the darkness surrounding us, and the one within us, by looking unblinkingly — intense, shining eyes that disperse mists and miasmas.

He worked as a lens grinder until the day he died at forty-four, of a disease of the lungs, probably silicosis, exacerbated by the glass dust he inhaled while plying his trade.

He died early trying to help people see.

Like many of the writers and musicians I admire, he never married. Probably died a virgin.

I always assumed that Spinoza lived the life of a hermit after the cherem, but I recently found out that wasn't the case at all. He had a good number of friends who visited him, and some even supported him financially. So I know that my idea of who he was isn't accurate, but I still hang on to my myth. Now, if he hadn't written *Ethics* — if he hadn't developed the concepts of religious freedom, freedom of the press, democratic republicanism, and a secular morality detached from theology — I wouldn't claim him. The fact that he wrote that masterwork is what makes him a genius.

The fact that he was, and that I consider him, a pathological outsider is what makes him my favorite.

We so desperately need a Beiruti Baruch, a knight to slay the ecclesiastical dragons, or at least declaw them.

When I run across his name in one of my readings, as in the brilliant novel I mentioned earlier, *Sepharad*, by Antonio Muñoz Molina, butterflies flap their wings about my heart as if I've encountered a lost lover or rediscovered an intimate, an almost sensual experience.

The heel of my shoe lands on hard ground, the pavement tile, but the ball of my foot encounters no support and I lose balance. I gather myself quickly so I don't fall forward. A hole in the pavement gapes at me — a hole big enough for a mining dwarf to slide through. I try to look in to gauge how deep the mine is, if only to guess how many leg bones I'd have broken had I stepped in it. Nausea overwhelms me, and I back away. The small hyperactive church bell rings in my ears again. A few meters away I stop, lean against a building's wall in order to breathe and settle myself, to allow the miasma of memories to seep out of my head.

I must keep walking. Onward.

Two giant residential buildings are being erected on this tiny street. Billboards featuring ridiculously wealthy Western-ers shopping, swimming in private pools, and getting facialed in spas cover the construction sites. One slogan proclaims WE'RE BEIRUTING AGAIN. Hundreds of these buildings are going up all over the city, none of them less than super ultra deluxe.

Not long after I was married off, the family of which I'd suddenly become a superfluous part moved into the apartment that my mother and my half brother the eldest's brood live in now. The change of residence, one street over, was an upwardly mobile one, but not by much, from two bedrooms to two and a half—the half being my mother's cell. The tiny building with the tinier apartment I grew up in was leveled and replaced by a twelve-story complex with a sushi boat restaurant on the ground floor where our home used to be. I've never eaten there.

I don't ring my mother's doorbell (my half brother the eldest's). I pause briefly before knocking on the pinewood door. Hearing nothing, I wait. It has been such a long time since I've stood on this spot. Scratches, scrapes, and dents make the door look like the bottom of a litter box, but the copper knob is polished to a shine by the touch of many a hand—many a hand but not mine, not in a while.

I refuse to touch it, refuse to turn it. I notice that my hand is fiercely clutching the black wrought-iron railing that surrounds the landing. I let go.

I wonder what Murakami would think about strangers slicing tuna where he once slept, where now a series of dispirited miniature boats connected stem to stern goes around and around forever.

No one seems to be answering my knock. I lean into the door, hoping to hear no sound within the apartment. I won't be disappointed if no one's home, for I can most certainly return another day. I can climb these seventeen shallow, steep stairs once more if I want to, if I choose to. The wood presses the scarf against my ear.

I ring the doorbell. A rustle of steps inside, then more steps. A young girl in a T-shirt, jeans, slippers, and clumsy makeup opens the painted pine door. Thirteen, I'd say, maybe even fourteen in spite of the ludicrous pigtails. An obstinate ridge of pimples occupies the lower right quadrant of her chin. Her eyes hide behind lids that droop heavily, giving her an appearance of permanent apathy that belies a shadow of astonishment, possibly even excitement, over this seemingly rare occurrence of a stranger at the door. Her T-shirt screams KENZO in sparkling gold letters.

She is so very young. I try to hazard a guess as to whom she might be, what our relationship might be. There is a resemblance, of that I'm sure. She's family. I'm stumped.

"I would like to see my mother," I say as a formal announcement.

She obviously has no idea who I am or whom I'm asking about. She calls her grandmother, loudly and a bit too insistently. She waits at the door, guarding it, not exactly preventing my entry, but standing slightly aside as if she expects me to offer her a tip or at least a keepsake as a souvenir of our encounter.

Her grandmother is none other than my starchy sister-in-law, all shortish height of her. The bewildered look on her mousy face may be worth whatever nasty surprises are lurking within this household. She looks tired, haggard and tattered, overworked and overwhelmed. The poor woman is inexperienced in either repose or solitude.

"I want to see her," I say. "Please don't allow your hopes to rise. I'm not taking her with me. Don't even think about it. I simply wish to pay a visit."

She recovers her sour composure quickly. "Now?" she says. "You come to visit now? After all that's happened?"

A conversation in short bursts of question marks? Why such irritation? Such antipathy?

I am inoffensiveness incarnate. I don't expect people to love me, like me, or feel anything at all toward me. I never wanted to be prominent enough to have enemies. I'm not suggesting that I'm congenitally shy, or that I'm a wall-flower whose deepest desire is to bloom into a scandalously fragrant tiger lily, just that I try to live without interfering in the lives of others because I have no wish for them to interfere in mine.

Why does my sister-in-law dislike me? I've never caused her harm. I don't even remember many interactions with her. I understand that she wishes me to take my mother off her hands, but she must know that her wish is unreasonable. She moved from her parents' house to my parents' house and has been living with my mother ever since. She knows my mother better than I do.

I haven't been involved in my sister-in-law's life for years, for decades. She shouldn't hate me.

"I thought my visit might help."

I take a small step back, ready to pack up my intentions and leave. She doesn't say anything but takes a bigger step back. Both she and her granddaughter make way for me, parting the sea, so to speak.

The girl unwraps a piece of bubblegum and stuffs it in her mouth. I can't tell whose daughter she is, which of my half brother the eldest's children. I should ask but I don't. Come to think of it, I can't recall any of his children or how many he has. I walk into the apartment, past the two doorkeepers, glide through the scents of youth (gum, cheap perfume) and old age (sweat, slightly stale body odor).

The apartment hasn't changed much since I was last here. When was that? So long ago that I can't remember.

It has always been stuffy, dark and dank. In the corridor, I walk under a strip of flypaper hanging from the ceiling; it's probably as old as I am, brown now, covered with darker spots—carapaces, one presumes.

My half brother the eldest isn't home, for which I'm exceedingly grateful. He's probably playing boyish games with his buddies. I don't ask about him, nor does his wife offer any information on his whereabouts. She leads me through folding double doors, deeper into her den. I note the miniature ladder running through her dark stockings.

The wallpaper has lost all semblance of color or texture. Last time I saw it, if I remember correctly, it was peachy pink with embossed vertical stripes. Now it's dirty beige. Two walls in the living room are decorated by carpets, giant machine-made Turcomans, to which age has added nothing of interest or worth. Life-sized portraits litter a third wall, black-and-white photographs of plump-looking men, all mustached, none smiling, all keeping a reproachful, stern eye on me as I enter the room, all of them dead. The portraits ensure that the walls will always be more crowded than the living room, that the dead outnumber the living.

My mother looks dead in the living room, but her chest murmurs. She breathes.

"She's not dead," my sister-in law says.

My mother's head and arms fold into her body like commas; because of her diminutive size and the droop of her head, the floral-patterned armchair (roses and dahlias, thorns and leaves) looks as if it belongs in *Alice in Wonderland*. Her shoes, low black heels, do not reach the floor—she's always hated slippers. The strip of white in her

hair seems to have expanded. Light from a small window
hits her face, but it doesn't bother her. We are all children
when we sleep.

*I sit by the window. And while I sit*
*my youth comes back. Sometimes I'd smile. Or spit.*

"I can wake her," my great-niece says. "It's not difficult
to make her stop sleeping."

I tell them, my sister-in-law and great-niece, that I don't
want to disturb her, or them either. I can wait for a while. I'll
be out of their way. I drag over a nearby high-backed chair
and sit facing my mother, the window behind me. The few
leaves on the ficus tree next to me are wilted and scorched,
whether from lack of light, or of blessed watering, or of loving attention, I can't tell. There doesn't seem to be another
potted plant in the apartment.

The armchair's back faces the rest of the living room.
You can watch television without having to be disturbed by
the sight of my mother. She can stare out the window toward
the world, but not toward her family. Maybe she's the one
who made the choice. Maybe she's the one who wanted to
keep looking out, not in.


There must be a word in some language that describes the
anguish you experience upon suddenly coming face-to-face
with your terrifying future. I can't think of one in any of the
languages I know.

Maybe it exists in Swahili or Sanskrit.

Maybe I can make one up, like Hamsun's *Kuboaa*.

Maybe the word is just *mother*.

There is a word I know: *litost*. In Czech, according to
Milan Kundera, litost is a state of agony and torment created by the sudden sight of one's own misery.

The more I observe my mother, the more I think she
looks like a Chekhovian character resting before a long journey, possibly a train trip, though God knows we no longer
have passenger trains in Lebanon. Like a constipated creek
in dry summer months, the drool of sleep flows leisurely and
intermittently from the left corner of her slack mouth as her
head falls southeasterly forward. Her breathing comes at
me in jagged intervals, a whispery snore.

I don't wish to be here. She's contagious. My breathing
becomes as serrated as hers.

There's a milky gash in the dark chestnut coffee table
next to her, a table that hasn't felt the smooth pampering
of a coat of varnish in at least a decade. On it, alongside an
inopportune desk lamp, sits an old, round, ticktocking alarm
clock with a spherical skullcap for a bell. But what captures
my attention is another object on the table: a mother-of-pearl-
encrusted music box, hand-sized, that I remember well from
my childhood. I recall the day she bought it as a gift to herself.

I control my breathing because I feel a flood of emotions
rising. I haven't seen that music box since I was married off.

*"I begged of you, O Memory, / to be my best assistant,"* wrote
Cavafy.

I assess my surroundings. My sister-in-law isn't in the
room. She's making blustery, demented chopping noises in
the kitchen, but her granddaughter spuds on the couch in
front of the flickering television while banging the keys of
an older-model laptop, studying me out of the corner of her
eye. I must restrain myself.

My mother bought the music box because of its odd-ness; it had two twirling ballerinas, not just one, a pseudo-Sapphic pas de deux. It was Russian, or appeared so, and we all assumed the music it played was Russian too. It isn't. I may not recall what I had for breakfast this morning or whether I had breakfast at all, but I can whistle that tune note for note, even though I probably haven't opened the box in sixty years.

The twisted red coils of the heater in the far corner emit a steady electric hum that feels ominous in this situation. I begin to perspire again.

The tinny piano-imitating tune interred within the box is Chopin's Waltz no. 2 in C-sharp Minor. I had forgotten all about this box, forgotten it even existed. I'd dismembered it in my memories. I'd disremembered it.

No wonder I was so easily infected. The Chopin virus was already latent in my system.

I desperately wish to sneak the Russian box into my handbag, but I resist my shameful urge. There are things I just won't do, as much as I want to, if I intend to live decently with myself afterward.

I'll listen to Rubinstein the Pole play the waltzes when I get home.

I distract myself by gazing at the barely perceptible steam rising off a damp pink sweater that's draped over the top of the heater. The girl must have come in not long before I did, wet from the rain. She chews her gum loudly.

My mother used to call me a praying mantis (the term in Arabic translates to "prophet's mare," which is beautiful, if you ask me) because I was tall and scrawny. I think she meant a stick insect, but whether as a child or as a woman,

I rarely disabused her of her incorrect assertions. Yet as I
sit before her, I realize she's much thinner than I ever was.
She's gone from Rubens to Schiele.

Many suggest that we close the circle as we age by
growing childlike. The way she sits, folded upon herself,
I'd go as far as to say that she's shrinking to fetus form.
Her appearance has changed as well, and I don't mean
just the intense reticulation of lines and wrinkles, the true
stigmata of life. She wears someone else's skin, someone
much larger, a hand-me-down skin. A bluff of short spiky
hairs sprouts on her upper lip, sparse Hitlerian. Her face
is both gaunt and puffy; its muscles are completely slack.
It has no discernible angles. My mother's countenance has
turned androgynous.

This is what I have to look forward to.

In slumber, my mother is melancholia in human form.
I wonder, though, whether I only see this in her because I
expect it. For all I know she may be dreaming of flowers and
wheat fields, butterflies and Swiss Alps, chocolate and Chanel.
Maybe that mind of hers is happy in its insanity. Devoid of
worries and responsibility, of mundane earthly concerns, she
may have reached Nirvana, without guru or Sherpa.

But the mournful words of Thomas Jefferson loop
through my head. In a letter to a friend in 1825 he wrote,
"All are dead, and ourselves left alone amidst a new generation whom we know not, and who know us not."

Jefferson obviously had no Sherpa.


My mother wears a hearing aid that circles and penetrates her
left ear, a recent addition but not a recent model. What seems

at first to be the manufacturer's logo behind her ear fails to sustain the illusion on closer inspection. It is formless Roman script in purple ink that reads, when I lean forward to see, AU SECOURS! I don't have to wonder long who did this: as soon as I lean back in my chair, I notice the Kenzo potato blushing, avoiding eye contact by staring at a television commercial.

The slam of the front door distracts her. The density of the air changes faintly, allowing me to note how stale the room smells, a brew of ancient cigarette smoke, naphthalene, and armpit sweat. I worry that it's my half brother the eldest, but a sloppy teenage boy walks in, a year or two older than the girl, who must be his sister. His eyes are covered by unattractive sunglasses that feature, incredibly, cheap-looking silver tassels behind each ear. He stops when he sees me. He stands with arms ceremoniously akimbo, directly in my line of sight.

"Who're you?" he snaps, not maliciously, but with a certain air of privilege.

His sister shushes him, points toward my catatonic mother. I don't reply. He shrugs with the honed nonchalance of ungracious adolescence, trudges with lazy steps into the kitchen. I'm sure his grandmother will explain who I am.

I, on the other hand, can't explain who my mother is. Who is this woman before me? This thought drifts like smoke through my head: *Do I know you?*

I've been so busy thinking about how my mother saw me that I've had little sight left to look upon the grande dame, her holiness herself. This is my mother. I rack my brain. What do I know of her? What do I remember?

I remember incidents, patches of a life — actually, minor patches in a long life, and only when they intersected with mine. I see scenes—images and scenes. I know my mother only in sepia.

Isn't someone's life more than a collection of scenes? Isn't she more than the images I have compiled in my head? These questions may sound rhetorical, but I genuinely don't know. I can't tell whether my understanding of her is limited, if I can't get to know her because of a basic deficiency of mine, or whether this is as far as any human can understand another. The question that really bothers me is whether I know anyone else better than I know my mother. It seems I've always asked, with Lear, "Does any here know me?" but never "Do I know any here?" Trying to know another human being seems to me as impossible, and as ridiculous, as trying to grasp a swallow's shadow.

My mother lived, lives, in a hazy world, not my own.

Other people are hazy phenomena that become corporeal only in my memories.

Although I know the characters of a novel as a collection of scenes as well, as accumulated sentences in my head, I feel I know them better than I do my mother. I fill in the blanks with literary personas better than I do with real people, or maybe I make more of an effort. I know Lolita's mother better than I do mine, and I must say, I feel her more than I feel my mother. I recognize Rembrandt's painted face of his mother better than I recognize the real face of mine.


The girl pretends to watch television. It may be just background noise for her, but it isn't for me. Even though the volume is low, whatever show is on is in a language I don't understand, possibly Turkish, possibly Hebrew; the voice drifts as if from a distance, not the television, but a far-off land—a male voice, nasal, mingled with faint crackles and New Age string music. Most irritating.

"Turn that off," I snap angrily, much too angrily.

Surprisingly, the girl does, doesn't even hesitate.

What I would love right now is a massage, a gentle shoulder rub, anything to untangle my mess of muscles. Not that I've had many massages. I don't submit easily to a stranger's touch no matter how beneficial it might be, and I can't afford to pay for self-indulgence in any case. My shoulder muscles have spun themselves into worsted yarn, their numbness and ache locked deep between the blades. I tense my shoulders, count to three, and relax them, an exercise Hannah taught me once. It doesn't help. It never actually did.

A heavy vehicle causes the window to rattle and the spiderweb dangling from the chandelier to sway. The noise and clatter wake my mother. She opens her left eye first, then her right.

I brace myself. In my head I count the seconds—no, no, someone else counts the seconds in my head: one, two, three. I can't seem to restrain my thoughts. I count each wrinkle around her eyes without mixing either tally. I shiver as my mind skates from one bleak oblique thought to another. Will she recognize me? Has she ever rocked me in her arms? Does she hate me? Why did she never brush my hair? Has anyone taken her to a doctor recently? The voice of Karita Mattila singing the opening notes of the third of Richard Strauss's *Four Last Songs* echoes in my skull. My tongue and the insides of my cheeks feel dry. I note the little red lash marks on the palm of her hand, the earth-toned liver spots on the back of the other. Her eyes focus on me. They seem so very sane.

At the count of twelve, she calls my name quietly. "Aaliya," she says.

I acknowledge the recognition by smiling and nodding. My hands, still slightly clammy, unclench. I place them on my thighs. My heart beats just a little faster, just a little sharper. Her breathing is calmer, without stertor, less of a struggle than while she slept.

"You've changed," she says in a cotton wad of a voice.

"Yes," I say. "We all have. I've grown older."

"No," she interrupts me. "No, your hair is blue."

Has she ever rocked me in her arms? Hugged me? Whispered baby talk in my ears? I doubt it very much.

"Yes, that," I say. "Yes, it is blue."

She looks puzzled, and a little lost. She winces. Her face distorts a bit, as if she found my answer offensive, or maybe incomprehensible, or simply terrifying. I can't tell. She tries to move farther back into the chair, but that proves physically impossible—she is as far back as the chair will allow.

"It's all right, Mother," I say in as comforting a tone as I can muster. "I used coloring shampoo by mistake, more than I should have. It's not permanent. My hair will recover."

She looks more confused, breaks eye contact. She regards the ceiling as if she's watching some ghostly agitation up there. She pushes her hand under the shawl around her shoulders and scratches her arm. Her grimace becomes more pronounced, the corners of her mouth moving farther apart as if they loathe each other.

"Are you all right?" I ask, pointing at her.

I receive no response, verbal or non.

"She doesn't always answer," my great-niece says. No longer pretending to ignore my presence, she's on her knees, leaning over the side of the couch, trying to engage me. "Sometimes I know she's in pain but she won't be able to tell me what's hurting her. Other times she'll tell me it's her neck but she means that it used to hurt her years ago. You can't tell. She's not good at communicating."

"Neither am I," I say. "Mother, are you in pain?"

"She doesn't talk much, just hums most of the time." My great-niece underlines her words with an extravagant repertoire of hand gestures and facial expressions. "Old Arabic songs. Hum, hum, hum. Not Oum Kalthoum, not Fairuz. You'll never guess."

"Asmahan," I say.

"You guessed!" She sounds ecstatic, unable to control her glee. "Of course you'd know. You're her daughter. I try to ask her who Asmahan is but she keeps mumbling, 'They killed her, they killed her.' Then she starts humming again. Nonstop humming, always music in the house. It's like we have our own canary."

At first I feel hurt and want to object. That's an awful thing to say about someone. In a short story by the fabulous fabulist Sławomir Mrożek, a narrator attends a party at which the entertainment is provided by the household pet, a caged liberal, a humanist who has been reduced to nothing more than a singer of quaint revolutionary songs. My mother doesn't know any revolutionary songs, but she does Asmahan's. So I also feel a tickle of happiness, a flicker of joy, unrelated to the fact that I guessed the singer; that my mother hums Asmahan's songs makes me feel good. That my mother likes the singer who married and divorced three or four men, the scandalous actress who left her husband and family to pursue her career — an illustrious, titled family no less — allows my own heart to sing.

"Do you know who she is?" asks my great-niece.

"Who?" I ask.

"The singer," the girl says. "Do you know who the singer is?"

"Of course."

"Well?" she says.

She waits for me to say something. I am more experienced in waiting.

"Who is she?" my great-niece asks.

"You have that wonderful computer next to you. Look her up."

My mother whimpers, and a frisson of fear courses through me. Will she?

"Are you all right, Mother?" I ask.

She no longer seems to recognize me, but she quiets. I can't read her, can't tell whether she's in agony or simply distracted. She seems alone and fearful, her mind the only place in which she can hide. Her mouth is never still, moves from grimace to lazy smile to irritation in a matter of seconds, back and forth, sideways, up and down.

"You have to be more specific," my great-niece says.

She's off the couch now, standing beside me. If I stay a bit longer, if I continue to linger in her presence, I wonder whether she'll end up sitting on my lap.

"She doesn't answer if I ask a general question," she says, "but if I ask whether her back hurts, she might.

Sometimes I have to ask about every body part one by one."
She nods while speaking, as if she's agreeing with what she's
saying. Her voice seems to have an element of delirium.
"Before you came in, she answered yes to whether she was
thirsty, but when I brought the glass of water, she was asleep,
so I drank it."

My great-niece's excitement is so high that I wonder
if I should hold on to her so she doesn't launch herself at
the ceiling.

"Mother," I say, "does your back hurt?"

My mother pays no attention, as if I don't exist. I have
to control the urge to lean forward and smack her.

"How can I ask her anything if she doesn't hear a word
I'm saying?" I mutter.

"Hold her hand," my great-niece says. "She doesn't
always know you're speaking to her. Sometimes you have
to touch her, otherwise you might be sitting here for hours
and she'll be off in her own world."

She puts her hand on my shoulder, but withdraws it
when I instinctively flinch. She folds her hands into the small
of her back. What can I say? Judging from her enthusiastic
agitation, I'm afraid she'll go Ancient Mariner on me. "*The
guests are met, the feast is set.*" Let me be.

"Go on," she says. "Hold her hand. She won't hurt you.
She doesn't bite."

"Oh, but I might, so better be careful."

Can I get any sillier than this in my old age? Trying to
be funny for a teenager, my jokes as bad as Fadia's. Maybe I
should pick up Fadia's boisterous laugh as well. I'll ride out
on a lame horse toward a simulacrum sunset with a comedy
drum roll and cymbal crash.

"Haha," she says with amused sarcasm. "That was almost as unfunny as Grandpa's jokes."

In my hand, my mother's feels breakable; it is skin and bones—desiccated skin that lacks any semblance of elasticity. My great-niece is right, though. My mother looks suddenly alert.

"Does your back hurt?" I ask.

She shakes her head no. She removes her hand from mine and points toward her shoes with a skinny finger that looks surprised that it can hold itself aloft. "My feet," she says softly, gently.

"Your feet?" I ask, pointing toward her shoes to make sure.

"Her feet," my great-niece says. "Yes, it must be. She's never pointed to her feet before."

I now have a sidekick.

"Can I see?" I ask my mother. "I'll need to take your shoes off."

I don't know why I'm making such an offer. She's not wearing any socks or nylons under her low black heels. For all I know she may have callouses, and will I be able to help her with that? Contagious fungi, gigantic bunions, ingrown warts, lacerations, ulcerations? What if she's accumulated blisters on the bottoms of her feet like barnacles on the bottom of a boat—a boatload of blisters?

I bought my first pair of slippers after I left her house. She wouldn't allow me to take my shoes off until it was time for bed. For all she cared, the boys could prance around the house shoeless, sockless, barefoot, or wearing their underpants as freedom fighters' face masks—"boys will be

boys," that most insipid of phrases. Not her daughters. Ladies should never be without shoes.

My sidekick is wearing light blue slippers with sheep-
skin lining and a Hello Kitty logo. She sees me looking at
them and says, "She used to demand that I wear shoes, and
we used to argue all the time, but then she stopped a few
years ago—she stopped noticing."

No bunions, no blisters, at least not at first glance,
though an effluvium of foot odor assaults my nostrils. The
stench even penetrates my great-niece's defenses of cheap
perfume and bubblegum.

"Ew!" she says, quite succinctly, if you ask me.

I don't have to touch my mother's feet—I really don't
want to—to realize how dry they are. Her shoes have irritated the skin at the joints, making the toes look like they've
had a lovers' tiff. Her nails are clawlike, an eagle's talons,
which is what's probably causing her pain. She needs to
have her toenails trimmed.

"Oh!" my great-niece exclaims.

I like her monosyllabic.

My mother should have a pedicure. I can't take her to
a salon, not in her condition. Some manicurists visit your
home, but I don't know how to find one. I can ask my sister-
in-law; she might know.

"We have to do something about her toenails, Tante,"
my great-niece says.

"I know, I'm trying to think, and please don't call me
Tante. My name is Aaliya."

She proudly tells me her name, Nancy, and waits for
me to comment. I don't.

"Think quickly, Tante Aaliya," she says, "or we might suffocate in here. Should I open the window? It's cold outside, though. Should I get cologne?"

I'm surprised that I find my great-niece bearable. She seems to be able to change gears from shy to loquacious in microseconds, needs to have every thought heard and acknowledged. I usually find that incredibly annoying, if not insufferable. Not here, though, not now. I wonder if she too is lonely—if she too is in possession of that vast, heavy isolation that's so difficult to bear. If she would sometimes happily exchange it for any kind of interaction, however trivial or cheap, for the tiniest outward agreement with the first person who came along, even the most unworthy. If so, then today I happen to be my great-niece's first person, the most unworthy.


I don't want to give my mother a pedicure. Apart from the fact that I've never trimmed anybody else's nails, I find it— how shall I put it?—demeaning. I am not Jesus washing the feet of his disciples. I don't wish to be crucified tomorrow. I am not Mary of Bethany. If I dry my mother's feet with my hair, will they turn blue?

I am not the Magistrate. I am not the Magistrate. I am not the Magistrate.

*And now, what will become of us without barbarians?*

O Coetzee, O Cavafy, O beloved gods, what am I doing here?

"Can you help me, please?" I ask my great-niece.

Can she bring a tub of hot water, not boiling, but hot enough for a footbath? Green tea leaves if there are any in the house, black tea if not, even tea bags are acceptable. No, we're not going to drink the tea, it's a disinfectant, but if you want to make some, I'll share a cup—separate from the footbath, mind you. Rubbing alcohol, clippers, nail file, and a sliced turnip, or if there isn't one, a radish will do. Their juice is a natural deodorant. Can she get a pair of my mother's socks, please, and Vaseline to moisturize, since I doubt we can get our hands on spikenard oil?

Did Mary of Bethany use spikenard oil simply for its fragrance or does it actually moisturize? I should experiment with lavender oil, its sibling, to see.

How did I learn about the bacteria-destroying properties of tea, the odor-ameliorating power of certain root vegetables? My usual response is snappy: books, I read books—read, read, one can learn everything from books. Not in this case, however. I learned from watching my mother wash her feet when I was a little girl, as she probably learned from hers.

My great-niece needs the help of her brother, sans sunglasses, to carry the plastic basin of hot water—a red circular tub the size of a car wheel, with four Lipton tea bags floating like water lilies, their yellow tags conspicuous. My sister-in-law's chopping reaches mayhem proportions. I hope a juicy turnip is among the things she's torturing. The siblings bicker as they lower the water wheel to the floor, my great-niece insisting her brother should listen to her because she knows what we're doing.

What are we doing?

My mother's feet barely reach the water. Her toes dive below the surface and curl, wishing to drown; the arch of her foot retracts, wanting no part of this forced baptism.

"This won't work," my great-niece says. "She's too small. We have to move her forward."

"No," my mother says, quite succinctly, if you ask me. She is suddenly alert. "Go away." If eyes are windows to the soul, then my mother has a pretty angry one right now. "Leave me be," she tells my great-niece, her weak hand flicking in a dismissive, despotic gesture, "and tell your mother to find you a decent husband."

"She's busy," my great-niece snaps. Her upper lip curls inward, almost disappears — not so attractive.

Her brother considers this the greatest of jokes. "I can find you a husband," he says, "a big, fat, ugly one with no sense of humor."

Without thinking, I glare over my shoulder. He looks suddenly a little guilt-ridden, less enamored of himself than when he walked in, a disheveled quail of a boy; his hands behind his back, he rocks hesitantly on his heels. His sister bores into him with a homicidal stare, but that doesn't seem to be the cause of his concern. My mother holds him with her glittering eyes. Maybe she objects to the lack of humor in a husband.

"We can raise the basin," the boy says, his singsongy voice alternating oddly between high and low notes. "That'll solve the problem."

We place the red tub of water on a stool, and I kneel on the floor, luckily carpeted by an old cheap Turcoman similar to its sisters on the walls.

My mother's feet are broad, the toes stubby, the toenails corn yellow with kernels at the center, the ankles prominently veined but not swollen. Mottled discoloration runs the length of her legs, from the tips of her toes to the knees and probably higher. The pigments of her skin are no longer properly mixed.

She sighs as I guide her feet into the water.

The boy claims his sister's old spot on the sofa and begins a dialogue with the laptop. He lights a cigarette and within seconds fades into an uneasy cumulus of smoke. My great-niece kneels beside me, asks if she can help. I admit that I don't know what I'm doing. Wash her feet and trim her nails? She can take the right foot and I the left.

I lift my mother's foot out of the water, all bones and no meat. With my hand I wash the foot slowly, build a milky lather before passing the bar of soap to my great-niece. Once tectonic plates, her calves are now emaciated, striated with boysenberry-purple veins. She used to have the strong legs of any of Javier Marías's female characters. I knead the tendons and knots around her anklebone, massage her toes, run my fingers through the gorges between them. I feel the flow of her blood.

My great-niece mimics my every step. We arrive at a gentle rhythm, slow and anodyne, the rocking of an old porch swing on a summer afternoon.

My mother's eyes are shut, her lips as well, and probably her ears. Calm spreads over every wrinkle of her face. She cares little that I'm the one who's washing her feet. She cares even less about my bleating conscience. More than content, she seems happy. She's no longer present in the room. I don't know what to do with her, what to say. I continue with my menial task. She is lost to me once again.

"Maybe I'll dye my hair blue," my great-niece says.

Rain streaks the small window—lazy, untroubled rain, sure of itself, which tells me I should reconsider my plan to walk home.

*The troubled sky reveals*
*The grief it feels.*

O Longfellow, what will happen to me if I live long enough that I lose my ability to walk long distances? Will I still be able to wash my feet?


My mother's foot balances on the side of the basin, but I feel its weight on my thighs, a tight knot in the back of my neck, a burden on my shoulders. Up her foot, down, across, the water remains warm; my fingers turn pruney, their folds and furrows more intricate than their counterparts on my mother's.

A few ulcerations on the carpet hanging to my right catch my attention. I didn't notice them at first. It seems that someone sewed the tears with a timid thread and then covered them with cheap paint. There is a portrait hanging on the fake Turcoman itself, an old picture of my uncle-father. Now I remember what he looks like. The cataract subsides, if momentarily.

He is younger, the way he was when I was a child. He wears a suit and a fez, trying without much success to appear respectable for eternity. An odd photo, his skin is a dovish hue, but I can't tell whether the grays have deteriorated through the years or whether the photograph was developed in those unnatural tones. Tufts of black hair protrude from his nostrils to mix with his mustache. He has too long a chin and a cucumber nose. He and I have a similar protruding brow, which probably means he and his older brother looked alike. I can't tell whether we have the same eyes because he's squinting at the camera as if trying to read it. I remember that he needed glasses but never owned any, or visited an ophthalmologist for that matter. He lived and died squinting at the world.

How he managed as a tailor's assistant is beyond me.

He looks displeased, as if something is irritating him. Maybe he knows that the photograph will make him look peculiar, maybe he believes his face is unattractive; he seems, I don't know, discontent with the sum of his features. I remember him as irascible but not unreasonably so. He looks like someone who is ready to leave the party, forever disgruntled and wishing to return home.

I remember him now.

I flash to a memory of him holding my hand to cross the street. I must have been ten or eleven, old enough to be conscious of what he was thinking. There were cars, buses, trams, and mule carts on the street, hence the need for handholding. I held his right hand, my half brother the eldest his left, but all of a sudden he switched us around. I would be the first to encounter oncoming traffic.

Could I find fault with that? I was his stepchild — his brother's daughter, his wife's child, not his. I most certainly blamed him then.

On the other hand, I remember that he used to make my half brother the eldest kiss the leather strap he was going to use to whip him, but not me — my stepfather never punished me.

"I didn't even know she had another daughter," my great-niece says. "Grandfather hasn't mentioned you either. He might have when I wasn't around, but I don't think so."

I pare my mother's toenails, we both do. We allow the clippings to drop into the water. I massage a thin layer of Vaseline onto her skin and cover her foot with a sock that catches on a small, sharp protrusion. I should have filed the toenails smoother.

I'm not that far from home. The rain has halted, but the lowering, evil-looking clouds threaten, their congealed masses pushing across the sky, their color mirroring that of my stepfather's skin in the portrait. I will risk walking in the cold. I need to clear my head, dispel the ant farm once more.

Does one have to fulfill a promise made to an unconscious person? I told my mother that I'd return, but she couldn't possibly have heard me. My great-niece was a witness, though.

Nancy? What an odd name. Who would have thought someone from this family would give a daughter a Western name?

Beirut changes its dazzling accessories more often than its society ladies do; she certainly has more color highlights. She sparkles. According to the time of year, the time of day, the weather, and numerous other variables, her streaks of light morph. The sparkle — real, not metaphorical — is a result of location, between iridescent Mediterranean and mountains. A headland breasting the sea, Beirut stands as a gaudy sentinel, Horatio and Marcellus bedecked in shiny baubles. Élisée Reclus once called Byblos voluptuousness deified, but that's probably a more apt descriptor of my Beirut.

Whereas most people will tell you that they prefer the city on spring afternoons when she fills her lungs with briny air, when bougainvilleas, purple and crimson, and wisterias, lavender and white, begin to bloom, or during summer sunsets, when the water is decked with a panoply of gold and hyacinth so vibrant that the city practically rocks on her promontory, I prefer her in this subdued light, under roiling gray clouds, rain-filled but not raining, when the neutral air gives contrast to the authentic colors of the city. These clouds prevent me from seeing the brilliant new white on the mountain peaks, but they offer spectacular city sights as compensation.

I am old enough to remember when this neighborhood was nothing more than two sandstone houses and a copse of sycamores, their carpet of tan leaves acting as their garden. The development of our metropolis began in the 1950s and went completely insane in the 1960s. To build is to put a human mark on a landscape, and Beirutis have been leaving their mark on their city like a pack of rabid dogs. The virulent cancer we call concrete spread throughout the capital, devouring every living surface. I'm not sure how many sycamores remain, how many oaks or cypresses, but I can now walk for half an hour without encountering a single tree, and when I do, it's usually a foreigner, a eucalyptus, jacaranda, or bottlebrush—nice but not satiating. If I happen to come across a garden these days, I burst into bloom.

I mention this now because, miraculously, one of those two houses has survived. Amid the proliferation of unsightly buildings, this crumbling Ottoman house with its triple arcade and red tile roof stands out as starkly as a woman in parliament. There are a few of these houses strewn here and there in the city, but none is as decrepit or as defeated as this one, none as beautiful.

*Here I stand, your slave,*
*A poor, infirm, weak and despised old man.*

Unlike the homes that look down upon it, the house is uninhabitable, and hasn't been lived in for at least a generation, definitely not since the beginning of the war in 1975, probably even earlier, not since 1972, the year Hannah passed away. Pockmarked and perforated, disemboweled, roofless and doorless, it allows entry to all manner of trash, yet it appears majestic, to my eyes at least. Encroached upon by bigger, taller, mightier armies, it is poor, infirm, weak, and despised, but unlike Lear, it remains defiant, remains regal, probably till the end. It stands alone.

I remember another wreck from long ago. In the early seventies I was walking to my bookstore, taking a route not far from here—not far at all. This Ottoman house was in much better shape then, of course. The war hadn't started yet, although signs of it were beginning to pop up here and there. I saw a bright orange BMW 2002 refuse to slow for stalled traffic, its driver probably a self-important young man who would soon be ordering his inferiors to murder, maim, and pillage. He swerved to the right to pass a couple of cars and ran right into the back of a mule-drawn cart full of vegetables, primarily cucumbers and tomatoes. No one was hurt, the mule unperturbed, but the wooden cart was crushed. The cart driver fell to the ground, his seat collapsed, fell on his buttocks as if he were in a Charlie Chaplin movie. The BMW driver, the militiaman to be, was covered in vegetables and embarrassment.

I was an hour late opening the bookstore because I couldn't force myself to leave the scene. Even then I realized that I was seeing something extraordinary: new Beirut crashing into old, young driver and old street vendor, modernity rushing in, an orange car covered in red and green, German steel jumbled with Lebanese pine, and everyone in shock. I was spellbound.

I leave the sandstone house behind me. I remember that on the top floor it used to have lovely arched stained-glass windows with abstract whorls and curls of bright red, orange, and deep-fried yellow. Whether they were broken or spirited away in the middle of the night, I do not know. They've simply disappeared. They live only in my memory now, my Proustian memory.

The last book that Hannah read was Proust's, which she didn't finish. She'd read *Du côté de chez Swann* very early on, but didn't pick up *À l'ombre des jeunes filles en fleurs* right away, not on her first try at least. Every time she decided to continue, she felt the need to return to the first volume and reread it in order to get the full experience. She'd begin rereading *Swann* every few years and give up before the second volume or during the third, always before reaching the end of all ends. I don't know which volume she was on by the time she passed away, but she'd gone further than she ever had before. I thought she'd be happy.

If during those last days she had written in her diary instead of going silent, I might be able to know whether Proust killed her, whether she encountered something in the text that unnerved her, something the great dandy wrote. I wish I could know. I desire more explication.

I do know that she wanted to finish all the volumes to please me. I'd read through the whole thing twice, and I used to go on and on: Marcel, the spectacular writer, my idol, and so forth. I used to blather endlessly about why I adored him, how he, the desperate socialite and party hopper, the inveterate pleaser, was actually the outsider par excellence, how he could be amid all the people he'd always dreamed of befriending yet remain alone in the universe, the loneliest speck of all.

But please don't think I'm suggesting that she killed herself because she failed to finish the gargantuan novel. That's silly.

Hannah aged prematurely; gray hairs began to sprout when she was in her early thirties. She appeared to be in her sixties while in her midforties. Many Lebanese women of her generation had similar problems; these days most resort to plastic surgery and no one is able to gauge how old anyone else is. I don't think she concerned herself much about it, at least I didn't think so in those days. Her mother had aged similarly. I remember her mother as being rather seasoned when I met her, and she was much younger then than I am now. In her journals Hannah wrote impassively about being elderly when she reached forty. She simply expected it. She jokingly wrote that as an old woman she could eat whatever she wanted without worrying about her looks, not that worrying ever stopped her from eating.

I can tell you that she suddenly began to have trouble sleeping sometime in her forties, and that caused a great deal of concern. Her most fervent fantasy was to experience an uninterrupted night of sleep. I began having similar sleeping problems in my sixties, not my forties. She first tried old folk remedies. Hot milk and honey, green tea, anise, chamomile — all were of little use. She placed a sachet of lavender under her pillow, she placed two, then three. She tried spending the night in my apartment instead of hers. Nothing worked. A doctor prescribed Valium, but as little as five milligrams turned her into a walking corpse the following day. She took Seconal, but that didn't induce slumber so much as grogginess and bewilderment. She told me she fought off sleep and spent the night terrified because she wasn't able to recognize herself or what she was doing.

She spent her remaining days and nights troubled by the lacerating paralysis of insomnia.

As she approached fifty in 1972, the Valium and Seconal pills would become part of her story, though not in the way one might assume. She plummeted — she dove into her abyss before Beirut dove into its own.

I was a fool. I was young, a child in my midthirties, but I shouldn't offer that as an excuse. I should have been paying attention. The end of the year was fast approaching and I was about to begin a new project. I was distracted.

She was changing. I thought it was temporary, a phase. She'd mentioned that she missed her mother, thought of her often, missed both her parents. I thought that perfectly normal. She still had her brothers, her nieces and nephews, and the full glory of the lieutenant's family. She was a moon orbiting a multitude of planets. She'd filled her life with people and relationships, people who were not in my life at all. She'd carved her name into many a heart, or so I had assumed.

That trumpery, hope, allowed me to dupe myself. I desperately wished her to be less alone, less solitary, than I was—alone as she had always been, alone as she would always be.

Hope is forgivable when you're young, isn't it? With no suspicion of irony, without a soupçon of cynicism, hope lures with its siren song. I had my illusions and she had hers—she certainly had hers.

Exactly a year before her first suicide attempt, the lieutenant's mother, my mother-in-law, had passed away. I had not considered associating the two events together until after Hannah's death. She kept vigil with the family at the dying woman's bedside. She told me that my ex-husband kept glaring at her, but wouldn't say anything because his mother had specifically asked for her to be there. It seems that Hannah was the last person the lieutenant's mother spoke to.

"You have given me, my dearest daughter," she whispered in a slow, raspy voice, "some of the happiest moments of my life. Your presence in our family has made the absence of my son bearable. I promise that once all three of us are in Heaven, I will not be forced to make the impossible decision of choosing between the two of you."

Hannah, happy as could be, relayed all this to me the following day. She so appreciated that on her deathbed, with her last breath, the lieutenant's mother acknowledged her as a daughter. She mentioned that last sentence but glossed over it, laughed it off even. Choosing between the lieutenant and her? What choice? Later, when I received the journals, I saw that she'd written down the first two sentences the dying woman spoke, but hadn't recorded that disturbing promise.

She moseyed along through her life for quite a while after that, nine or ten months, but I imagine that like a mosquito buzzing in your ear, that last sentence, vague as it may have been, wouldn't let her sleep. A buzz of doubt that became the roar of the crowd at the Colosseum?

Reality may have tempted her, the serpent may have offered her the apple.

She may have woken up one morning and realized that the lieutenant had never desired her. She may have woken up one morning and found one of Spinoza's lenses.

Flashing a light on a dark corner can start a fire that scorches everything in its wake, including your ever-so-flammable soul. Cioran once said that "one touch of clear-sightedness reduces us to our primary state: nakedness."

I am tired, always tired. An amorphous exhaustion smothers me. I wish to sleep. I wish I were able to sleep.


We had a dreary, curiously gloomy winter that year, cold but not freezing, with heavy rainfall. Hannah seemed to compete with the weather: Who is more overcast? At first the changes were gradual and practically imperceptible. She seemed a bit withdrawn, less talkative. It took me a couple of weeks to realize that she hadn't been writing in her journal. I asked her about it, but she dismissed my concerns with a flick of the hand.

In a strange way, I felt she was there but she wasn't there with me, or to put it another way, that she occupied her body, but not her soul. Does that make sense?

In the evenings at home I would make her a cup of tea, and at times it would sit before her untouched. I would remind her that it was turning cold.

"Silly me," she'd say. She'd take a sip and then forget about it once more.

One evening, as I sat across from her at my gaudy kitchen table, I caught her transfixed, studying a limpid pool of lentil and chard soup as if the bowl were a vessel for divination. Another incident really triggered my anxiety. It involved the knitting. I saw her fingers stop, just stop—the needles didn't move for at least thirty seconds. That was unthinkable, inconceivable. Hannah could knit in her sleep, an indubitably automatic motion for her. She could pick up her knitting and carry on a conversation, watch television, talk on the phone, the needles never stopping. She could read, only pausing briefly to flip the page. I saw her—I saw her stop knitting and stare out into the ether, her gaze fixed on a spot in the middle of my living room, and I panicked.

"What are you doing?" I asked.

"Thinking," she said in a conversation-ending tone.

We had an early spring in 1972; after the groaning winter, the temperature grew mild. Even a few butterflies dipped their wings into the air. One of those pleasant days, I was busy at the bookstore. I don't think customers bought much, but I had heavy walk-in traffic. By closing time, Hannah hadn't shown up, even though she'd told me she would. I assumed she wanted to be by herself to think of her deceased mother, of both her parents. I didn't bother her. However, she ended up missing three days in a row, and I finally telephoned. She admitted she was sad, yet she sounded rational.

We had a laugh when she inadvertently said I'd be cheerless as well if my mother were to pass away, then thought better of it. "Well, maybe not so much," she added.

The following morning Hannah entered my bookstore in flamboyantly high spirits. It was spring, she insisted in reply to my inquiries, the season of mad flowerings and lovely beginnings.

"Must there always be a reason for one to be happy?" she asked in feigned innocence. She sang her words—no, it was more that she spoke them in an exuberant cadence. Her face was dotted with color. She picked up books off the shelves and replaced them without looking at title or content. Her eyes gleamed with mischief, like those of a fox just discovering that she has the run of the chicken coop. I did believe her—believed that she was happy that morning, that her bubbling joy, momentary or not, was real. What I needed was an explanation—always with the causality. What makes *you* happy?

After much parrying—she answered most of my questions with a short burst of laughter—she told me she'd had a good night's sleep, the first in years.

How, what, why—an hour of evasions and obfuscations before Hannah confessed all, or at least what I thought was all. She'd felt terribly despondent the previous evening, she couldn't handle the weight of such sadness. She spoke of this melancholy in abstract terms (this heaviness, this pressure), she spoke of it as something outside her, something entering her, and now it had disappeared, a good night's sleep was all that was needed it seemed. But last night she hadn't been happy. No, she hadn't been. She didn't see a way out of the fog. Yes, she had been in a colorless midwinter fog, a peculiarly oppressive fog. The evening before, she'd been disconsolate, that's what it was.

"I was weary," she said, looking and sounding anything but. "I was wandering in my head, if you know what I mean, without any aim or plan, lost, unable to see what was in front of me."

She was tired, but not afraid, she told me. She spent at least three hours looking out the window in her room, looking out into the darkness, no streetlights. Not pitch-black darkness, mind you, not the deep world of darkness we dread. The city's electric grid was humming. Her brother and his wife watched television in the living room. She could have turned on the night lamp, but she didn't.

"Last night," she said, "I misplaced the light of God."

She wasn't herself, so she put on her dress of fine linen and purple, and she was cold, so she put on her black cardigan.

"I wanted to recognize myself," she said.

She took out the hated pills of so many years ago, the Seconals and the Valiums. She swallowed all of them, around thirty-five altogether, drank two full glasses of water so the pills would journey smoothly through her system. She told me that it had been years since she'd had more than a sip or two of water after eight in the evening. She had a thimble-sized bladder, which meant that anything more than a sip would keep her running to the bathroom throughout the comfortless night.

"I felt a tingle of guilty pleasure," she said. "Those two glasses of water almost made me regret my decision. I felt sinful with two glasses. Can you imagine if I'd had three? Now, my dear, don't mock me."

She lay on the bed, her head on the feather pillow, her eyes fixed on the ceiling, waiting for trumpet-tongued Gabriel to come calling for her. Everything was in its perfect place.

"I was ready," she said.

She woke up at eight in the morning, having slept wonderfully and deeply for ten continuous hours, her most fervent fantasy fulfilled—woke up refreshed and rejuvenated, with the minor inconvenience of a painfully full bladder.

"As you can see," she said, "I don't even have a single crease in my dress."

To say that I was aghast would be an understatement. I was horrified because I discovered then, and only then, how lonely she was, so late into the game, and that I had failed her. "How could you?" was the only phrase my voice could articulate. Why didn't you come to me when you needed help? Was I not your friend and confidante? Look for me when you misplace the light of God.

I shouldn't worry, she insisted. It was a misjudgment. She had to clear her head. She'd made a few vows that morning. She must fulfill them. I made her promise to return at closing. We would talk more that evening. I decided not to open the store the following morning. Instead I'd take her to a physician to make sure everything was in working order. She may have found the lost divine light, but I thought a medical doctor would see to it that she had a flashlight handy.

She suggested that we overindulge that evening, purchase two whole rotisserie chickens with full accoutrements:

pickles, lots of pickles, and especially pink turnips, her favorites, and at least two tubs of garlic paste. We'd kill insects
by breathing on them, she said.

   She returned to her room, and sometime in the following hour she packed all her journals in two boxes and wrote
my first name in florid Arabic script on yellow notepaper
that she left discarded atop them. She changed into her
most comfortable shoes, climbed the stairs to the roof of
the building, and jumped. The four-flight fall did not kill
her on impact, the poor thing. She died in the ambulance
on the way to the hospital.

   I should have realized that Hannah was going to try again
after her failed attempt. Her sister-in-law Maryam blamed
herself. She was in the house when Hannah was packing
the boxes and hadn't paid attention. She was in shock for
a long, long time. She brought flowers to Hannah's grave
weekly. Maryam is still alive, I believe, and since Hannah
died so many years ago, I assume she has quite recovered.
At times I think I have.

   I try to console myself with the thought that many
have killed themselves and their loved ones weren't able to
halt the proceedings. The incredible Italian writer Cesare
Pavese committed suicide, overdosing on barbiturates in
a hotel room in 1950, the year he won the Premio Strega.
Who would have expected that?

   Yet I could have been more observant. After the first
suicide attempt, I should have understood that the meaning
of her life, the meaning she'd assigned to her life, had come
detached from its moorings. The shrine of self-delusion had

crumbled. When she told me she'd swallowed those pills, I should have thought it through. I didn't know any better then. I should never have let her out of my sight.

I blame myself. When I wish to feel better, I blame other people: her family, since she lived with them and no one noticed; the lieutenant's mother, who couldn't take her secret to the grave. If Ahmad hadn't left me, I would have had him mind the bookstore while I stayed with her. I blame King Hussein and Yasser Arafat for Black September, which caused Ahmad to abandon me. I blame Hannah herself. I blame me again.

These memories — these memories make keen the pain that time has blunted.


As I walk toward home I hear the hollow, distant roar of commercial planes descending, so many of them at this time of day, so many of them at this time of year, bringing the Lebanese emigrants home for the holidays.

I blame Ahmad, the emigrant, or, more precisely, the exile. Somewhere in my apartment I have a photograph I clipped out of a newspaper of Ahmad leaving Beirut. He was among the throng of Palestinians forced out of the city in order to end the Israeli siege and their insane bombing. In August 1982, we had the great Palestinian exodus redux redux redux, etc. There were many pictures of the event. A few of Yasser Arafat from different angles, insincerely triumphant, broad smile, fingers of both hands celebrating victory like Nixon; weeping women bidding farewell, stoic mothers, children carrying posters and plac-ards. The photograph I kept appeared in the newspaper the following week. Surprisingly, it showed Ahmad, one of a dozen men ready to board the ships to Tunis, kaffiyeh on his shoulder, but no Kalashnikov. Some of his armed companions hid their faces behind the black-and-white kaffiyehs, but not my Ahmad. He and his cohorts seemed neither defiant nor ashamed, more resigned, their heads drooping like sunflowers.

That was the last I saw of him.


I walk a small street that ends at a perpendicular intersection. A gutter running from the top to the second floor of a nearby building pumps a torrent of excess rainwater to the street, an unnatural pastoral brook in the middle of the city. A troubling noise, I have to say. I didn't realize it had rained so much.

> *Water, water, everywhere,*
> *And all the boards did shrink;*
> *Water, water, everywhere,*
> *Nor any drop to drink.*

There is a wonderful story about Pavese, after his death. When he returned from exile in the late thirties, he worked for Einaudi, the leftist publisher, translating and editing books. The house of Einaudi published his works and supervised his estate after his death. On the day that the right-wing prime minister Silvio Berlusconi bought Einaudi, Pavese's old home was flooded. A pipe burst, destroying all of his papers. From his grave, Pavese would not let that rat-faced popinjay make a penny from his work.

I can continue on my way home by turning right or left, since bend after bend, street after street, there's not much to distinguish either route. What does distinguish this junction is the presence of three full-grown weeping figs, panniers of green, forming an equilateral triangle across opposite pavements, none of them having to fight human-built structures for air to breathe. I love this working-class neighborhood. The buildings on the street are architecturally contiguous and consistent—no modern monstrosities. They're not aesthetically beautiful—dull colors past their due date—but since they're organic and coherent, this part of town makes sense.

One building has a recent addition: its outdoor staircase, similar to the one in my building, is now covered in unpainted concrete. What used to be quite common before the war is becoming extinct. Like foals born ready to run, new buildings are born gated, protected, able to force the city out instantly with their cadres of doormen and security guards.

There is a Sunni mosque a mere half block away. Lebanese flags facing every possible direction drape across an electricity pole, making the green cedars, symbol of our pygmy state, look like they're tumbling in a slow avalanche. Each sect wants to prove it is more Lebanese than the next, which explains the recent rise of puerile patriotism in our neighborhoods. This one also bears a large poster depicting the ugly mug of the "leader of the Arabs," Gamal Abdel Nasser, against a Mao-red background. I haven't seen one of these in decades.

I may be able to explain the difference between baroque and rococo, between South American magical realism and its counterparts in South Asia and sub-Saharan Africa, between Camus's nihilism and Sartre's existentialism, between modernism and its post, but don't ask me to tell you the difference between the Nasserites and the Baathists. I do understand that this neighborhood can't be Baathist; Sunnis are anti-Syria these days, and the need to belong to a party, any party, is greater than the fear of appearing stupid once again, hence Nasser is the hero du jour. However, I can't figure out what the terms mean.

Samir Kassir, in his wonderful book about Beirut, differentiates them thus: Arab nationalists who converted to socialism and socialists newly alert to the mobilizing virtues of nationalism.

Decipher that.

Need I tell you that Baathists and Nasserites have killed each other by the busload?

One's first response is that these Beirutis must be savagely insane to murder each other for such trivial divergences. Don't judge us too harshly. At the heart of most antagonisms are irreconcilable similarities. Hundred-year wars were fought over whether Jesus was human in divine form or divine in human form. Belief is murderous.


After Hannah died, life became incomprehensible—well, more incomprehensible than usual. I confess that I went through some hard times, hard years. I grieved—whether I grieved enough is difficult to gauge. Life was crazy. Hajj Wardeh passed away that year as well, and I wasn't sure if Fadia would try to evict me. My mother harped about my apartment. My half brothers tried to break my door and my spirit. It was not pleasant, and then war, the ultimate distraction, broke out. I plunged into my books. I was a voracious reader, but after Hannah's death I grew insatiable. Books became my milk and honey. I made myself feel better by reciting jejune statements like "Books are the air I breathe," or, worse, "Life is meaningless without literature," all in a weak attempt to avoid the fact that I found the world inexplicable and impenetrable. Compared to the complexity of understanding grief, reading Foucault or Blanchot is like perusing a children's picture book.

I flag a taxi. I'll splurge. I must reach home. It is much too cold; the frost-laden wind is picking up speed, and there's a slight downward slant to the road that makes it slippery. I can't seem to feel the ground beneath these old feet. I must reach home.

The driver looks like he wants to talk. Whatever he has to say, I've heard it a million times before. Taxi drivers, the talkers, the storytellers of this chatty city, can never shut up once they get going. I take out Rilke from my purse and pretend to read. Community is not what I need right now.

The taxi makes slow progress in the coagulating preholiday traffic. All of Beirut is out shopping for the holidays. It has been so long since I've bought a gift for anyone. The sun falls, as does the rain; winter nights arrive without warning. Headlight beams refract on the windshield, creating mini rainbows. It takes the car half an hour to travel a distance I could have walked in the same amount of time. A far-flung flash of lightning, out of earshot, reminds me that the taxi was a good decision, even though I'm discomfited by the backseat's worn-out springs.

The taxi slogs and stalls a couple of neighborhoods before mine. My back begins to ache. A brand-new hotel, mus-
cular and gray, has sprung up on the street. I hear that one
can sit in a hot tub on the top floor and observe all of Beirut
through large circular windows, a sort of reverse submarine
effect. On the ground floor, there's an American diner and a
gigantic fitness center. I can't tell you how many people use
the latter, but I envy their health. This has been a long day.

No matter where I've been or how long I've been away,
my soul begins to tingle whenever I approach my apartment.
The sharp turn that leads to my street, the brown-and-gray
building that I call "the new one" even though it was built
in the early seventies and is certainly no longer new, are
signs that announce I am close. The pleasurable sensation
of almost arriving and the impatience of not yet being there
begin at those markers. My first act upon entering the apartment, after shutting the door behind me, is simply to drop
on my sofa and rest. My home.


*ô rage ! ô désespoir ! ô vieillesse ennemie !*

The troubling sight of the recalcitrant wrinkles on my
face holds me still. I stand transfixed before the mirror in my
bathroom. I reach for my glasses to see more clearly. What
happened to me? What happened to my face, so gaunt and
inexpressive? The person looking back at me is a stranger.
I've never had a flattering notion of my unprepossessing
physical appearance, but now I seem more insignificant than
ever, lifeless and without a spark or sparkle of intensity. I'm
a wholly nondescript human.

I should ask my mother if she has a picture of my biological father—must do so before she dies. I want to know whether I look like him. I must. I have my mother's nose, which these days looks like a scimitar buried in slain flesh. I try to reconstruct my father's face, but nothing seems to work, of course. I was much too young. I may have seen a picture of him at some point, but I have absolutely no recollection. I do recall my mother then, how she looked when he died, but since it was so long ago, I assume that's a reconstruction. I remember that my mother wouldn't raise her head, kept her eyes down, her gaze on the ground, lower even, toward the center of the earth where Satan dwelled. She must have felt guilty about her husband's death. If she had been a better wife, more competent, he wouldn't have been snatched away from her. Had we practiced suttee, she would have willingly dived into the pyre headfirst, a forward two-and-a-half somersault.

Can I possibly remember this, or is it a jigsaw that I've forced together from bits and pieces of how I think it went? I continue to drop the wooden pail into the brackish well of my memories. There was a meal. My mother concentrated on the food, on the plate. I don't think she ate. The memory seems both real and unreal, reliable and tenuous, solid and insubstantial. I wasn't even two when he died. I must have configured these images much later. Childhood is played out in a foreign language and our memory of it is a Constance Garnett translation.

My features have blunted with the passage of time, my reflection only faintly resembles how I see myself. Gravity demands payback for the years my body has resisted it. Not just my breasts and posterior, but somewhere along the line the slightly swollen curves of my lips have straightened. I've also lost quite a few eyebrow hairs. They're all white now. I've noticed the change in color before but not the sparseness. I used to have a pair of heavy lines for eyebrows. On the other hand, my melanin-deprived skin has accumulated a number of different colors. Two asymmetrical landlocked seas of purple and mouse gray spread under my eyes. A brindled barnacle clings next to my right ear. Temple veins and their tributaries are decidedly green.

I'm willing to swear that the bone structure of my face has shifted.

How can my breath hold out

*Against the wreckful siege of battering days*
*When rocks impregnable are not so stout,*
*Nor gates of steel so strong, but Time decays?*

I hear Joumana puttering in her bathroom above. If she's following her usual schedule, she's washing up before making dinner.

I must do something. I walk out of the bathroom to my reading room, to the compact disc player. I search for Chopin, find one of Richter's recordings. My head slowly clears. Richter's Chopin is inspiring.

Sviatoslav Richter refused to give a concert if his pink plastic lobster was not with him. I used to think it was red — I read it somewhere, a red plastic lobster — but then I saw a picture of it. It certainly looked like a crustacean, oversized pincers, but not like a lobster, or at least not like any lobster I'd recognize. And it was pink, a rose pink, not red.

"I find things confusing," he said on film.

In this film, *Richter: The Enigma*, he looked baffled and bewildered, befuddled by life. Bald, bony, ragged, and old, a face that couldn't face the camera, a face that fully understood what had been lost, what had been given up. He looked real to me. I don't know if he was a virgin, but he was a homosexual.

Richter spoke to this plastic lobster and felt lost without his companion. If you talked to him without his lobster, he sounded autistic. When he played, though—when he played he could liquefy your soul. He walked on water—well, his fingers did—liquid supple and fluid smooth, running, dripping, flowing.

"I do not like myself," he said on film.

Once more, I stand transfixed before the mirror in my bathroom. I take out a pair of scissors, shut my eyes for a moment, and cut off a handful of blue hair. As Richter works his mellifluous magic, I snip and weep, snip and weep. He tears my heart. I am a sentimental fool. I cut and cry. Blue hair falls around me, collecting in a wispy cloud on the floor, the halo of a saint encircling my feet.

"For if a woman does not cover her head," says Corinthians, "she might as well have her hair cut off." Since no one reads anymore, Bible or otherwise, everyone assumes that Muslims invented the hijab. "Every man who prays or prophesies with his head covered dishonors his head. But every woman who prays or prophesies with her head uncovered dishonors her head—it is the same as having her head shaved."

Without my hair, I am no longer uncovered. I begin to sweep up the blue clippings on the floor. Slowly, methodically, each movement measured, each distracted, my mind in a fog, I clean and sweep.

In Germany, cut hair used to be wrapped in a cloth that was then deposited in an elder tree days before the new moon. A similar ritual can be found among the Yukon Indians of Alaska. In Morocco, women hang their hair clippings on a tree growing on or near the grave of a wonder-working saint to protect themselves against headaches. In Saudi Arabia and Egypt, they stow the fallen hair away, in a kerchief in a drawer. I sweep it all into the dustpan and dump it in the garbage.

My hair is sheared, lopped off to be exact. It is now white, the frost of old age. I don't know whether I look like a cancer patient, a Red Brigade terrorist from the seventies, or an avant-garde artist, but I do look new. Since I only used scissors my hair is uneven and choppy. No, I don't look like any of the above. I look like a Catholic postulant or a novitiate of some obscure monastic order.

I feel lighter, though I know it's unreasonable to feel so. It's only hair.

*The albatross fell off, and sank*
*Like lead into the sea.*

This evening I will contemplate the world from my bathtub. I'll soak today away. I'm going to wash my mother right out of my hair. Wash her out, dry her out, push her out, fly her out, cancel her and let her go. I will fill the tub to the brim with cleansing water, rattle the pipes, conduct the Schoenberg symphony of glockenspiels once more. I'll light a couple of candles for mood. I can't retrieve those in the maid's room, so I'll make do with a couple of stubby ones lying around the bathroom, ugly and functional. Fire and water, I'll end up with baptism, cleansing, and rejoicing all around.

I will shorten the hours of this evening, for I am tired. I will read, though. I am still more or less sane because of my evening reading.

I will continue with *Microcosms* this evening.

I sit by the window in my living room. The sky puts on its darkening blue coat. My socked feet join me on the couch, my hands interlock around my knees. Even though I rubbed it dry with my good towel after the bath, my hair still feels wet. Phantom hair syndrome: I touch my scalp and my hair feels dry, but a minute after my hand grasps its partner around my knees, the sensation of wetness returns.

Out my window, all I see is a small section of my street, a cropped rectangle of the building across the way, and my lonesome lamppost. When I was a little girl I wished for a window that would overlook all of Beirut and its universe. Once I was married and in this apartment, my dreams shrank to more reasonable dimensions; I wished for a window on a higher floor, maybe the fourth—Fadia's apartment instead of mine on the second—wished for a marginally more elevated, slightly more expansive view. These days I wish only that a Finnish or maybe Chinese company would invent some inexpensive utensil to clean the city grime off the outside of my window without my having to strain my back.

I should reread Johnson's *The Vanity of Human Wishes* and be admonished once again.

It is fitting that I'm allowed only a glimpse of Beirut's vista through my window, a thread of a sliver of a slice of a pie. Nostalgists insist on their revisionist vision of a hospitable, accepting city—a peaceable kingdom where all faiths and ethnicities were welcome, a Noah's ark where beasts of every stripe felt at ease and unthreatened. Noah, however, was a son of a bitch of a captain who ran a very tight ship. Only pairs of the best and the brightest were allowed to climb the plank—perpetuate the species, repopulate the planet, and all that Nazi nonsense.

Would Noah have allowed a lesbian zebra aboard, an unmarried hedgehog, a limping lemur? Methinks not.

Never has my city been welcoming of the unpaired or the impaired.

I never cared for the story of Noah or Edward Hicks's stilted paintings of Stepford animals.

From what I read tonight in *Microcosms*: "Why so much pity for the murderers who came after and none for those before, drowned like rats? He should have known that together with every being—man or beast—evil entered the Ark."

Say what you will about the God of Israel, but consistency is not His forte. He hasn't been fair to my kind. The One God is a Nazi.

*I sit in the dark. And it would be hard to figure out which is worse: the dark inside, or the darkness out.*

I must try to sleep tonight. I must.

❁     ❁     ❁

Of course I don't sleep. I don't recall the entire night's affair, so I may have dozed off a bit, my usual fare. I bend down to pull on woolen socks and feel every vertebra crack in order as if in a roll call: C1, here; C3, present; T4, yes; L5, I'm here; coccyx, ouch, ouch. All that's missing is a reveille-playing bugle.

It is much too cold. A chilly tremor runs through my shoulders, chasing away any inclination to sluggishness. I scratch my scalp. Still shorn. I'm not sure I can risk the bathroom mirror this morning.

A night of storms and heavy rain, of bumps and sounds in the dark. I heard floods and sirens outside. Comfortably tucked under three blankets, I heard a ghoul scratch his fingernails on the windowpane, a militiaman fire his machine gun into street puddles. Above me, I heard Joumana murder someone, probably her husband, and drag the corpse around the house in circles over and over while hitting the skull with a Tefal frying pan. Nothing else could have made those night noises.

*I am aweary, aweary, I would that I were* . . . warmer.

I wear my robe over my nightgown and top it off with the burgundy mohair overcoat. I trudge to the kitchen to begin my early morning tea ritual. The apartment smells of damp and rain. The radiators diffuse sputtering heat in spurts. Indoor winter winds interrogate my ankles.

I'm hesitating again about the new project. The novel *2666*, incomplete though it may be, is too big, and this morning it interests me less. However, I'm not sure I have enough time to come up with a new book to translate this late in the game unless I pick something short and easy. Can I risk missing the rite of beginning a translation on the first of January? I wonder if I'm able to break my own rules. The rules are arbitrary. I recognize that, but I also know that they make my life work; my rules get me through the day. If I have to, I can begin the translation on another date and the world will not reverse on its axis. I'll not lose any more sleep than I already do if I postpone. Still, I prefer to stick to what I know, creature of habit and all that.

Maybe my epiphany is that I can begin a translation in the second week of January this time. Maybe this epiphany will excite me after I have my tea.

I light the flame under the kettle.

I decide that I must make a decision this morning about which book to work with. Uncertainty is unsettling.

Whispery light begins to disperse the shadowy forms outside my windows. A garbage truck leaves my street and takes its howling ruckus with it. Nothing to be heard now but the childish pitter-patter of rain. The streetlamp flickers its bulb in a short tantrum, gathering a blush of carnation pink and russet before turning off for the day. The air in the kitchen still feels somber and damp. I carry my tea to the reading room, sit in my armchair, and drape the quilt over my legs under the mohair coat.


My doorbell rings and I am disoriented. I must have fallen asleep in my chair. How long has it been since that happened? I can't tell what time it is, can't read the clock without my eyeglasses. The light is high. Eight o'clock? The doorbell buzzes once more. I put on my glasses. The cup remains on the side table, next to the vase and the seven books of the

Muallaqat, the tea untouched and obviously cold, not a wisp of steam rising from its surface. I'll not open the door. Not this time. I'll not let the world in. Is this going to be a daily ritual? Let's disturb Aaliya's morning, jumble and upend it. Tous les matins du monde.

Whoever is outside knocks on my door, an insistent knock. It's not my half brother the eldest, though. This knock is well mannered.

"Aaliya," I hear Joumana's muffled voice call from outside. There is urgency to her call. "Open up, please!"

I jump out of my chair—well, what would be considered a jump at my age. My knee buckles, almost sending me sprawling across the carpet. I steady myself at the reading room's door. My hand leans against the jamb and I find myself face-to-face with the unframed circular mirror. I avert my eyes, of course, but I make a decision to clean it before the day is done, at least dust it off.

"She must be inside," Marie-Thérèse says. "I didn't hear her leave this morning. I'd know if she did."

I rush to the door. I hear Fadia on the stairs, coming from below, not above. The world is upside down today, topsy-turvy.

"I've shut off the water," says Fadia, the loudest of all. She has yet to reach my landing. I hear the hurried stomping of her clogs approaching.

"Aaliya!" she screams just as I open the door. My face encounters the full force of her voice, and of December's cold.

The three wet witches jostle into my foyer, they speak together, all at the same time, high-pitched Disney-like chatter, and I'm flummoxed and confused. If Fadia's housedress swept the floor the last time she was here, today her purple one mops it. The hem is so damp she looks as if she's just waded out of a river. But I hear the word *flood*, and just above the bridge of my nose, just under the skin, I feel a nerve snap. A lump grows in my throat, an anchor weighs down my heart. I feel my ears shut off. I do not wish to hear.

Haphazardly soggy, the witches surround me, orbit me like planets on Dexedrine, talking, talking, talking. A water pipe—maid's bathroom upstairs in Joumana's apartment—flood—no danger anymore—plumber's been called—they hope I don't have anything valuable stored in my maid's room.

Anything valuable? Valuable? My crates, my crates and crates, my life—they know nothing of that.

I run—yes, run—through the kitchen to the maid's bathroom. I smell the damp before I open the door, like a woolen sweater in the rain, like the smell of Nancy's damp pink sweater draped over the top of the heater, steaming, I'm steaming. Nausea punches my stomach from inside and out. The knob doesn't turn all the way on the first try because my hands are too clammy. I swing the door open and witness the damage. The stink assaults me physically, and I recoil and stagger a step; the stench wallops me, bashes my nose, sour, musty, my mother. My heart behaves strangely, wishing to object. I feel an urge to regurgitate.

*Hail horrors, hail*
*Infernal world! and thou, profoundest Hell.*

My neighbors sidle up to me, too close.

There is some water on the floor, but not too much. Most of what has passed through the maid's bathroom continued on its journey toward the swale of the drain. The water that insisted on remaining, though, chose to do so among my papers. Every crate is wet.

There's no longer any need to panic. It is done.

*If it were done when 'tis done, then 'twere well*
*It were done quickly.*

It was most certainly quick.

On wobbly legs and exhausted knees, I walk through to the maid's room. There is no hope. Dark though the maid's room is, I need not see. The smell of water damage is acute. The seven mouths of the Nile have poured their wares in here. My soul screams, my voice is mute. I am now destitute.

Who among the angels will hear me if I cry? I stand in the dank and the dark, amid my wasted life, not knowing what to do, unable to make any decision, and weep. My hopes were extinguished a long while ago, and now any tinder of dignity follows suit. Whatever remains of my self-worth seeps out of me, flows out of me, and follows the water down the drain.

Everything has gone and left me and I don't know what to do.

I face a battle that has been over for a long time. I accept defeat with no white flag to wave, with no strength even to unsheathe my sword.

*Into the valley of Death*
*Rode the six hundred.*

Degradation is my intimate. Like Job's, my soul is weary of my life. Snot falls from my nostrils; I wipe it and the tears with the sleeve of my mohair coat—the sleeve of my tattered, unwearable coat.

I don't know how much the three witches can see, but I'm horrified that they know I'm crying, which makes me cry more, and louder.

My soul is fate's chew toy. My destiny pursues me like an experienced tracker, like a malevolent hunter, bites me and won't let go. What I thought I left behind I find again. I'll always be a failure, then, now, and forever. Fail again. Fail worse. I witness my life's collapse.

*Shadow that hell unto me.*

Cursed is this world and cursed is all that is in this world. Cursed is this age of relentless humiliation and slapstick. Here's your damn epiphany.

The women surround me once more, lead me by my hands and elbows out into the light. One of them, probably Marie-Thérèse, the shortest, gently pulls on my arm, forcing me to bend a bit, and wipes my face with a tissue — a tissue moist with sanitizer gel. She must have one of those miniature antibacterial bottles on her person at all times. My hands, of their own accord, escape the women's clutches and dive into the coat's pockets. The only thing in my pockets is a bent pair of reading glasses.

My eyes, with a will of their own, stare ahead, concentrate on the small pan I put under the radiator when I let the air out. A rusty water drop hangs on the pipe above it, waiting patiently to join its sisters who have stained the aluminum.

The kitchen is noisy, the city drawing in its morning breaths, horns and traffic and rain on the street, and Joumana talking softly, talking to me.

"What's in the boxes?" She repeats the question a few times in response to my silence. "We should get them out of there and see what we can salvage."

How can I explain my esoteric vocation, my furtive life? This is the private source of meaning in my life. "Translations," I say. "I'm a translator." I hesitate. What I said doesn't ring true in my ears. I sound like a liar. "I was," I add. My heart feels too exhausted to beat. "I was a translator."

Joumana looks confused, her eyebrows arch into question marks. Her eyes concentrate on the lower half of my face as if she intends to lip-read. If I'd said I had bags of heroin in the cartons, she'd have been less shocked. She is a decent woman who isn't used to deciphering the mutterings of monsters.

"Let's get to work," she says in a commanding tone. "Let's get them out of those rooms."

As soon as I try to move, I teeter like a giraffe that's gorged herself on fermented fruit. Marie-Thérèse of the kind face wraps her arm around my waist and steadies me. My forearm rests on her shoulder. I feel both helpless and shiftless. I wish to escape all this and return home, except I am home.

"Sit," Marie-Thérèse says, leading me to my armchair. "Catch your breath for a minute. We'll clear the boxes out." She hesitates for a moment, as if she intends to ask a most portentous question. "Do you have a stepladder, or should I get mine?"

I'm upset at myself, not just for blubbering in front of strangers like a little girl during kindergarten recess, but for blubbering at all. I try to control myself. In my comforting armchair, I observe the three women hustle. I try to stand up; my thigh muscles quiver, my legs give way, and I sit back down. Only for a minute, I tell myself, less than, I lie to myself. I feel like a slimy toad pressing into the mud, unblinkingly eyeing my nothingness. Spinoza has little if anything for me this morning.

Fadia had gone up to her apartment and returned with two large bedsheets and at least eight towels. Now all three sally back and forth, carrying out soppy crates one by one. They seem synchronized, as if they've been clearing out flood-damaged translations all their lives, as if they grew up in one of the villages on the banks of the Euphrates where this kind of work is not unusual. One of them enters the dark, another exits carrying a box from the underworld. I notice for the first time that Joumana's feet are as flat as a duck's. The smell of rot wafts through the apartment, the scent of decay permeates my home. Sadness and frustration well up inside me. I should stand, but I can't yet. As they work, I can do nothing but twiddle my thumbs.

I must get stronger, fortify myself. O Flaubert, show me how to seal my chamber, send me your mason. Fear, sorrow, keep out these marauders and pillagers, this anger, this guilt, this hopelessness.

I feel nostalgic for my once arid heart that knew how to cope with such loss.

Non fui, fui, non sum, non curo.


In silence, I help my neighbors move the crates out of Egypt. I am able to reach the high ones more easily. Ahead of me Fadia steps on the Israeli landmine, a hand's width

south of the drain. I avoid the spot, still think my slip-
per will be soiled if it hovers anywhere near where the
stain had been. The damp cardboard feels like boiled
cabbage in my hands. We line the crates up on the towels and bedsheets, in the kitchen, in the living room, in
the reading room, caskets of war dead being returned
home. I should stand at attention and salute—so many
national anthems, so many countries in the pile. I wish
to fire twenty-one guns.

Finally, Joumana kneels before one of the coffins, a
mourner of sorts. As her left knee lowers, it knocks the
English version of *The Encyclopedia of the Dead* off the side
of the box (English version on the left/west, French on the
right/east); the book falls a few centimeters to the floor with
a minimal thud. She hesitates, but only for a moment. An
airy gasp escapes my throat.

*What unaccustomed sounds*
*Are hovering on my lips.*

Joumana's knees rest on the towel and cradle the crate.
Her left hand gestures for me to calm down, her palm extended. Her right hand holds my chef's knife. She saws
through the masking tape in four places.

The manuscript is wet, of course. The first page is legible since it contains only the title, Danilo Kiš's name, and
mine. Joumana lifts the title page and sighs. Underneath,
the pages are damaged. There seems to be a dry section in
the middle of each, the size of a young woman's mittened
hand. But the rest of the page, the rest—the smudging,
the discoloring, the smell—death, as it always does, creeps
toward the core. Mine certainly does.

I can't help myself. I begin to weep again, silently though, less embarrassingly. Joseph Roth ends *Flight Without End* with the sentence: "No one in the whole world was as superfluous as he." I beg to differ. No one in the whole world is as superfluous as I. Not Franz Tunda, Roth's protagonist, no. I am the one who has no occupation, no desire, no hope, no ambition, not even any self-love.

From out of nowhere, it seems, Fadia's hands reach up from behind and gently massage my shoulders. I resist the urge to go Merkel to her Bush. I allow her hands to touch me.

I can't help myself. My mind leads my thoughts to death on a leash.

Arbus slashed her wrists, as did Rothko. Woolf walked into the river and drowned herself. Hemingway shot himself in the head, of course. Plath, Hedayat, and Borowski put their heads in the oven. Améry swallowed an overdose of sleeping pills in 1978 and didn't wake up the next day refreshed. Neither did Pavese in 1950. Gorky (Arshile, not Maxim) hanged himself. Levi allegedly jumped to his death.

Then there's the strange suicide story of Potocki, who shot himself in the head with a silver bullet. Every morning for a few months, he worked at filing off the strawberry-shaped knob of a sugar bowl his mother had given him, until he freed it and used it as a bullet. Paging Dr. Freud.

No composer of note, or at least none that I know of, committed suicide. You would think if anybody would have, it would have been Schnittke, but he didn't. Schumann jumped, but he had bipolar disorder, and as if that weren't enough, syphilis spirochetes were rejoicing in his brain. In any case, he didn't die from the attempt. Tchaikovsky may or may not have intentionally drunk that bad water. I wouldn't count those two. Music seems to be the healthiest of all the silly arts. I should point out, though, that composers tend to die at a younger age than the average human, whereas conductors die older. I don't know why that's so, but it intrigues me.

Syphilis spirochetes felled both Schus, -mann and -bert.

Fadia notices that I'm feeling calmer and more collected. Her hands drop to her sides.


"I can read most of this," says Joumana. She riffles through the pages of Danilo's and my collaboration.

"Please don't," I say.

"I mean it's legible," she says, a little amused. "I'm able to read it, not that I'm going to." She puckers her lips and blows on the page in her hands. She waves it back and forth, trying to fan out the dampness, but stops, probably worried that the page will disintegrate.

"We must separate all the pages," Marie-Thérèse says, "and dry them. It's the only way we can salvage them."

She occupies the floor in the center of the room and constantly checks up on me while pretending not to. Today she doesn't look like Pessoa's imaginary girlfriend, Ophelia, more like the older Eudora Welty, though with dyed black hair.

"It'll take a long time," I say, "much too long."

"We have the time," Marie-Thérèse says. Kneeling, she blots her wet hands dry on the towel on the floor before

her. "It's the holidays, after all. I don't have anything better
to do."

"If we don't dry the pages," Fadia says, "we'll have fungus growing all over the place. Fungus spreads like fungus.
All over the place, all over the building. I can't have that.
What if it gets under your nails? It's highly contagious. Who
knows what would happen to mine? Look, look." Fadia's
voice hoots and shrieks as she shows us her nails. "I can't
risk structural damage to these. We need an emergency
intervention."

She does repeat her unfunny jokes, which for some
strange reason sound funnier the more I hear them.

It rains and rains. My soul is damp from hearing it.
It drizzles, then showers, then drizzles, then showers. The
day's sorrow is pouring itself out. The window groans from
being battered. Through it, the sky seems frozen.

"I'm not sure they're worth salvaging," I say, returning
to my chair. Standing exhausts me.

"What a silly thing to say." Fadia shakes her head
in mock disbelief. "This is a lot of paper. It can't all be
unimportant."

She settles next to Joumana and grabs the chef's knife
from her. She, the vivisector, slices through Javier Marías,
opens him up to examine his insides. Her use of the knife
is more skillful, of course: she's both a better cook than
Joumana and less sensitive, less meticulous.

Marie-Thérèse begins to put up laundry lines. Her
deceased husband, who was obsessed with hunting, fishing, and trawling, left behind a boatload of line spools. She
strings crisscrossing clotheslines across my entire apartment,
tacking them to the wall with pushpins. When I suggest that

they might not hold, she reminds me that all we're hanging
are sheets of paper. Even before she finishes, I know there
won't be enough lines for my pages.

Fadia and Joumana begin to hang, sheet by sheet, in
meticulous order, as Marie-Thérèse finishes stringing the
lines. They use plastic clothes pegs, even paper clips. My
reading room begins to brim with ghostly Tibetan prayer
flags.

I want to help. I stand up again, rejoin them. I pick up
a page to hang on the line. Fadia and Joumana leave a space
for me, but by the time I finish they are six or seven pages
ahead of me. My mind is mired in turbid swamps. I see the
three witches in the room, I interact with them, but it's as
if there's a thin layer of Saran Wrap between us — only the
rare molecule passes through.

"This won't be enough," says Joumana, still hanging
the Danilo Kiš manuscript.

"No," says Fadia.

"We'll need something else."

It's raining hard, raining harder, raining harder still,
the drops like mourners goading one another into a rising
frenzy of laments. It rains as if the whole world is about to
collapse, as if the sky is going to plummet — Noah's revenge
upon my kind. He has finally broken through into my home.

"Where's your blow dryer?" Fadia stands before me, a
paper line between us, our faces between the pages.

"My blow dryer?" I ask. Why does she suddenly want
to dry her hair? I explain that I don't have one, that I've
always dried my hair with a towel, that I haven't had one
since my husband left and took his with him, that it was
one of his prized possessions, which didn't make any sense

because his coiffed hair was always covered by his sopho-
moric hat.

Suddenly garrulous me.

All three stop what they're doing. If I'd said that I ride
with the Valkyries every morning after breakfast, that I gave
birth to a million jinn on the shores of the Red Sea on Sunday
the twenty-second of June, that my secret lover is Zeus in the
form of a shower of gold—anything but the fact that I've never
owned a hair dryer—they would have been less surprised.

"Your hair was nice," says Fadia. "It had so much possibility, but you never dyed it, and when you did, you had
to dye it blue. I don't understand you."

She's standing much too close to me. They all are. I
can smell them—each wears a different cologne; Fadia also
reeks of French cigarettes.

"Fadia!" her companions yell simultaneously.

"Oh, be quiet," she tells them. Then, to me, "What was
up with the blue hair? Why did you do that?"

"It was an error in judgment," I say.

"It was certainly that." Fadia waves her hand to signal
her co-witches that they should not interrupt her. She knows
when they're about to meddle in her meddling. "And why
in the name of all that's holy did you shear off your hair?
Couldn't you have gone to a salon and had it fixed? A little
coloring and brushing and you'd have felt like a new woman.
You look like a nun without her habit, and not the pretty
one, not Audrey Hepburn, more Shirley MacLaine."

"Fadia!" her companions cry.

"How can you say such a thing?" Marie-Thérèse demands. She tries to pull Fadia away, but Fadia shrugs her
off like someone flicking off an irritating housefly.

"She's not Shirley MacLaine," Joumana says. "You are. You're just as loud and inappropriate as she is. What happened to your manners?"

"They aged," Fadia says. "They grew old to keep me young."

"You don't look like Shirley MacLaine," Marie-Thérèse tells me. She reaches out to me, her right palm cupping my left elbow.

"Well, she doesn't look like what's her name in *Rosemary's Baby* either," Fadia says. "That film scared me. All I have to do is think about it and I need adult diapers. Let's not think about it. Wait, wait. Do you remember that French film with the mustached American actor who looks like a raisin left in the sun too long? The actress had short hair. Not Annie Girardot, another one."

"Just ignore her," Joumana tells me. "We always do. She hasn't made any sense since 1998. That was her last good year."

"I'll get my hair dryer," Marie-Thérèse says. "Maybe we should all get ours. We can dry the papers faster."

"Something in the rain," Fadia says. "The movie had an interesting title, but I can't remember. It's from the sixties. You don't really look like her, but the French actress had very short hair."

"Get your hair dryer," Joumana says as she drags Fadia off by the hand.


I want to lock the door and keep all of them, the entire world, out, but the dank smells almost suffocate me. An imperious humidity hangs thick in the apartment, an oppressive tyrant. I leave the door to my home open. I let the air in. It circulates briskly in the apartment for a moment but is soon vanquished; it grows heavy and stale.

I look for *Anna Karenina*. Where is she? She's all I need. I step from one coffin to another, but I don't see her among those in the reading room. I retrace my steps just in case. I move into the kitchen. On a damp blue-striped bedsheet covering the floor, Anna's box looks like a small, broken dwelling about to implode, like abandoned trash on the sidewalk. She's all I need. I must inspect her.

This was one of my earliest translations, probably the third or fourth. I love Anna, but that's not the only reason she's important. *Karenina* was the first project where I began to feel I knew what I was doing. I shouldn't say that. I'll say it was the first translation where I didn't feel as inadequate, where the struggle was no longer as arduous or titanic, where the translating itself became enjoyable — just as pleasurable, if not more so, than the anticipation of finishing the project. *Anna Karenina* was the first time I allowed a book and its world into my house.

Dampness has crimpled the first page and all underneath, softened and thinned them. If I'm not careful, I might easily tear a sheet in half when I pick it up. When the pages dry, they'll turn brittle and crinkly. Ink was less permanent when I translated these pages. Arabic words swim on the sheets; some drown, some float. Some pages look like a Rorschach, a faint blue Rorschach. I see a big dragon eating a pig. I see my mother eating a pig. I see a squashed butterfly. I see my life circling the drain. I see water damage everywhere. I see words, not all disconnected. I can rewrite these pages with an Egyptian pyramid's worth of effort. I'll have to be painstakingly conscientious and cautious, but it can be done. I'll probably die before I finish transcribing. The newer translations are probably less damaged than Anna, the ink being less fugitive. I can also throw the whole pile in one of the dustbins of history. Why would I want to resuscitate this rotting cadaver? It's nothing if not unnecessary.

*I am nothing.*
*I'll always be nothing.*
*I can't even wish to be anything.*
*Aside from that, within me I have all the dreams of the*
   *world.*

Álvaro de Campos, Pessoa's bisexual dandy poet, wrote that. He is welcome in my home anytime.

I am nothing. I should aspire to become a speck. I assign importance to literature and poetry, plate the arts in dazzlingly bright gold to bewilder my vision so as not to see what is plain to all humanity: I am nothing, I'll always be nothing.

In order to live, I have to blind myself to my infinitesimal dimensions in this infinite universe.

Kneeling on Fadia's ancient linen on my kitchen floor, I separate Anna page by page, placing each in order around me. As I extend my arms, I realize I'm genuflecting, as if I'm praying. This is my religion.

My handwriting hasn't changed much in all these years, but the water damage makes the pages look like a stranger wrote them. Everything is written in a foreign language that I must translate — retranslate. Letters are thickened randomly, some word endings are extended. In a few instances, the tip of the Arabic letter *r* runs like a river tributary until it either dries up or pours itself into the lake of the letter that follows.

A short scream escapes my throat when I see slippered feet almost touching Anna's farthest sheet of paper. Marie-Thérèse has entered without my noticing. She apologizes for startling me, though she doesn't need to since it's my fault. She informs me that the plumbers have arrived. They're going to be breaking into the wall in the maid's bathroom upstairs. It will be noisy but it shouldn't take long.

"We'll have our water back in about an hour," she says. Sheep-colored wool tufts crawl from inside her low-heeled slippers. "Joumana is making coffee while Fadia argues with the plumbers. They'll be down with their dryers shortly." She extends her arm, and her hair dryer's electric cord sways like a drunken pendulum. "I can start while we wait for them to join us."

Suddenly the ceiling and the kitchen walls behind me convulse. The plumbers must have dropped a heavy load. I feel as if something is shattering in my brain, but I pay it no mind.


Not for the first time, I notice that Marie-Thérèse has an alarmingly fragile appearance, more substantial than my mother's, but also more brittle, as if she wouldn't survive a minor fall without a major break. A baby blue nightgown calls attention to itself from under the collar of her housedress.

"It hasn't been our usual morning," she says. "I haven't had time to make myself presentable."

She touches her hair, which is bursting out of its clips. What was a meticulous bouffant after the salon visit is now massive and unkempt.

I should say something. I must have been staring.

"I'm less presentable." I gesture to the burgundy mohair overcoat. "How unattractive is this? It's repulsive." Sorrow seems about to envelop my world once more. "Who wears something like this? Who?"

"I would," she says.

"It's unsightly."

"It looks warm."

Marie-Thérèse gathers the early pages of *Anna Karenina* and sits at the red-and-yellow breakfast table. She plugs the blow dryer into the wall socket, but before she turns it on she adjusts her eyeglasses and glances at the title. Her face bursts into life.

"Thank the Lord," she exclaims. "I've read this. I was worried because I hadn't even heard of the others. I felt so small. In all the other piles not one name I recognized. I felt inadequate."

"Don't," I say. "I'm the one who should feel so."

"But I've read *Anna Karenina*," she says. "I read Tolstoy and Dostoyevsky as a young girl. It's been a long time, but I did."

"It's been a long time for me as well." Those were the books that led me down this path, the books responsible for both the peak and the abyss.

"I remember quite a bit of it," she says. "I loved it so much. All my friends did. It was what all of us had to read. Such different times then. I wonder what young girls read these days. I adored Count Vronsky."

She smiles to herself. I can imagine her memories of the novel, or, more likely, of who she was and how she felt when reading it. She blushes.

"I fell in love with a character in a book," she says. "When I first married, I couldn't understand why my poor husband didn't behave like the count. I know it's silly. My husband loved me, cared for me, provided for me, but I still wanted all the frivolities that Vronsky offered. I wanted my husband to be as handsome as I imagined he was."

"I understand," I say, and I do. I also understand that you have to lie to yourself to survive in a bad marriage, you have to delude yourself if you want to carry on in this life.

"Oh my," she says suddenly. "I'm sorry. I shouldn't be talking about romantic husbands."

"That's quite all right," I say. "Husbands mean so little to me."

She laughs.

"Did you fall in love with Vronsky as well?" she asks.

"No. I loved Anna."

Hearing Joumana and Fadia enter the foyer, Marie-Thérèse announces, "We're talking about Anna Karenina and husbands."

The women greet this pronouncement as if they heard that one of their children was getting married. The expression on Joumana's face is that of a woman about to ululate. Fadia holds three hair dryers in her arms, one the size of a cannon, Joumana a tray with her sacred coffee kettle and four cups. I am touched by their thoughtfulness. I have only two cups in my apartment.

✿   ✿   ✿

We have to drink a first cup of coffee before turning on the hair dryers; Fadia wants a noise-free one. They missed their ritual this morning because of the commotion. Fadia doesn't get her wish, though, because as soon as she takes a sip, the plumbers begin to bang upstairs. In my reading room, the walls of books tremble in anticipation. My hair dryer nestles in my lap like a prehistoric bird, its open beak hungry, waiting.

The coffee cup is like a thimble in my hand, makes my fingers and thumb look gigantic. I bring it to my lips and take a sip. The coffee is ambrosia, a flavor of heaven. I am stunned. I have never tasted anything like this. Had I known that coffee could taste so good, I would have gotten drunk on it every day. I want to ask them if this is how it tastes all the time or if it's a unique brew. Do they use a special ingredient, a pinch of salt maybe, or eye of newt? I wonder where they buy their beans. I don't know how to ask. I consider the possibility that I find it delicious because of the condition I'm in.

Marie-Thérèse adds to the plumbing racket by directing her dryer at the first page of *Anna Karenina*. Joumana begins with Hamsun's *Hunger*. Their faces harden with concentration. Joumana sucks in her lips till her mouth resembles a solitary line laid down by Klee, or by Matisse, who wanted nothing more than to be like everyone else. I don't ask the question: Are we going to blow-dry every single page of my thirty-seven manuscripts? I don't believe any of us are young enough to finish the task. We don't get to find out. Fadia turns on her hair dryer and the electricity shuts off.

All four of us look at one another. Fadia stands up in a huff as if the tripping of the circuit breaker is a personal affront, as if Beirut's foibles and idiosyncrasies exist only to irritate her.

"I'll switch it back on," I say, moving forward in my chair to stand up.

"Don't worry," she says. "I know where the fuse box is."

The apartment's circuit breaker is only able to handle two hair dryers. Whenever Fadia tries to turn hers on, the breaker trips.

Joumana suggests that one of us can iron the pages dry, or to be more precise, run a hot iron over a towel covering the damp sheet of paper. I do have an iron and a board.

"I'm not ironing," Fadia announces. "Blow-dry, yes; iron, no."

Marie-Thérèse sits on the love seat, in the same position and in the same spot where Hannah used to sit all those years ago. That was where she sat. That was where she knitted a red-and-pink scarf for her nephew, a scarf she never saw him wear, which caused her no little irritation. That was where she listened to me read Beauvoir aloud. From that love seat, she shared her stories with me. Always prim, always proper, but her dresses never fit quite right, and the cardigans she loved rarely matched them. That was where she wrote in her journals. How many years did she sit there? I should be able to count the years. How many evenings? All I have now is her writing and my memory. Who will keep her journals when I am gone?

"I like this," Marie-Thérèse says. She holds a page in front of her glasses. "You write well."

"I didn't write it," I say. "It's a translation."

"Your handwriting is small," Fadia says. "I can't read a thing."

"Eyeglasses," Marie-Thérèse says.

Fadia is the only one of us who isn't wearing glasses. I can't recall her ever wearing a pair.

"Has anybody read these translations?" Joumana asks.

I don't know what to tell her. No one has, of course. I see her hesitate; as tactful as she's trying to be, her curiosity isn't easy to mask. Fadia is as jumpy as a horse a few seconds before a race begins.

Joumana tries a different angle. "Have you considered publishing all this?"

"No," I say.

The look on her face confuses me. I wait for her to say something or ask another question, but she doesn't. She keeps looking at me, discomfiting me. Then she nods her head slightly, a small downward and forward jerk, and I understand. She wants me to continue.

"I'm not that good," I say, "and I'm not sure anyone would be interested in reading my translations."

"You're not sure anyone is interested in reading *Anna Karenina*?" Joumana asks.

This look, disbelief, I can decipher.

"Anna is one of my earliest. It has been translated into Arabic. I'm not sure mine would add anything, not sure if it's of any significance at all. I created a system to pass the time. This is all a whim."

"A whim?" Joumana shakes her head.

"A whim?" Marie-Thérèse asks.

"A whim." Fadia smiles.

"A whim," I insist.

Joumana looks at each crate on the floor; her eyes settle on one for a second or two before moving to the next. "Don't you want people to read your writing?"

"My writing?" I have to say I've never thought of my projects as writing. "I'm translating. The writer is Tolstoy. It's Sebald, not me."

"Your work, then? Don't you want your work to be read?" Joumana talks to me as I imagine she does to her students, patient and mentoring.

"I don't know," I say, which is as honest an answer as I can muster. I want her to understand, I want to understand.

"Don't you wish to keep a record of everything you've translated?" Joumana asks, pointing to all the boxes. "These writers, I've never heard of them. Pessoa? Hamsun? Cortázar? Hedayat? Karasu? Nooteboom? Kertész?"

"Wonderful writers," I say, "even a couple of Nobel Prize winners."

"More to the point," she says, "I'd like to read them. Others would as well."

"You can read the English translations," I say. "Wouldn't that be better? The original translation can at times convey the subtleties of the writer's language, its diction, its rhythm and rhyme. My version is a translation of a translation. All is doubly lost. My version is nothing."

"I can have a few graduate students from the university transcribe all this."

"Why would they want to do that?"

No one is working anymore. The blow dryers remain quiet, perhaps wanting to overhear the conversation.

"Because serfs do what I tell them to," Joumana says.

"I'm joking," she adds when she notices that I don't get the joke. "They'll do it because it's research. Library science students, or maybe from the Arabic department. It doesn't matter. I'll get them."

"I'm not sure I'm ready," I say.

"How long have you been doing this?" Fadia asks.

"Fifty years."

"And you haven't thought of changing your system in fifty years?"

I'm not sure I understand and I tell her so.

"You've been doing the same thing for fifty years, the same exact thing. Did you not once consider adjusting something?"

"I haven't been doing the same thing. I translate a different book every year, different writers, from different parts of this world of ours. I make a point of taking on dissimilar kinds of novels. I like distinctive novels with an atypical voice. Every project has been unique. I think—"

"But have you not considered trying a new methodology?" she persists. "Changing tactics?"

"She's explaining," Marie-Thérèse tells Fadia. "Every project is different. Let her speak without interrupting."

"It seems the same to me," Fadia says.

"Let me translate what she's saying," Marie-Thérèse replies. "You change the color of your nails regularly, but you don't vary how you put it on. You have a system, but you don't use the same color."

"I don't have a system," Fadia says. "I have a manicurist."

"Don't pretend you don't know what I'm talking about," says Marie-Thérèse.

"Look," says Fadia. "I don't have the same manicure every time. It's not just the color I change. I change the

brand, I change the kind. Sometimes I have a morning manicure, sometimes an evening one. Sometimes the manicurist
comes to me, sometimes I go to her. Why, every now and
then, I even change manicurists."

"I should have a manicure, right?" I say.

"Oh Lord, yes," Fadia says. "I'll try to be gentle here.
Yes, you need a manicure. I can't think of anyone who needs
one more, maybe Russian wrestlers or East German swim-
mers. Now, please don't tell me you don't care about how
you look and that there's more to you than your appearance.
There are two kinds of people in this world: people who
want to be desired, and people who want to be desired so
much that they pretend they don't."

"I'm not sure that a manicure is going to make me
desirable."

We work all morning. I run the iron in one corner of my
reading room. Fadia and Marie-Thérèse blow-dry. The three
of us form a triangle, or three points on a circle, within
which Joumana moves. She performs triage: she organizes
the piles, decides what needs resuscitation first, which page
for ironing and which for hot air.

I develop a system: press forward and backward twice,
then lift the blue towel to check if the page is dry. Most times
I have to go over it once more. Naturally, I don't need to
use the iron's steam functions.

We settle into a silent routine. Fadia talks to herself, but
no one can hear her above the din of the blow dryers. Marie-
Thérèse concentrates on the task before her, but Fadia treats
it as some kind of game. Joumana asks her to give each page

more of her attention, and she does for a minute or so. Still, the weird sisters are coordinated. Yes, it's as if they've been resuscitating manuscripts all their lives. Without realizing it, I begin to fall in with their cycle. I look up after finishing each page, making sure I can move on to the next.

I consider asking them to stop, to give up, but I can't bring myself to. I feel guilty that they're working so hard for my benefit; I'm imposing. I also feel uncomfortable in their presence; they're imposing. This situation is simply not right.

I must ask them to stop. My back hurts; at least two knots throb next to the left shoulder blade. The ironing board isn't high enough, of course, forcing me to stoop a bit, and I've never stood over it for so long. I open my mouth to speak, but Fadia beats me to it. Both she and Marie-Thérèse have turned off their dryers at the same time.

"We have to consider lunch," she says. "Shall I make it?" Her tone implies both infinite choice and no other at the same time. She stands up and stretches.

I stop moving the iron back and forth, lay it on its side. I'm exhausted and drained.

"Let me check your kitchen to see what you have," Fadia says.

The look of panic on my face must be out of proportion, because all three women laugh.

"She's teasing you, my dear," says Marie-Thérèse.

"She can't cook anywhere but her own kitchen," says Joumana.

"Definitely not your kitchen," says Fadia. "In the fifty years you've lived here, I've never smelled anything enticing coming out of your kitchen. Not one thing. Surely a record of some sort. I figured you must eat only boiled rice. Or maybe you learned to cook from an Englishwoman or something."

"I'm sorry," says Marie-Thérèse. "We probably shouldn't be making jokes at a time like this."

"At a time like what?" asks Fadia. "What happened?"

"Are you smiling?" Joumana asks me. "What's amusing you?"

"Nothing much," I reply. "What Fadia said reminded me of my dead ex-husband. He used to accuse me of smelling like onions when he returned home. Almost every evening, onions, onions. He blamed that for not being able to be around me."

"You didn't cook with onions, did you?" Fadia says.

"I've never chopped one in my life."


I am alone again. My home is quiet, as I like it. My neighbors have left, taken a break for lunch. We'll all return, Joumana insisted. After lunch, Marie-Thérèse thought. Probably after a siesta, added Fadia. I tried to excuse myself from lunch, but they would have none of it. Marie-Thérèse is going to make sure I accompany her up to Fadia's when lunch is ready.

We haven't made much of a dent in the drying process. In three and a half hours, we barely finished two manuscripts, *Anna Karenina* and *A Book of Memories* —two fairly long manuscripts, true. Only some of the pages are legible all the way through. When we start again, we'll do *The Book of Disquiet*. I need to save it next if it's salvageable. It will take forever. Maybe I should take Joumana up on her offer, have a passel of students air out the pages, create a serf assembly line to move the enterprise along more quickly.

Tolstoy would be upset with me for using the term *serf*. Or I could just throw everything out, discard the weight of years, shrug off the albatross. Choices.

My apartment is a hellish mess, damp boxes and loose sheets of paper in the kitchen, in the living room, in the reading room. Only Joumana knows where everything is now. This is her system. How will I ever clean my home once we're done? How will I be able to clean the wet disaster that is the maid's room and the maid's bathroom? I'll need someone to change the lightbulb. A serf?

I'm losing my manners. I must ask Joumana whether she's heard any more news from her daughter. Joumana has been kind, as has Marie-Thérèse; even Fadia, crazy Fadia.

The crazy witch is right in a way. This destruction is an opportunity to break free from the rules I've set for translating, or from some of them, at least. Like a teenager, I too can rebel. Maybe I can translate a book written in English for a change. Miss Spark — I'll translate Muriel Spark's *The Prime of Miss Jean Brodie*, or, better yet, the crème de la crème of short story writers, Alice Munro. I can live in Alice's skin for a while.

Forget the industrialized countries; I can work with writers from the third world, Ireland! Edna O'Brien, Colm Tóibín, or Anne Enright.

The subcontinent and its diasporas: *A House for Mr. Biswas* or *Midnight's Children*.

A farrago of possibilities.

Coetzee! I would love to do Coetzee; yes, I would.

I can translate *Mrs. Dalloway*. I can if I want to. I'll spend that famous day inside Clarissa's head as she prepares to host the party. Or work on *A Room of One's Own* in a soggy apartment of my own. Maybe I should translate Hemingway's *For Whom the Bell Tolls*. The pain might induce a religious ecstasy.

No, I can translate a French book. I can spend a year with my darling Emma Bovary.

If English and French are the limits of my language, the limits of my world, then still my world is infinite. I no longer need to translate a translation. Not all has to be doubly lost. I've been studying the water while snugly nestled within the safety of a boat, but now I will swim in the murky waters of Flaubert's French. I don't have to work from a language once removed; I don't have to translate from a distance. Aaliya, the above, the separate, can step in the mud.

Am I experiencing an epiphany?

Forget Emma. I'm going to translate my Marguerite. *Memoirs of Hadrian*, my favorite novel. Marie-Thérèse may have wanted Vronsky for a husband, but I wanted Hadrian. I wanted someone to erect monuments in my memory, build statues. I wanted someone to dedicate cities in my name.

Where is my Aaliyopolis?

Hadrian or Emma, Emma or Hadrian, a French housewife or a Roman Caesar? Choices, limitless choices — well, almost limitless.

If I translate Yourcenar, I can be my own Hadrian. I can build my own city. I can be emperor for a year, ruler of the universe, arbiter of life and death. Call me Emperor Speck.

But I would love to translate Coetzee and his impeccable prose, shorn of all excess. I'll do *Waiting for the Barbarians*. After all, I'm no longer a feet-washing virgin. The book is magnificent, a perfect jewel.

I can try to capture Coetzee's lapidary English in Arabic. Can I discover how to convey his precision and incisiveness? Or Yourcenar's French, which she tamed, making it sound more Latin, as if Hadrian's old, shaky hand wrote it with a quill? I don't know if I can share her expansive formality of language or Coetzee's beguiling subtleties, though I am a better translator than when I began fifty years ago. I can try.

Should I be Hadrian or the Magistrate?

I'll use waterproof ink—permanent, nonfugitive ink.

*That in black ink my love may still shine bright.*

I hear Marie-Thérèse coming up the stairs—time for lunch with the witches. She promised to stop at my door.

Should I translate Yourcenar or Coetzee?

Marie-Thérèse reaches my landing. If she rings my doorbell, my next project will be *Hadrian*, if she knocks, then it's *Barbarians*.

I take a long breath, the air of anticipation.

# Acknowledgments

Thank you:

Reading and editing: Asa DeMatteo, William Zimmerman, Madeleine Thien, Joy Johannessen, and Elisabeth Schmitz.

Generosity and a great place to write: Beatrice Monti della Corte and the staff of the Santa Maddalena Foundation.

Inestimable faith and support: Nicole Aragi, Christie Hauser, Duvall Osteen, Amy Tan, Colm Tóibín, Silvia Querini, John Freeman, Tony Chakar, Andrea Laguni, Teri Boyd, Sasha Hemon.

Translation of Antara's poem: Fady Joudah.

Randa, Rania, and Raya, of course.

Thank you.